One Night Stands
and
Lesson Plans

Book One of the Marchfield Middle Series

M. Jayne LaDow

This work contains content that may be distressing to some readers, including paternal deaths occurring in childhood and some references to what it was like in Afghanistan during the war. Additionally, there are sex scenes described in detail and occasional use of strong language and profanity. This novel is not intended for children. Readers are advised to proceed with caution if they may be affected by any of these themes.

For Lauren, who laughs at all the jokes

Playlist and Book BINGO

The main character, Audrey Freemont, experiences life through a living connection to music. Celebrate her radio in a box mindset by listening to her playlist on Spotify. You can scan, click here, or find the list on my website: mjladow.com

My book club adores Book BINGO, and we have two ways of playing it. Sometimes, we play it for fun during happy hour or other occasions after we've finished the book. But more frequently, we play it concurrently while reading, jotting down page numbers in the boxes as we read. Talking about it afterward is always fun.

Below are two boards for your enjoyment. You can also grab them on my website: mjladow.com

Educational Bingo

Pop Culture BINGO

Chapter 1: Audrey

Brass Monkey

"How did you ever convince me to come tonight?" I shouted. Travis Tritt pumped through the speakers and offered me a quarter to call someone who cared. I debated taking him up on it and calling an Uber.

Normally, I would have taken my bestie Val's shrug and grin as a challenge and plunged into a debate on the misnomer of happy hour. But my mind was on overdrive, bouncing between ideas so much that logic was impossible. I was wearing myself out pinging from one thought to another.

Panic rose up from the pit of my stomach. School started for teachers tomorrow, and I swallowed down the growing sense of doom. Summer's end heralded the start of the annual pressure and stress that turned free time into parent phone calls, meetings, detentions, afterschool activities, and hours of preparation for every class.

I'd pushed away the dread all day, but I couldn't avoid it. Even here in Sharky's Pub, with dozens of teachers, custodians, and office assistants all celebrating one last night of freedom, I stared at my undeniable failure of a summer more morose than previous years.

Back in June, I felt like the world was my oyster! *School's Out for Summer* by Alice Cooper filled my head, drowning out Travis Tritt and the bar noise.

I had big goals.

I might even call them HUGE goals.

It would be my summer of indulgence. After nine years of teaching summer school to twelve and thirteen-year-olds, I promised myself I'd set aside three months to work on myself.

My entire life to this point revolved around school - going to school, graduating, and then teaching. Don't get me wrong; I love teaching kids, but was it wrong to want more? Devoting myself to education day in and out was exhausting.

Does it pay well? Nope. Does society at large respect me? Not really. I'm lucky to have a two-bedroom apartment with enough left over to feed my cat.

For eight years, it had been enough. But last year, I started wanting more.

Loud laughter nearby made me jolt. Val passed me a cold beer. "It's called networking. You gotta put yourself out there more."

Her so brown it was almost black hair was piled on top of her head, and her green glasses glinted under the bar's lights. Val knew damn well that I'd tried to break out of my shell all summer and failed miserably. If you Googled couch potato, my name would be the first result.

She patted my back. "Loosen up. Unwind. Have fun. Otherwise, you'll become a Pauli Nelson."

Pauli taught algebra at our school for four years, but she'd cracked last March and cried every day until June. She quit on the last day of school, moved back home to her parents, and got a job managing a Waffle House, making more money than I do.

"It didn't turn out too badly for her," I grumbled. "She's marrying her high school sweetheart in May."

Val nodded. "We're gonna dance barefoot at her reception, drink free booze, and party all night."

I shrugged. "I'll probably skip it." Going would feel like rubbing wedding cake into the wound during open heart surgery.

"Girl, you have to go."

"Going will only remind me of the mess I've made of my life." Or my lack of life. I couldn't even find a summer fling.

She tossed her long, dark hair over her shoulder. "You just need to find a man and get laid. Pauli has more brothers than toenails. Pick one and let the guy drive his hot dog truck into your Taco Town all night long until he runs out of hot sauce."

"It's just a dry spell." In reality, I hadn't been on a real date in the eight years since college, and my last long-term boyfriend, Jonathan, broke up with me during my senior year of high school. The well was bone dry.

Val shook her head. "It's more like the Sahara Desert!" Val has a mean streak. I love that about her, but right now, I considered punching her.

"Why is it so hard to find a clean, reasonably handsome man to have some no-strings-attached fun with?" Just saying it made me feel old. I didn't need to look in the mirror to know I was starting to resemble one of those old-fashioned spinsters with the bun and the reading glasses.

"You could be a cougar. Fierce, powerful, and strong. Pauli's little brothers..."

"My spicy salsa is too hot for them."

She laughed, "Then find someone who can. You're only thirty-two. Stop acting eighty."

If only it were that easy. I couldn't even find a single acceptable guy interested in having sex with me. Did I need to wear a sign?

A saccharine sweet voice interrupted. "Audrey, I'm so happy you're here. It's so rare to see you at a faculty function."

I tried not to grind my teeth together. My eyes met Val's. Why hadn't she warned me Pricilla Henesey circled me like a shark dressed in summer linen? I carefully wiped the irritated expression off my face and turned, attempting a smile.

"Hey, Pree, did you have a good summer?" I forced a smile, hoping Priscilla would answer in one word.

We'd started teaching the same year at Marchfield Middle. It only took me a few months to discover Pree has a competitive streak which turned her into a pit viper. If I were named the Spotlight Teacher of the Week, she had to be nominated the next week. When I was given two advanced classes in eighth-grade, she had to have two in sixth. Honestly, I could ignore all of that, but the fake, sickly sweet Southern charm she always spat in my direction annoyed me.

Pree laughed. Her perfectly cut and styled platinum blonde hair barely moved as her words gushed out. "Oh my gosh, it was a whirlwind! I traveled to Africa and joined an eco-safari. We were only supposed to go for two weeks, but Ned wanted to photograph the big five, you know – lions, leopards, elephants, rhinoceroses, both black and white, and African buffalos, so we stayed an extra two weeks to check it all off his bucket list."

"Ned?" Val asked, "Is he your boyf–"

"Fiancé!" Priscilla shrieked. Her smile was full of impossibly white teeth as she flashed her manicured left hand, wiggling her fingers to make the light bounce off her large diamond.

"Wow!" I said searching for words. "That's gotta be…"

"Five carats!" Pricilla cut me off with a girlish giggle. I looked away, trying not to laugh.

"I would have said heavy. But, wow, five carats! Cool! When did you meet Ned?"

"Oh! He goes to my gym. We trained together for the Shamrock Marathon in March. He's a sustainability architect and rich, rich, rich." She fanned herself with her hand as if the thought of his money made her hot.

I struggled to find words and ended up blurting out, "Is that diamond sustainably sourced?"

Priscilla narrowed her eyes and huffed, "Maybe? Who cares? I'm engaged!"

Val's left eye twitched. Her face turned red from holding back her laughter.

My eyes clashed with Val's, trying to communicate my desire to cut this conversation short, but she just smiled wickedly. "When's the wedding?"

Priscilla gushed. "Oh, we were thinking about spring break, but Ned reminded me the Rock-n-Roll marathon is the same weekend, so you know, we can't miss that. Have you ever run a marathon, Audrey? The endorphins! Oh, my God! They are *amazing*! Better than sex." Priscilla fanned herself, her sparkling diamond mocking me.

My first thought was Ned needed to work on his game.

My second... No way in hell could Pree ever convince me that running was better than sex. Some people ran for enjoyment, and I watched *Chariots of Fire* on Netflix.

I rubbed the piercing ache developing above my left eye, searching for any excuse to get out of this conversation. If Priscilla gushed her happiness over me for one more minute, I'd vomit or cry. My hand tightened on the beer in my hand, and I did something I hadn't done since college. I drained it in one swallow.

"I'm going to go get another drink," I lied, trying not to burp. "I'll catch you later, Pree." I turned my back on Val, leaving her there as retribution for her poor performance as my emotional support person.

I steered through the happy crowd, waving to co-workers and colleagues on my way to the bar. Marchfield Middle had a staff of about seventy-five, and it looked like almost everyone had turned out for Happy Hour. Once again, I debated calling an Uber and getting the hell out of there, but I'd stupidly bet

Val I would stay for at least two hours. I couldn't throw in the towel and lose the bet.

Spying a group of eighth-grade teachers sitting together at a table, I sidled up and grabbed a seat.

"Yo, Audrey." Keith Payt, a special education teacher, welcomed me with a grin and slapped an arm around my shoulder in a loose headlock. "How was your summer?"

"Short." I glanced over my shoulder, hoping Val had shaken loose of Pree and followed me. She knew random social chit-chat was not my forte. Introverts of the World Unite Online. I bought the T-shirt and wore it proudly.

"Ain't they all?" Keith commiserated. "I taught summer school, so it flew by."

"I took the summer off, but I wasted it all."

"That sounds like a story I'd like to hear. Let me buy you a drink, and you can tell it."

I tried to tell him not to bother because my misery didn't need company, but he disappeared into the crowd of teachers.

Science teacher, Dee O'Malley, smiled and patted Keith's empty chair. "Good to see you, Audrey," she said as I slid over.

"How is the baby?" I asked. Other people's babies were one of my weaknesses. I loved buying tiny clothes, socks, and hats, and don't get me started on those sweet-smelling snuggles.

"Oh! Wanna see some pictures?" Dee pulled out her phone and began scrolling through candid photos of dogs, children, and her husband splashing in the pool, building sandcastles, and playing at the park.

"Conner's getting so big! How old is he now?" The pictures, an endless supply of frozen moments of joy, created an emptiness inside me. My phone was full of cat photos.

"He's two. And the terrible cliché is spot on." Dee grimaced.

"I've heard that two-year-olds are remarkably similar to 8th graders."

"Pretty much," Dee chuckled and put her phone down on the table. "What did you do this summer?"

"I watched *Game of Thrones*."

"Oh, I've only seen bits and pieces. Hard to watch with little ones in the house." Dee shrugged.

"I watched the whole thing. All eight seasons, on the big screen, full volume. And then I re-watched it three more times."

"Impressive." Dee gave me a weird expression.

I glanced around. No sign of Val. Scanning the crowd for Keith and my beer, I spotted him giving my drink to a cute, new teacher. He caught my eye and shrugged. Keith was a huge flirt and would date any breathing woman. He and Val had dated a few times, so he and I steered clear of one another.

"I need a drink. Want anything, Dee?" I asked.

"No thanks." Dee blushed a pretty pink. "I'm preggers again. Due in April."

I gaped at her. How did people do it? I mean, I know how they do that, but come on! I couldn't find a man to save my life. Dee was pregnant, and Keith probably had a date for later. I wanted to scream.

Dee didn't seem to notice. "I'm hoping for a girl this time, but I'll be happy if it's another boy."

I smiled dumbly while Dee glowed in that pregnant way women do. My uterus clenched with envy, but I ignored it. I was just horny, for God's sake!

"I need a shot." I stood and took a few steps toward the long wooden bar. I could see the bottles of whisky on the shelves behind the bartender.

Maybe?

I considered him for a few seconds and then dismissed him. I imagined I was old, but he was definitely in his upper sixties. But maybe I'd brush my hand against his just to see if there were any sparks.

Everyone around me laughed, having a great time. My mind jumped from one thought to the next but finally settled on getting drunk.

I knew I'd regret it tomorrow. Being hungover would be a terrible idea as I sat in a faculty meeting watching summer become a memory. The principal would introduce this year's many mandatory initiatives, and the weight of them lands on every teacher's shoulders.

The stress and the worry came flooding back, but I refused to acknowledge it. I marched over to the bar and ordered.

The bartender's scarred hands produced no spark as he passed me my drink. I spun to observe the crowd and spotted Val across the room talking to some sixth-grade teachers. Lifting my glass, I toasted her, tossing back the amber liquor. It burned its way down my throat, but blessed, warm numbness spread through my body. I ordered two more.

"Mixing whisky and beer is a surefire way to make terrible decisions before tomorrow's teacher workday." But Val picked up the second shot.

"Good decisions are overrated." I raised my glass. "To May weddings, new babies, and sustainably-sourced fiancés."

Val clinked her glass to mine. "And to of all the sweet, innocent new teachers everywhere."

I drank my shot and slammed the glass down on the bar.

Val observed me closely. "Are you okay?"

"Fine, fine. Want another drink?"

The D.J. amped up Garth Brooks' *I've Got Friends in Low Places* and the whole crowd cheered.

Val squealed! She sang along, shimmying her hips to the beat. "Dance with me."

"No." I gestured to the bartender who poured me another shot.

"If you won't dance to Garth, I'm not sure we can be friends."

I shrugged, and she ran to the dance floor, joining the mosh pit of twerking teachers singing the chorus.

I motioned for another drink but sat holding it for a minute. My head felt swimmy with the effects of my drinks. When had I last eaten? Breakfast?

I smiled, lifting the glass up to my lips. Mission accomplished. I was drunk. I'd just finish this one, call that Uber, and go home.

Pat and Danny, two P.E. teachers, who were both married with grandkids, walked up to the bar shooting the breeze about baseball. *Enter Sandman* by Metallica, one of the best sports intro songs of all time, played loudly in my mind.

My dad always said I was a walking radio station. One of my favorite memories is singing Michael Jackson's *Beat It* with him in the car. Similar to a photographic memory, once I hear a song, it gets filed away until something triggers a connection.

Danny smiled at me. "You're really tossing them back tonight, Audrey."

"I'm celebrating." The words came out a little slurred— *Shellibrating.*

Pat nodded. "You sure can't drive. Can I call you an Uber?"

I nodded. Here was the perfect opportunity to leave being handed to me.

He unlocked his phone and opened the app just as the door to the bar opened and I glanced over.

The sun was hanging low in the sky, and light poured in, temporarily blinding me. A tall figure filled the door frame. He stepped into the bar, and it was like a ray of sunlight lit up his features.

And time stopped.

I watched as the stranger scowled, looking around the room. His hunky solidness sent shivers of awareness down my spine. His wide, mouth-watering shoulders made me want to climb him like a leopard. I hummed low in the back of my throat. His red T-shirt stretched tight across his chest, showcasing his yummy strong chest. How often did he work out? Errmmmagoddd!

My mouth dropped open, and drool pooled at the corner of my mouth. This Adonis ticked every one of my boxes. He was the filling to my Reese's Cup, the Han Solo to my Princess Leia. I wanted to take Def Leppard's advice and pour some sugar on him. I blinked. Was he a mirage in my sexual desert?

Heat swept over me. Some women are into a man's eyes or their hands, but hard, muscled shoulders are my kryptonite. Add to that his short, wavy blond hair and chiseled chin, this guy might as well have been wearing a gift tag saying for Audrey.

My alcohol-soaked brain cells caught up with my body and began clamoring for action. Tossing back the last shot, I stood.

"Thanks, Pat. I think I'll stay a little longer." If he responded, I didn't hear him.

Mostly steady on my feet, I sent a silent thanks to my two older brothers, Kyle and Jack, for teaching me how to hold my liquor even on an empty stomach every crazy holiday since I turned seventeen. I paid my tab and scanned the bar.

Priscilla Henesey stood only a few feet away, looking at me with disapproval. I smiled and waved, turning away before she could react.

He was still there, just inside the door. It was a sign. I focused hard on The Shoulders of My Dreams and started across the room. I felt drawn to him as if pulled by a tractor beam. A few feet from him, I paused. Nice chin and enough stubble to give a girl a good scratch.

I stepped closer. My body almost brushed his.

He smelled of the ocean, and my tongue itched to taste the saltiness of his skin. I squinted at him, trying to pick the right color to describe his eyes. Were they gray or hazel?

And that's when I noticed. He was staring at me as if he'd been struck by lightning.

Chapter 2: Oz

Perfect Strangers

My buddy, Bobby, had texted me non-stop most of the day about showing up at the school happy hour.

5:00 PM **Bobby: We're at Barrel. Come down and meet everyone.**

5:23 PM **Bobby: Sarge, come on. You're late. Happy hour is at Barrel on 15th Street.**

6:03 PM **Bobby: Dude, you promised me. I'll cover all your drinks.**

6:46 PM Bobby: Oz, seriously. Where are you? Don't leave me hanging.

I knew I should text her back, but it had been a hell of a long day. Why did I ever think I could move from New York to Virginia in one weekend? Sure, spending the extra time with Mom and my little sister on vacation in Delaware had been worth it, but hauling furniture and boxes had destroyed all my desire to socialize.

I'd been to enough awkward office happy hours to know it was the worst way to meet your future colleagues. A bunch of teachers cutting loose at a bar is remarkably similar to a cluster fuck of platoon soldiers on leave. I've been there and done that.

After leaving the Army, I still wanted to serve my country, so I chose middle school math. Eighth-graders are still young enough to be goofy and funny but not so young that I have to take them to the bathroom or hug them if they cry. I taught for two years in New York, but I wanted to work in a smaller school. When Bobby told me about the job opening at Marchfield Middle, she didn't have to nag me too much before I applied.

I've known Bobby forever, but I met her in Afghanistan. I'd been sweating it out in the moon dust for a month when she got stationed at the combat outpost near Kandahar. She had a lot of piss and vinegar, and even though she was a Southern girl, she swore like a New Yorker. Fighting back-to-back in the disgusting heat of the god-forsaken desert had built a strong bond between us.

So yeah, I'm late to the party, but I'm here. You show up for friends.

I parked my truck next to a neon green Fiat. What possessed people to paint cars to resemble slime or vomit? I glanced around the lot, not seeing Bobby's red Mitsubishi. She'd probably taken an Uber. Steeling myself for the worst, I marched to the door.

Stepping inside, my eyes took a second to adjust from the evening sun to the darkness of the bar. I stopped inside the threshold, letting the door close behind me. Out of habit, I scanned the crowd and located the exits. Once a G.I. Joe, always a Joe. Looking for Bobby's short black hair, my eyes skidded to a screeching halt on the redhead at the bar.

She tossed back a shot, not the first from the looks of the scattered glasses in front of her. She slouched on the stool, and I could almost visualize them skimming over her tight butt. I wished she would stand so I could see if reality equaled my imagination. I caught a glance at her profile as she pushed the mass of red hair to the side.

She looked lost in unhappy thoughts. Normally, I'd move on. I don't need to borrow any more problems because I have enough of my own. But there was something about her. I'm not sure why she kept my attention, but I learned long ago to listen to my instincts. They'd kept me alive for six brutal years in the military.

My blood started moving south before she even turned. And when she looked right at me? Damn, I felt my knees go weak. Sparks jumped across the room, hitting me like a concussion blast. I couldn't tear my gaze away.

She spoke to the bartender, paid her tab, and climbed off the stool. God bless those skinny jeans hugging her legs. I got a brief glance at her butt; the fabric skimmed tight over those perfect cheeks. Her pink top dipped in the front, showing a hint of cleavage I wanted to explore. She floated over to me, her body small and curvy. Her red hair floated around her shoulders, and a misty sunrise set against her creamy skin. Damn, she was hot.

She stopped in front of me, so close I could feel the heat of her body and smell the sweet, flowery perfume on her skin. The top of her head reached my shoulder, and she craned her neck up, a long, kissable column of soft, pale skin. Her gaze scalded, hot across my neck and face. When her green eyes finally met mine, I felt unsteady.

Her full pink lips curved and then parted in a naughty angel's smile. She put her hands on my shoulders to steady herself. Maybe she felt the ground shake, too?

"Are you married?"

I cocked my head at the sound of her husky voice. "No, ma'am."

"Dating anyone seriously?"

I smiled, looking down at her as she slid her hands across my shoulders, giving me a peek down into her shirt. "No, Darlin'. I'm new in town."

Her lips spread wide in a sloppy smile. "Can I kiss you?" She stretched up on her toes, her breasts brushing across my chest, and kissed me, playing with the collar of my Yankee's shirt.

"Well, now," I hedged even though I wanted to taste those pink lips.

She leaned in. The warm scent of vanilla and flowers teased my senses, and then her lips moved across mine. Her tongue tasted of whiskey and cinnamon.

The shock of being kissed by a stranger lasted about five seconds, and I kissed her back. My hands found her hips. I lifted her up, holding her against me, making it easier to explore her mouth. It was hard to say how long the kiss went on because I sure as hell didn't check the clock. Red's hot body clung to mine, demanding all of my attention.

Loud laughter nearby brought reality crashing in. She pulled back. I hooked my finger in her belt loop, keeping her close. A man at a nearby table balanced a full pint on his forehead to the amusement of about ten women. The pint teetered; somebody was about to get doused.

"Come with me." The red-headed siren tugged my hand.

And I followed. The sun had set, painting the clouds the same red as her hair. Enough blood returned to my brain as she tugged me toward the ugly green Fiat next to my truck. I cleared my throat. "I'm Oz."

She stopped, looking over her shoulder at me. The fading light made her eyes big and her hair dark as midnight. "Can you drive?"

"That thing?" I gestured to the green slime. "Well, yeah, but..."

My words stopped as she slid her hand into her jeans pocket. My eyes were glued to those fingers digging deep into the tight denim.

She held her keys out to me. "I'm Audrey. Wanna take me home?"

Audrey. It was an old-fashioned name. Her actions were bold, but her voice held a touch of uncertainty. I was ninety-five percent sure she didn't bring strangers home often.

She jingled the keys, the question echoing in her eyes. I closed the distance between us and kissed her, backing her up against the ridiculous neon side of her car while I drank from her lips.

My mouth crushed hers. Whatever blood had made it to my brain plunged south again. My hands slid from her waist and moved higher. Audrey moaned low in her throat, moving closer. I brushed the side of her breasts with my thumbs, and her moan turned into a groan.

A horn honked nearby. Instinctively, I shielded her body with mine as a boy's voice called out, "Hey, is that Miss Freemont?"

The horn honked again, and she buried her head into my shoulder at the sound of laughing boys. A second later, the light changed, and the car sped away.

Audrey jerked away from me and made her way unsteadily around the side of the car to slide into the passenger seat. I opened the driver's side door, pushing the seat as far back as possible to squeeze my legs under the steering wheel.

She gave me a sidelong look as I adjusted the mirrors. "What'd you say your name was?"

I laughed, turning toward her in the tiny car, and held out my hand. "I'm Oz."

Her warm hand clasped mine, and I sucked in a breath. I wanted this woman with a passion that surprised me.

"Will you take me home, Oz?"

Smiling, I turned the key and started her pitiful excuse of a car. "Anything for you, Darlin'."

Chapter 3: Audrey

Girls Just Wanna Have Fun

Darlin'. He'd called me Darlin'. I pressed my hand against my belly. The Southern charm and the intimacy of it made me want him even more.

Oz drove my car toward my apartment as *Born to Run* came on the radio. The lyrics resonated. Who was I to argue with The Boss? I wanted to wrap my legs around something for sure.

I tried to talk myself out of the ludicrous idea. Taking a stranger home because I was horny could end badly. He could be a sociopath or a murderer. But then I'd peer over and melt a little.

His big, tan hands on the steering wheel... melt.

His shoulders, way too large for my car... melt, melt.

His short, messy blonde hair pressed against the ceiling... melt, melt, melt.

And when he looked at me, acknowledging my directions with a slow smile... I turned into Olaf on a summer day.

A tiny moan escaped my mouth, and he glanced over at me, his eyebrow quirking up.

I love that. Every sexy movie hero in the world can quirk an eyebrow. Chris Hemsworth, Will Smith, Ryan Gosling—all of them can quirk. It's probably in the screen test. 1, 2, 3! Quirk! You're hired!

The silence felt heavy between us. I squirmed in my seat, needing to say something. I twisted my hands together. "Are you a serial killer?"

His eyes cut to me for a second before returning to the road. "Are you?"

"No, nope, not me," I babbled. Did he really wonder if I was a murderer?

"Me either." He smiled. "Of course, that's what a serial killer would say."

"Probably," I laughed weakly. "It seems counterintuitive to admit it straight off."

He smiled. "Want me to give you some references? Yelp reviews? Maybe look at my resume?"

I giggled helplessly. "Will they testify to the fact that you're not a psychotic murderer?"

"Only the ones I didn't murder." Oz had one relaxed hand on the wheel while the other tapped a beat on his thigh. "Seriously though, my best friend would love it if you asked her."

He stopped at a red light and reached for my hand. His thumb rubbed across my knuckles, sending sparks trailing across my skin. I sucked in a breath and asked, "Do you have any pet peeves?"

"About sex?" He flashed me a grin. "Not really. Am I gonna need a safe word?"

I opened my mouth to respond but my witty repartee was drowned in whiskey. Only one word popped into my mind, "Asparagus?"

He must have seen the blush which started on my cheeks and took over my whole face.

"Relax, Red. There's no pressure."

Red. Obvious yet accurate. A secret part of me loved it. Tonight, I was a rebel.

I smiled at him. "Are you this nice to all women?"

He flashed a smile back. "Only the cute ones who kiss me in bars."

I struggled to find a response. Flirting required a clear mind and less alcohol. Retreating back to safe conversational topics, I directed Oz to pull into my apartment complex and park in my spot. He killed the ignition, gave me the keys, and returned his hands to the steering wheel.

"If you've changed your mind, I'll walk back to the bar after I've seen you to the door." His eyes met mine, eyebrows quirking.

Oh, Hell. No.

He thought I wasn't interested anymore! I turned in my seat to meet his gaze. Lifting my eyebrow, I put the question back in his corner. "Do you want to go?"

His mouth split with a grin. He popped open the car door and awkwardly edged himself out from behind the Fiat's steering wheel. His tall frame spilled out as his arm accidentally hit the horn.

His scowl of disgust was priceless. Even I'll admit my baby's horn sounded like a squeak toy crossed with a sick cat's sneeze. I nearly fell out of the car, laughing.

"Don't frown at my baby! Green Lightning is sensitive." I scolded him, wiping tears from my eyes.

His burly, muscular arms crossed over his chest. The fabric of his T-shirt clung to his biceps, outlining every yummy detail, and I tried hard not to drool. "That is a poor excuse for a car, and that horn isn't fit for a bicycle."

His wide, innocent eyes and mischievous grin made my belly flutter. "All your middle school teachers must have hated you. Acting all cute and innocent while getting into trouble."

He shrugged. "All the kids loved me."

"Yeah, I'm sure they did."

Using my best sassy, butt-swinging walk, I led him to my apartment door. The heat of his body radiated against my back as I unlocked the door. Leaning back against him, I wiggled my hips. He moved so fast that I barely blinked before Oz swung me around and had my back up against the closed door.

Marvin Gaye crooned *Let's Get It On* in my head, and my hips began to sway to my internal playlist. I shivered as Oz's calloused hands ran up my arms. His mouth trailed down my neck, setting fire to my blood.

"Red, something's rubbing around my legs. You double-jointed or something?"

I laughed, "Oz, meet Stevie, my cat. Go away, Stevie."

Reaching up, I pulled his mouth back to mine, drinking in his masculine taste. Mint with a hint of dark chocolate became my new favorite flavor. I was addicted. Craving his touch, I arched into his hands. "More, harder."

Oz leaned back and looked into my eyes for a moment. He must have seen the want, no, the need in mine because he kissed me hard. I reveled in the roughness of his whiskers against my skin. When he brushed my nipples with his thumbs, I cried out, groaning and crushing my fingers into his hair.

I broke away from him, out of breath. "I should probably tell you. It's been a long time for me."

Oz grinned as his fingers continued to make sweeping circles across my breasts. "Do you need a refresher course?"

"Are you offering?"

He picked me up like a swoony romance novel hero. I wrapped my legs around his waist so my body aligned with his. I rubbed my clit against his thick cock, my pussy memorizing him, welcoming him. My breath hitched. I felt out of control, and when Oz groaned into my mouth, I felt powerful.

I wildly gestured toward the bedroom and kissed him again. I tugged his hair, then raked my nails down his back, feeling the strong muscles of those never-ending shoulders tighten in response to my touch.

His mouth broke away from mine, breathing harsh and out of control. "We need to slow down."

His words, his voice rumbled through me. I paused. We were eye to eye as he held me as easily as a doll.

"No."

"No?" Oz repeated. I felt him pulling back, easing away from me. I clutched at him, refusing to let him go.

"I don't want to slow down. I want you, Oz. Now."

I watched the hazel of his eyes darken and his pupils dilate. He took a deep breath, nostrils flaring, and started down the dark hall past the kitchen with me clinging to him like Jane in a Tarzan movie.

I pulled Oz's Yankee's t-shirt over his head just as Stevie set a feline roadblock in the hallway.

"Wait! Stop!" I cried.

Partially blinded, Oz grunted, struggling for balance. He braced his hand against the wall. I wrapped my legs tighter around his waist, holding on.

Beneath us, Stevie wound through Oz's legs, heading back toward the kitchen. He looked back with large, yellow eyes in the dim light and meowed innocently.

"We're a little busy, Stevie. Go take a nap," I suggested and pulled Oz's shirt over his head. Circling my hands over his hard shoulders, his skin felt as hot as a furnace.

"How much do you work out?" I muttered against his neck while breathing in the salty scent of him.

His wry laugh vibrated through his chest. "I had a lot of free time this summer."

When we reached my bedroom, he lowered me until my feet skimmed to the floor. Glancing around, I prayed I hadn't left anything embarrassing out. I loved my Muffin Mixer but didn't want him to see the big pink vibrator.

Oz reached down to lift the hem of my pink shirt, and a new worry took its place. Closing my eyes, I said a little drunken prayer. *Please, let me be wearing my matching navy lace underwear and not mismatched granny panties and a sports bra.*

His eyes were hot as fire as they fixed on my breasts, wrapped in satin and lace. His mouth fell open, and that powerful feeling rose up in me again. I lifted my arms over my head. His fingers dragged across my skin, following the straps of satin from my shoulder down, down, down to the tiny white bow between my breasts. I lowered my arms, squeezing my breasts together, lifting them, and accentuating my cleavage.

Oz stepped closer, his chest brushing against me. My nipples hardened at the contact. He unhooked my bra, lowering the straps and peeling the fabric away from my skin. He wrapped one arm around me and guided me to the edge of the bed.

He sank onto his knees. His hands were on me in an instant, thumbs brushing against the peaks of my nipples. Taking one and then the other into his mouth, he adored them with his tongue and teeth, mixing pleasure and pain until I knew only him.

His thumbs hooked in the edge of my jeans, peeling them down my thighs until they pooled around my ankles and fell to the floor. He traced the lace across the top of my navy panties. I shivered as he tugged them over my warm skin. The soft mattress dipped as I sank down into the softness of my bed; his fingers trailed through the red curls between my legs, found me, and slipped inside.

My back arched, and I groaned, grinding my hips against Oz's fingers. "I need..."

He growled, low and husky, "What, Red?"

I almost didn't recognize my voice when I panted, "I need more."

"Tell me." His thumb rubbed softly across my clit.

Unable to find the words, I pounded my fist against his shoulder, but he effortlessly held me still. For a moment, I wondered if I should be scared.

"Do you want me to stop?" His hooded eyes searched mine, and I shook my head. "Then tell me what you need."

I pouted a little. Why couldn't he read my mind? "I need you inside me. I want to come with you inside me."

He yanked a condom out of his wallet and unfastened his pants, letting them tangle with mine on the floor. "You're so beautiful, Red. I want to be in your wet pussy."

My body felt hot and tingly at the sight of him naked. Before he could move, I sat on the edge of the bed, taking his length in my hand. The heat of his body drew me to him, tempting me. I kissed his hard belly and then lower, inching my way down, my hand moving over him.

"Red, stop. You're killing me," Oz panted. He jerked away before I reached my target. His fingers left a trail of sparks across my body, and I wondered if we would set the mattress on fire.

Burning Down the House clicked into my mind until his fingers danced across my core, and I forgot all about the Talking Heads, thinking more about giving head at this point. I fell back onto the pillows. The fire in my blood grew white hot.

I reached for him, and he rolled on the condom.

His hands and mouth roamed over my breasts and down my body. My heart pounded in my ears. It was time to take what I wanted. Sitting up, I pushed him down onto the pillows. In an instant, I straddled him, squeezing his hip bones with my thighs. His cock rubbed against my center as I lowered myself eagerly onto him.

His hard body flexed beneath me as he pushed deeper, stretching muscles I'd neglected for so long. I gasped. Tiny spasms shivered through me as sensations swept over me like a whirlwind. The force of it drove me beyond thought until there was nothing left but his body inside of mine.

The orgasm washed over me like a tidal wave. Oz's hands and mouth were my anchor as my body arched tight. Lightning bolts surged through me in a never-ending wave. I moaned, shuddering, never wanting it to end.

He groaned as my pleasure triggered his. He bucked his hips, the muscles of his neck tight. His teeth clenched, and he came.

I collapsed on top of him. My head nestled into his shoulder. I panted as if I'd run a marathon. Marvin Gaye crooned about sexual healing in my head. I sang along, feeling Oz's rumbly laugh in response.

He squeezed me tightly and brushed his lips on the top of my head. "Red, that was amazing."

I felt a rush of awkwardness.

My mind felt fuzzy, the ideas tangling together. What should I say? *Thanks* felt too polite, and *Yes, it was* seemed redundant. I could barely remember words

"I've never come like that."

"Yeah?" He kissed my neck, nuzzling me with his stubble. It tickled and made me laugh.

"The teen inside me wants to give you a high five."

Really? Did I actually say that?

He smiled, and his eyes fluttered closed. I felt him relax. His hands slowed, then stopped stroking, resting heavily on my back. His mouth opened slightly, and a soft snore escaped.

I lay on top of him, savoring the warm hardness of his skin. My inner teen did a few cartwheels. I had a sexy man in my bed. But as the minutes stretched, I wondered about the etiquette of these situations. Should I wake him?

Wake Me Up Before You Go-Go popped into my mind. I stared at him, squinting a little. Did he resemble a short-haired George Michael? Teen me squealed. George Michael had been my first celebrity crush. My heart swelled a little.

I shook my head, admonishing myself, and rolled off of him. The last bit of my buzz slipped away, leaving me chilly. I pulled the sheet up while scolding myself. It was way, *way* too early for heart swelling. Catching feelings for him would be a mistake. I didn't even know him. He could be a total jerk or a slimeball politician. He was nothing more than a whim.

A glorious, sexy, yummy, delicious whim.

I lay against the pillows and sang along with Wham in my mind until Stevie pounced on me. Silently, he stomped across my naked boobs, making sure to center his weight so each paw felt like a spike driving into my chest. I shoved him off, but he returned to sit on my pillow. Shooting me disdainful glances, his gray and white tail flicked back and forth, hitting me in the head.

"Alright, you monster," I whispered, sitting up.

I pulled back the sheet and peered back at Oz before I stood. All that tan skin and hard muscle called to me. I trailed a finger down the middle of his chest, following the line of blonde hair lower. He sighed in his sleep.

I leaned closer and kissed his cheek. Reaching up to rub the spot with his hand, he almost whacked me in the face with his wrist before rolling onto his side. Damn, he had a great butt. It was firm and round, two shades lighter than the rest of his skin.

I reached out to pinch it just as Stevie clawed me on the knee hard enough to draw blood. I tucked the sheet around Oz and got up with a sigh.

I grabbed underwear and pajamas out of a drawer. "Party pooper," I muttered as Stevie led the way to the bedroom door.

When I returned, he slept dead center in my bed, his head on my favorite pillow. Was I crazy to think it was cute?

I pulled the sheet back. His chest rose and fell slow and steady, mesmerizing me. I shifted to the edge of the bed, gauging the six inches he'd left me. Maybe I could slide in and snuggle up to him. He'd wrap his strong arms around me and shift over to give me more room.

Ready to live out my internal fantasy, I eased my legs onto the mattress. I pressed up against him, my butt dangling off the edge of the bed. As I stretched my hand out to wrap around his waist, he let out a grunt in his sleep. And rolled.

I grabbed the sheet as it slid off of him and wrapped around me, twisting like a boa constrictor. He yanked at his corner in his sleep, ejecting me from the bed, and I landed with a thump. Grunting, I struggled out from the fabric as he settled back into the middle of the bed with a sigh.

I no longer thought it was cute.

I gave his shoulder a shove, and he snored. Marveling that even in sleep, his muscles felt like heated steel, I pinched him, but even asleep, he was fast. He swatted me like a bug, pushing me away hard. I tickled his armpit, and he rolled over flat on his stomach.

His butt called to me, and I ran my hand over the curve and gave his balls a little jiggle.

"Go away," he grumbled.

I stalked to the bathroom, a queen with my flowery sheet trailing behind me. I needed time to think. After showering, I put on granny panties because he wasn't getting in my pants again tonight. Then I pulled on soft, comfy cotton pajamas splashed with drawings of llamas and books. The words scrawled across my chest pronounced me a LLAMA READING MAMA.

My brain cued up Rascal Flatts crooning *Walk the Llama Llama*. Glancing in the mirror, I felt armored from head to toe. Oz had stolen my bed. This might not be war exactly, but it wasn't an invitation. No silk nighties for him.

Sitting on my sofa, I wondered what to do. He'd wake up soon, right? We would have a civilized and awkward conversation. He'd be embarrassed. I'd thank him, and he'd leave. Then I'd change the sheets and get some sleep. I assumed that's how these things worked.

My head pounded. I should never have mixed beer and whiskey. I guzzled a bottle of water and took some ibuprofen. Afterward, I texted Val.

10:48 PM **Me: Sorry I bailed. I have a story and your $20. See you tomorrow.**

I tiptoed into my room and peeked at him. If I were a painter, I'd have set up my easel and created "God in Repose." What did I look like sleeping? I'm sure my painting would be titled "Drooling Red-Haired Demon."

Returning to the sofa, I Googled *how to get rid of a man*. The results were not helpful.

An hour later, I was thoroughly irritated. I decided I'd give the clown in my bed thirty minutes before I jumped on the bed while blasting an air horn sound effect on my phone. I'd call him a Uber and hand him his clothes. He could wait outside for his ride.

Decision made, I lay down on the sofa to wait. Stevie jumped up and purred, fluffy and warm, on my lap. I patted him three times before I drifted off.

Chapter 4: Oz

Back to December

I'm not sure what woke me. One minute, I was out like a light, the next, I was up and ready. I sat up, looking around. Flowery throw pillows on the floor by the bed made me wonder. An orange and red sunset watercolor painting of the Atlantic Ocean hung on the wall.

And then it hit me, the bathroom was in the wrong place. I could see a yellow, smiley face night light glowing between the mirror and the shower.

This was not my bed.

I was not in my house.

I sat up, and it all came flooding back—spending all day moving my stuff into a new place, appeasing Bobby by going to happy hour, and Red.

I'd been struck by a lightning bolt of lust. I'd been a fucking easy slut, and Red had been primed and ready to go. Her sweet mouth and little body had been intoxicating, and I'd lost my mind. Together we'd been so hot I was surprised we didn't set the damn bed on fire.

I stretched my stiff muscles, realizing I was in the middle of her bed. Hogging the whole mattress like an insensitive pig and leaving no room for her. The sheet was balled up in a twisted heap by the bathroom. Had I dumped her on the floor? Where was she?

I located my jeans, inside out and balled up at the bottom of the bed. What can I say? I'd been in a damn hurry. Pulling them on, I glanced at the clock on the small table by the bed. Two AM.

I couldn't believe I'd fallen asleep. Sure, I'd been exhausted from the long drive and moving all my furniture and boxes full of everything I owned. Add in damn good sex, and it was a recipe for disaster. No woman wants the man she picked up in a bar to fall asleep in her bed. It was just rude. No, it was worse than that. It was downright disrespectful.

And surprising as hell for me. I had trouble sleeping even in my own bed. After being in the Army, I had a hard time relaxing, and the slightest sound could wake me. I had to sleep with a white noise machine to drown out all the usual night sounds.

It was the worst of all multiple-choice questions. I had never in my life fallen asleep in a woman's bed unless she:

1. Asked me to stay.
2. Fell asleep first.
3. Was someone I liked and knew well.
4. Had red hair, smelled of fresh flowers, and had a pussy that sucked my cock dry.
5. All of the above

I found her on the sofa with the cat sprawled out on her chest. Her eyelashes rested against her pale cheeks, and her red hair fanned out across a half-dozen throw pillows. My eyes were drawn to her nose, sprinkled with freckles, and her pink lips, which were relaxed and parted as she slept. Her hands were tangled in the cat's fur as if she were still petting him. She was wearing pajamas with books and llamas printed all over them.

I felt my body react. Despite the flannel pjs and the embarrassment of falling asleep in her bed, I wanted her again. What was wrong with me? Sure, she was cute lying there in those ridiculous pajamas. But alluring? Not really. So why was I getting hard? Calm the hell down, Tarzan!

The cat raised his head and looked at me with glowing green eyes. They narrowed to a glare. He stared at me for a few seconds and then lowered his head to rest on top of her breast.

"Hey, Red?" I touched her shoulder lightly. "Audrey?"

She lay there. A stone sculpture, breathing lightly, not moving. I watched her chest, and the cat on it, rise and fall. It was as hypnotizing as following a clock pendulum swinging back and forth.

I pictured her waking up with me staring at her breast like a pervert. I could practically hear her screaming, calling 911, and then the slamming of prison bars. What was wrong with me?

I retreated to the bedroom and got dressed. After tying my running shoes, I paused to look around.

She had photos of family and friends on the walls and in frames on her dresser. Smiling, happy people. I could practically hear R.E.M.'s *Shiny Happy People* playing.

A photo of her as a child with an older man hung in the middle. Probably her dad. She might have been six or seven. The two of them were laughing and dancing. A record player was in the background of the photo.

There were no other pictures of the man. I thought of my own Dad and how pictures stopped with his death. I was closing in on the same age as he'd been when he died. None of the men in my family lived much past 40. It was a dark cloud of DNA coming closer. Always reminding me that time is short.

Shaking off the bittersweet feeling, I finished tying my running shoes and went out to the living room. Audrey hadn't moved.

I didn't want to leave without talking to her, so I sat down on the coffee table facing her. The cat stood and stretched, jumping down and padding away toward the kitchen.

"Hey, Red?" I shook her shoulder and ducked as her fist shot out toward my face. I stared down at her. The girl had a mean right hook.

Her eyes didn't open, but she said it loud and clear. "Go away, Kyle."

Filled with annoyed frustration, I wondered who the hell Kyle was. Irrational feelings fluttered through my belly. Had I read her wrong? Was she in a relationship with another man?

Was I jealous? Why the heck should I be jealous?

She rolled toward me, her breasts almost tumbling out of the neckline of her pajamas. My mouth watered a little. The naughty side of me wanted to slide down her top and taste them. She sighed, falling deeper into sleep. I felt like a sleazeball, drooling over her body while she lay there defenseless.

I should go home.

I wasn't an asshole, though. Audrey and I needed to talk. I saw her phone on the coffee table, but it felt wrong to pick it up and find her number. Looking around, I found a sticky note and a pen on her desk, and I stood there thinking. What were the right words for this situation?

I could Google it, but what would I search for? Notes to leave when running out on a woman after she picked you up at a bar? No. Notes to leave a woman after excellent sex? Hell no. Ways to apologize for falling asleep after sex? Fuck no.

I scribbled my phone number and Call Me After 4. Feeling like a jerk, I stuck it to the door as I let myself out.

Standing in the parking lot, I dug in my pocket for my keys only to remember my truck was back at the bar. Her ugly green Fiat laughed at me under the half-lit moon. My damn truck was back at the bar.

I pulled open my phone and opened the Uber app to call for a ride.

Chapter 5: Audrey

Cheap Sunglasses

I dreamed of a white sandy beach where I sipped Mai Tais on a lounge chair under a cheerful rainbow-colored umbrella. The warm ocean of blue crystal-clear water called to me. I swam out to a faceless man whose shoulders were so huge and brawny they blocked out the sun. Skimming my hands across his wide chest, I ran my fingers through his blond hair and dragged my lips over the contours of his muscles, tasting the salt of the sea on my tongue. As I pulled his head down to my breasts, sharp teeth sank into the arch of my foot.

Jerking awake, I fell off the narrow sofa. My legs were numb, and sharp pins and needles radiated throughout my legs and feet. My neck was stuck at an unnatural angle, and I heard the snaps and groans of protest as I stretched. Sunlight streamed in the kitchen window and directly into my eyes. It burned a hole into my brain which pounded like a bad college drumline.

Squinting, I sat up gingerly, praying the earth would stop spinning and I wouldn't throw up. I winced as Stevie let out a yowl and paced on the sofa cushions.

"Did you bite me, you fiend?" My mouth was dry, and my tongue felt swollen and covered with fuzz.

And then it hit me. *The Imperial Death March* stomped through my mind. Dread and doom washed over me as if Darth Vader walked in. School started today. There were faculty meetings, data presentations, and technology workshops all starting in—I looked at my watch—45 minutes!

"Shit," I jumped up. My stomach heaved, and I stood still for a second, breathing in and out slowly.

I could practically hear the sands of time whispering through the hourglass of my life. Swallowing hard, I ran down the hall only to skid to a halt outside my room.

What if—what was his name? Oz?

What if Oz was still here?

I peered past the door frame to my bed. My rumpled den of iniquity was empty. He wasn't in my guest bedroom or the bathroom. Unless he was hiding in a kitchen cabinet, Stevie was the only man here

My mouth was so dry. Had I swallowed a bucket of sand? I downed a tiny Dixie cup of tap water in the bathroom—and then another and another. Maybe I imagined the whole thing. I looked down at the llamas on my pajamas. Could I have dreamed it? An alcohol-induced fever dream? It was possible.

I threw on a red Marchfield Middle staff shirt and jeans. The more I moved, the more I panicked. The more I panicked, the more my head pounded. Too much thinking, and it would probably explode.

My phone beeped while I was brushing my teeth. Val was texting me.

8:25 AM Val: Where are you? The meeting is starting.
8:27 AM Me: Almost out the door. Be there in 10.

I grabbed my purse and keys, stuffing my phone into the back pocket of my jeans. Reaching the door at a jog, my brain sloshing around in my hungover skull, I skidded to a stop in front of it.

An orange sticky note was hanging on the door. Written in silver Sharpie marker was a phone number and the words CALL ME AFTER 4. I stood there dumbly, hearing Carly Rae Jepsen singing *Call Me Maybe* and staring from the note to my desk and back again. Dreams do not hunt through your desk for markers while you're sleeping to leave you cryptic notes.

A part of me wanted to rip up the note and throw the pieces in Stevie's litter box. Another part whispered just go ahead and add the number to my phone contacts. Time was a ticking bomb. I shoved the note in my pocket and ran out the door.

When I got to school, I parked in the last spot available, which, unfortunately, was the farthest from the door. I ran to the front entrance, grabbed the handle, and pulled, but the door didn't budge.

Damn! It was locked! Bruno Mars commiserated with me, singing *Locked Out of Heaven* in my head. I smoothed my hair back with my hand. Had I even brushed it before leaving the house?

I'd learned a long time ago that my brain was different from other people. My doctor called it Attention Deficit Disorder, and I'd lived with it all my life. I could spend hours being distracted by one thing after another. The constant playlist of songs in my head and the towering pile of unfinished novels by the sofa were examples. But I also fixated on things. I could worry over a problem for days, playing every scenario over and over. I might consume every novel by an author in a month or play a video game for an entire weekend, and it also meant I sometimes forgot to put deodorant on or brush my hair.

Pasting a smile on my face, I prayed I didn't look too much like a hungover bum while I pushed the button by the door to talk to the security staff.

"Yes, ma'am. How may I help you?"

Ma'am? Jesus, how old was this guy? I smiled harder into the camera. "Hi, I'm late, and I must have left my ID in the car. Can you let me in? I really need to get to the meeting."

"Sorry, ma'am. If you don't have your ID, I can't let you in the building." His voice sounded smug. Was the security guard pulling a power trip on me today, of all days?

My hate for the adolescent security dude grew as I sprinted back to Green Lightning. My head felt as if it would split open. My left eye began twitching, and my empty stomach was rolling menacingly. That asshole in security was going to pay for this.

Running my hands under the front seat, I pulled out the ratty red lanyard, a gift from the school administration last year. My ID was slightly sticky but attached.

Ignoring the fact that I was out of breath and soaked in sweat, I let myself into the school with as much dignity as I could muster. I glared at the young man—was he even eighteen? He shrugged and lifted his hands like it wasn't his fault.

I struggled to find enough professionalism not to flip him the finger and hurried down the main hallway. Yello was chanting *Oh Yeah* as I ran like Ferris Bueller past the office and the teachers' copy room to the library, hoping to avoid the principal.

Slowly, oh so slowly, I pressed the metal bar to open the door, praying that it would open silently, and I'd be able to sneak into the meeting. The metal latch snapped open with a deafening CLACK, I jumped, losing my grip on the handle, and the door swung wide. In slow motion, I tried to grab it but missed. In horror, I watched it slam against the inside wall, and so did every teacher in the library.

A short woman in a black skirt and jacket was addressing the faculty. "Now this year, all Professional Learning Communities will be expected to keep notes on all their meetings in their PLC notebooks."

The short woman paused and turned to the door. Her eyes narrowed, zeroing in, and she took in the whole breathing hard, sweaty, green around the edges package. She winced and said, "Good morning, Ms. Freemont."

I straightened my spine, focusing only on Val, who was waving and gesturing to the vacant seat at the table next to her. I murmured, "Good morning, Dr. Winters," and hurried over to sink miserably into the seat.

Our principal, Dr. Penelope Winters, was pretty typical for most of the people I'd worked for. Her job entailed keeping both teachers and students in line. She had a few favorites, teachers she gushed about and compared to everyone. She left the rest of us alone unless we messed up.

She cleared her throat. "A reminder to everyone that school starts for all teachers at 8:45 and ends at 4:35."

Val pinched me. "Stop blushing, Audrey. Actually, keep blushing. It makes you look a bit less green."

"Shhhh," I whispered as Dr. Winters's eyes honed in on us, and I wished the floor would open up and swallow me.

Priscilla sat at a nearby table, wiggling her fingers and flashing her big diamond. Dressed in a pink suit, she stood out against a sea of jeans and staff shirts. I caught her studying me with her lips pursed thoughtfully and wondered what that was about.

Dr. Winters nodded directly at me, "I see we have a lot of energy this morning, so let's get right to the icebreaker..."

"Oh God, why?" Keith buried his head in his hands and let out a deep sigh from across the room.

Several teachers laughed, drawing Dr. Winters's attention away from me. She clearly felt we were all children testing the boundaries.

Her spine was stiff as she said, "We have a lot of new faculty this year, so this will be a chance to get to know each other. Priscilla, will you help me attach these cards to everyone's back?"

Pree jumped up eagerly and began taping index-size cards to people's backs. Val and I looked at one another. Our thoughts were clear. She was the Principal's Pet.

"It's important that no one tells anyone or gives any hints about the cards until the game begins. Let's begin." Dr. Winters paused, and everyone sat in dreadful silence while Priscilla finished up the last few tables.

"Everyone in the room has a partner. You need to find your partner by asking each other questions and figuring out what is on your back. Then continue asking questions until you find the person with the matching card. It is taboo to tell anyone exactly what is on a person's back. For example, if it's a spider, you cannot say spider. You must give a hint like it has 8 legs or many people fear it. Does anyone have any questions?"

No one said a word, but the agony in every teacher's posture was clear. Why were we being subjected to this torture? Did principals meet together to discuss the most cringy icebreakers?

"Alright, then. Let's begin." She nodded to Priscilla, who hit play on the sound system. Pharrell Williams began belting out *Happy*.

I grabbed my head, feeling queasy. While other teachers began reluctantly rising and wandering around like zombies, I debated ditching the whole thing and running for the restroom.

Val touched my shoulder. "Are you okay?"

"I'm fine. I think I'm going to go to the restroom. Tell my perfect match I'm sorry."

I turned toward the door, hoping to make a more graceful exit this time. Keeping my eyes down, I started quickly in that direction and ran into a warm brick wall. I bounced off like a rubber ball, staggering. The wall's warm, calloused hands landed on my shoulders, steadying me. My slow brain took a second to catch up—not a wall—a person.

I looked up. "I'm sorry. I–" My words dried up. My eyes skimmed up past very familiar shoulders.

It was him. The guy. What *was* his name? What was he doing here? My stomach lurched. His blank face met my frown. Why was this happening? Mick Jagger drowned out Pharell with "Surprise, Surprise."

Dr. Winters walked up. "Are you both okay? That was quite a collision." She laughed lightly.

I nodded automatically. Then I shook my head. I felt clammy and hot at the same time. Goosebumps broke out on my arms while sweat pooled at the base of my spine. I gestured toward the hallway and the bathroom beyond. "I need to–"

Dr. Winters began introducing us. "This is Oswald Taylor."

Did she not see that I was getting greener by the second? I was going to hurl all over Dr. Winters's ugly brown shoes.

"We've met–" I clapped my hand over my mouth and began backing toward the door.

"Oh?" Dr. Winters was still clueless as to my predicament.

"At happy hour," Oz explained. "Audrey, are you okay?"

"NO!" I ran for the door with my hand over my mouth. The end of the world was chasing me.

Later, I decided it could have been worse. I could have thrown up in front of the faculty or on my boss while my one-night stand, who was somehow also my freaking co-worker, watched.

Chapter 6: Oz

Cherry Bomb

I watched as Audrey flew through the library doors, letting them bang shut behind her. What the hell? What were the chances that the woman who had jumped my bones and rode me like a rodeo star worked at the exact same school I did? But of course, she did—it had been a Marchfield School happy hour! This is what I get for thinking with my dick and not my brain.

Should I go after her? We probably needed to come up with a game plan.

Dr. Winters cleared her throat as she stepped away. "Yes, well, I need to circulate. I'm sure Audrey will be back soon."

As I took a step toward the library doors, a sharp elbow in my ribs stopped me.

"You've got a wiener on your back." Bobby Nooney bounced up and down in her Doc Martens. She smirked at me, a cross between a teacher and a teenager. Reading glasses nestled on top of her short brown hair. She was wearing a t-shirt that said "Never Trust an Atom: They Make Up Everything" under a big flannel shirt. No matter how long we'd been out of the Army, she always surprised me. This elf of a woman was the same person who could shoot a bottle cap off a beer at 100 yards.

"Huh?" I forced myself to focus on Bobby.

"The card? On your back? It's a wiener." Her forehead wrinkled in confusion, and she looked at me strangely.

"I have a penis on my back?" I said, bewildered.

Bobby laughed and shook her head. "Nope. It's a wiener."

I leaned back on the nearby table, anchoring my hands to the edge to keep from pulling out my hair. "What the fuck?"

Bobby dissected me like a bug under a microscope. She knew me better than almost anyone. The strong friendships that develop between soldiers are the only good that comes out of war.

"What's going on with you? You seem more tense than usual." Her tone was light, but she continued to eye me as if I'd grown horns. "You didn't come to happy hour. It might have done you good."

"Yeah, well, the thing is–" I debated whether I wanted to tell Bobby everything. She would find it highly amusing. Especially the part about me falling asleep.

Luckily, I was saved from responding. The library door clicked, and Audrey appeared in the entrance. She entered furtively like she wanted to hide behind a bookshelf for the next hour. Her face was pale, but the green tinge was replaced with pink embarrassment. A dark-haired woman rushed over to her, and they started to whisper.

I felt Bobby watching me as I watched Audrey. "That's Audrey Freemont and Val Bellini. Audrey's the English teacher on your team."

"What do you mean, on my team?" I asked slowly.

Bobby's eyes widened in surprise. "You teach the same group of students and work together to help them become the best little brats that they can be."

Audrey and Val both turned to look at me across the library. The whispers between them turned more heated, and the dark-haired woman threw her hands up wildly.

Bobby was watching the women, too. "That gesturing thing is Italian, for what the hell is wrong with you?" She turned toward me. "What have you done?"

"I'll tell you later," I whispered quickly as Audrey squared her shoulders.

Across the room, the dark-haired woman took a few hesitant steps toward a nearby group, but her eyes flashed between Audrey and me. I was back in high school, watching the girls talk about what I dweeb I was.

Her face was pale as she marched across the room with her lips pressed together.

"Hey, Audrey." Bobby seemed unaware of the mental daggers Audrey was throwing at my head.

Audrey's eyes cut from Bobby to me then narrowed. "You guys know each other?" She and her cat had the same green eyes, and she looked like she was ready to use her claws to tear into me.

Bobby's eyes widened as she looked from me to Audrey and back to me. Her head tilted just a touch to the side. I could almost hear the truth click in her mind.

"Who? Oz?" Bobby laughed. "We were in Afghanistan together. He wouldn't be here without me."

"What do you mean?"

"I told him about the job opening and put in a good word with Winters. We're besties."

Bobby laughed, throwing an arm around my back. Red stared for a second and then her mouth parted in a smile. Just for Bobby.

It felt a little like a needle jammed under my thumbnail.

There were two things I knew at this moment. One, I had fallen into some weird loophole where the hot redhead from last night was also my co-worker. Two, I had no right to be jealous.

Pale skin was tinged blue under Red's eyes. Damn it, no, it was Audrey. I needed to wash my brain out with soap. She was my co-worker and the fact that we'd had great sex last night meant nothing.

I shifted my weight from one leg to the other, leaning toward her. "How are you feeling?"

She searched my eyes for a second, and I wondered what she was looking for. More proof that I was a jerk? Wasn't falling asleep in her bed enough?

Glancing away, I caught Bobby staring again. She smiled at me like a crocodile and turned to Audrey.

"I'm sorry I didn't get over to talk with you last night. You were drinking pretty hard."

She groaned and rolled her eyes. "Don't make me talk about it, Bobby. Reliving it might make me throw up again."

Bobby nodded. "I can bring you some Ibuprofen and water after the meeting."

"I'll take it, but only if I live through this icebreaker."

"I'll let you get to it then." Bobby took a step away from us, but Red—damn it, Audrey—called her back.

"Wait, no! Don't go."

She reached out to grab Bobby's arm. Was she that desperate not to be alone with me in a crowded room?

"I haven't heard how your summer was yet?"

Bobby grinned broadly. "I have some good news. Mel and I are moving in together

A year ago, Bobby called me. She'd met the love of her life. She'd gushed on about the sweet, sexy, new guidance counselor, and it wasn't long before she'd worked up the nerve to ask Mel out. They'd been dating ever since, but Mel wanted to take it slow. It was news to me that they were making this big step, but I was so happy for my friend.

"We've looked at houses and everything." Bobby did a little victory dance.

I hugged her hard. "That's awesome, dude."

"I'm so happy for you both." Red, *damn it, Audrey,* hugged my best friend, and I dismissed the stab of the jealousy needle.

"She's making a respectable woman out of me." Bobby waved to Mel across the library where she helped a few new teachers find their partners.

All around us teachers participated unenthusiastically in the icebreaker. It was obvious no one wanted to participate. Many stopped trying to find their partners and were in small groups.

"I know I can count on you, Oz, to help me move." Bobby poked me in the belly.

I narrowed my eyes at her. "Like you helped me yesterday?"

Bobby shrugged. "We were visiting her parents."

I studied Bobby disbelievingly, raising my right eyebrow.

Audrey's cheeks turned pink. She groaned and hung her head. What was that all about? Couldn't a guy even quirk an eyebrow without upsetting her?

Bobby gave us a calculating look, "Is there something I'm missing here?"

Audrey and I shook our heads simultaneously.

"Nope," I said innocently.

"Uh-uh," Audrey added.

Bobby didn't look at all convinced, but she said, "Okay, I gotta go find my partner. I'll see you guys later." She winked at me before sauntering off to join Mel and the new teachers.

Alone again with Red, *no Audrey,* I took a peek at the card on her back. It was a picture of a short dog with a long body, like a hot dog with feet. Bobby's comment clicked into place. A wiener dog? What were the odds? Audrey was my partner.

The silence stretched between us. I could feel the heat radiate from her body as she stood close to me. My hands itched to touch her. I wanted to tangle my fingers in her hair and kiss and feel her smooth skin. I leaned in and smelled her skin, light and sweet—like apple blossoms in the sun. It was intoxicating.

"Do you know what we are supposed to be doing?" Audrey's voice washed over me like cold water. What the hell was I doing?

"Hell if I know, Red. I was hoping you knew." We laughed together, and I felt hopeful for the first time since she ran into me today. I smiled my slow smile at her that I'd used to get out of trouble since kindergarten.

Then I took it too far. I winked at her.

Audrey's face went from pink to purple in a second. Her hoarse voice was pure rage. "Don't! Don't you dare smile and wink at me!"

I spread my hands wide. Of course, she was right. I needed to apologize first. "I'm sorry about the way it ended last night, Red. I'd spent the whole day driving here and then moving into my house. But falling asleep was-"

"Shut up. Shut up!" Audrey's voice rose. "Don't call me Red! We're at school!"

"It slipped out. I'm trying to think of you as Audrey here, but you were Red the moment I met you."

I put my hand on her shoulder, but she wiggled out from underneath it. How had we gone from laughing together to open hostility with one wink?

"Don't touch me!" Audrey hissed, her face red. "Look, last night was great and all, but now that I know who you are, well, it was a mistake."

She was blowing this all out of proportion, and it irritated me worse than sand in my scrotum.

"Since we have to work together, we'll have to pretend it never happened." She twisted her hands together as she talked.

I narrowed my eyes and crossed my arms over my chest.

She looked at me defensively. "I've been at this school for eight years. It's my second home. People know me here, and I have a good reputation. I will not jeopardize all of that because we slept together once."

She stood there in the school library, lit up from inside. She radiated light like an angry Celtic goddess. Her words were filled with passionate fury. Her arms wrapped her arms around herself in a fierce hug like a cloak of indignity and scorn. I was struck by her beauty.

A smart man would have walked away, but I was pretty sure I was an idiot. All I wanted to do was unwrap her.

I knew I should have reined it in, but my mother always said I have a stubborn streak a mile wide. Give me an ultimatum, and a light bulb clicks on in my brain, and I have to storm the castle or charm the gatekeeper.

In middle school, I got in a lot of trouble. I couldn't let a dare go without acting on it. By high school though, I got away with a lot of shit just by turning on the charm. I was Captain of the Debate Team and Varsity Soccer. If I couldn't talk my way out of trouble, I just head-butted my opponent.

In the military, I used the same skills to convince soldiers to be braver and fight harder than they thought they could. By the time I was twenty-five, I could charm a snake oil salesman into giving me free merchandise. And it was a handy skill for teaching middle school math to kids who thought algebra was boring.

But right here. Right now. Audrey so easily pushed me to my limits. "Now, Darlin', you need to calm down."

"Don't Darlin' me either! And don't tell me what I need!"

"There's no reason to be so angry, sweetheart. No one here needs to know what a dirty girl you are in bed."

"Shut up," she whispered. Her eyes were round and shocked, but her nipples were hard against the thin material of her staff shirt.

"I'll be your secret lover," I whispered.

"Fuck you!" Her voice was loud and angry, and it cut like a knife across the library. Both Audrey and I became aware of a sudden lull in the conversation around us, and the fight seeped out of us as embarrassment skulked in. Everyone turned toward us: sharks smelling blood in the water.

Across the room, Dr. Winters was holding her hand up as a signal for silence. Almost all of the other teachers were raising their hands in acknowledgment of the principal. But all eyes were on us.

Audrey's face was practically purple. I heard her take in a shivery breath, and she looked ready to cry. I immediately felt guilty. What had gotten into me? I didn't argue with women about sex. I had fun and moved on when things got sticky.

But if I were honest with myself, I'd recently been thinking it was time for a change. Time for me to settle down, find a woman, and make a few kids before my genetic time bomb blew up. If I was going to do it, it needed to be soon, but it didn't need to be with Red.

I met Bobby's gaze from across the room. She was standing by the dark-haired woman who was Audrey's friend, and there was murder in her eyes. I was an asshole, and everyone knew it.

The principal lowered her hand and coughed lightly. "Well, now that you've had a chance to find your partners, I thought it would be useful if you talked about what you do for self-care. It's so important that you take the time to put yourself first in this profession; otherwise, you might burn out. Please discuss this with your partner."

All the teachers looked at one another and hastily split into pairs. The silence in the room was palpable. This was the dumbest icebreaker in the world. What could I possibly say about self-care? I lift weights? Sometimes, I eat a whole pint of Ben and Jerry's *Americone Dream*. I masturbate? Fuck me!

I looked at Audrey, an apology on the tip of my tongue. All the fight drained out of me.

"Why are you such an ogre?"

Was she calling me a monster? She'd picked me up in that bar, and now she was turning it all around. My own anger kicked in, but I buried it in humor.

"Me?" Maybe there was still some fight in there after all. "There's nothin' wrong with me, honey. You're the high-strung one."

She did not find it funny. If steam could come out of a woman's ears, Audrey would've been running the closest nuclear power plant. Her eyes actually crossed before she closed them.

She breathed deeply, her chest rising and falling. I stared at her rosy-pink lips as they began silently moving, counting to ten. I was mesmerized, and it wasn't because I was a math teacher.

When Audrey opened her eyes, the green was dark and cool, reminding me of a pond on a hot summer day. She held out her hand. "I apologize for my outburst. I have acted immaturely, and I promise to keep things professional between us. I'm sure you feel the same."

I left her hand hanging there.

"I don't feel the same," I growled, "And you are treading on my nerves, Red. We had sex. We teach school. These things aren't mutually exclusive."

I enjoyed the anger that flashed in her eyes, "Me!" she spluttered. "YOU!" Audrey was being irrational, but the fire in her eyes made me hungry for the woman inside. For Red.

Audrey jabbed her finger in the general direction of my face. She opened her mouth, and I knew she was going to shriek like a redheaded banshee. I set my stance, ready for the battle that was coming. Looking forward to it.

A polite cough interrupted us.

Dragging my eyes up over Audrey's head, I met Dr. Winters's angry glare."Ms. Freemont. Mr. Taylor. I need to see you in my office. Now."

Chapter 7: Audrey

Jamming

"This is the worst start to the school year! I've already been called to the principal's office for a chat about my behavior! *MY behavior*, Val! I should have given you the twenty bucks and skipped happy hour." My voice was muffled from inside the bowels of the copy machine. I lay on my back, looking up under the copy drum, wiggling my fingers into the tight places where misfed paper might be lurking.

Val provided moral support from the top of a nearby conference table. I could see her legs see-sawing back and forth over the edge like she was on a swing.

"I need context. How does your meltdown during the icebreaker connect to happy hour and our bet? And by the way, do I need to beat up the new guy for you?"

"No," I said quietly. I'd told Val during the icebreaker that Oz had called me a hung-over drunk. I regretted it immediately because Val wanted to stalk across the library and smack him. "But happy hour started it all, and now my life is ruined."

I sat up reflexively and hit my head on the manual paper feed. "Ouch, damn it!" I rubbed the sore spot and winced.

My bestie frowned and waited for me to continue. When I maintained my silence, she said, "Go back to the beginning. We were at the bar together. I left you for one dance. When I came back, you were gone."

I loosened a lever and squinted into the mechanism. "It's really all your fault, Val. If you hadn't left me alone at the bar, inebriated–"

Val laughed. "Whoa, whoa, whoa, girl. It was a happy hour. Last time I checked, you were an adult capable of making your own decisions."

I sighed, sitting up and rolling the copier away from the wall. Moving behind it, I opened the door in the back. "I was irrational! And completely wasted! No one should be held accountable under those conditions!"

Val's legs stopped swinging. Her voice grew serious. "Audrey, what did you do?"

"I picked up a guy, Val, and I took him home," I said into the machine without daring to look at her.

A minute passed in silence. Sammy Kershaw twanged *Third Rate Romance* in my head while I pushed and prodded the levers and buttons, searching fruitlessly for the jammed paper. Seconds ticked by slowly, and my anxiety grew until I couldn't stand it anymore. I ducked my head out to look at her.

Val was gaping at me. Her mouth moved as if she tried to breathe air underwater. Finally, she managed, "WHAT?!"

I snorted at her expression. "It was irrational and completely unlike me. But I was blindsided, Val. He came into the bar, and he had these shoulders. Massive shoulders!"

Val gasped dramatically. "Oh no! Not SHOULDERS?!"

I glared at her. "You know my weakness."

"I do," Val nodded solemnly for a moment. "So what happened?"

"I asked him to drive Green Lightning to my apartment."

"You never let anyone drive her! Not even me," Val pouted.

"He didn't even like her! He said she was ugly!"

Val's hands fisted, and she hit the table. "Outrageous! What a jerk. I can't believe you let a jerk drive her!"

"I'll say it again. I was both wasted and irrational."

"And hot for a bologna pony, apparently," Val responded wryly.

I wiggled my eyebrows. "I may have offered to ride his stick shift."

Val hugged her belly, laughing. I returned my attention to replacing the cover on the back of the printer. Opening the side panel, I hid my flushed cheeks. Rehashing this whole story was giving me a headache, so I changed the subject. "This thing is a beast! Who just leaves the copier jammed and walks away?"

"Maybe it was jammed all summer," Val suggested.

"Possible," I agreed.

"Finish your drunk sex story," she demanded. I should have known it wouldn't be that easy to distract her. Val had the tenacity of a pit bull.

"I don't remember any of it. It's a blank void," I lied.

Val wiggled her eyebrows at me. "Oh, hell, no, honey. I don't care if you have to make some shit up, tell me a story!"

Even though my head was in the copy machine, I could practically see the determined set to her jaw and the tilt of her head. I'd been friends with Val for five years. On her first day at Marchfield, we teamed up to play *Minute to Win it* Faculty Style, threw more M&Ms into a two-liter bottle than any other team, and won victory for the 8th grade. We've been besties ever since. I don't keep secrets from her. I sighed, knowing I wasn't leaving this room without spilling the tea.

I untangled myself from the copier, walked over to the conference table, and sat next to her. "Well, Val, what would you want to hear?"

Val smiled wickedly. "I have a few clarifying questions. Was it great sex? Did you feel a magical connection? Did the stars align, and the birds sing? Did you turn into a Disney princess?"

I laughed despite myself. "Stop. I'll tell you the truth. It was really great sex. Phenomenal sex. Crazy, howling at the moon, wild monkey sex."

Val clapped her hands in delight. "Now we're getting somewhere! Go on."

"I swear, Val, I heard Marvin Gaye and Barry White singing a duet."

Val doubled over, her shoulders shaking. "You're making me jealous."

"Maybe I was just primed after my epic dry spell or completely drunk, but I think it might have been the best orgasm I've ever had."

Val pursed her lips. "You'll have to take him for a second spin." She paused, eyes widening. "Or did you? Is that why you were late today? You dog!"

I slid off the table and stuck my head back into the printer, trying to act casual. "I actually didn't have time for a second test drive. He fell asleep on me."

"You were late because you were trapped all night under him?" Val's eyes twinkled with humor." And it wasn't until this morning that he rolled off? Poor you."

"Val, I worry about your sick sense of humor sometimes." I sat down on the floor in front of the machine. "He fell asleep after we had sex, so I climbed off him—"

Val cheered. "Riding him like a cowgirl, huh? Juicy,"

"Stop." I rolled my eyes at her and went back to fixing the printer.

"So he paddled up Coochie Creek and then fell out of the boat. Not the best first impression. So what did you do?"

Checking the last possible location for the jam, I stalled coming clean to Val, my fingers finally touched the crisp edge of the paper. "I found the jam."

"Is that what they are calling it now?" Val laughed, lying back on the table, legs dangling while her shoulders shook.

Tugging on the warm, crumpled paper, I eased it out a few inches. "You're terrible. Worst friend ever."

Val sat up and shrugged. "I'm funny, and you love me."

60

"You're absolutely hilarious," I added flatly.

"Keep talking, sister." She tapped her foot impatiently.

"Well, after he fell asleep, I tried to snuggle, but he rolled over and kicked me out of my own bed."

Val sang the nursery rhyme. "'There were two in the bed and the little one said, Roll over. And he rolled over and you fell out?'"

"Exactly. So, I took a shower, put on my pajamas–"

Val gasped and jumped off the table. "Hold up! Tell me you put on the sexy lingerie I made you buy last year."

"I wanted to be comfortable."

"Please, I'm begging you. Please, say you did not put on the llamas!" She dropped to her knees, praying for my good fashion sense.

I kept my eyes down on the sheet of paper, slowly unfurling from the copier. "Well..."

She groaned, slapping her palm into her forehead dramatically. "I'm burning those things the next time I come over! Honey, the Llama Reading Mama pjs are not for overnight guests of the opposite sex."

"He. Was. Asleep," I argued. "I felt stalkerish, so I waited for him to wake up in the living room. But then I fell asleep on the sofa, and–"

"The sofa?! Girl! You had a man in your bed for the first time in years, and you put on your llama pajamas and slept on the sofa?" Val threw up her hands. "Have I taught you nothing?"

I heard good old Frank Sinatra singing *The September of My Years*. I sighed. "You know what? It doesn't matter. I'm giving up on relationships. They're not for me. I'll be a spinster

English teacher for another 40 years. Then I'll retire, adopt three dogs, and tend my garden year-round."

"You better buy a good vibrator, too." Val sat back down on the table and chewed her lip thoughtfully.

"Great idea! Send me your recommendations." I gave one last pull, and the paper came loose from the printer. I closed the panel and restarted the machine.

Val sighed. "Does he want to see you again?"

My verbal response was lightning-fast, "No!"

But I remembered the sticky note on my door, and I could hear him offering to be my secret lover. "I don't know. Maybe."

"I swear you're driving me crazy, Aud! What does that mean?"

"He left while I was still asleep, but–"

"BUT?" Val prodded. "You might as well tell me the whole thing. You know I'm like a badger and will dig out all of your dirty secrets."

"He left me his number," I sighed.

"Great! You should call him. Better yet, let me call him."

"I'm not calling him, and neither are you."

"Why not? Maybe he took his contacts out or has terrible eyesight and didn't see you in those llama pajamas."

I dreaded telling her this last part. "I'm not calling him because when I saw him again, he was a real jerk," I hedged.

"You saw him again? How is that possible? When?"

Gritting my teeth, I said, "Today."

Val gasped. "OH MY GOD!"

She jumped up off the table and danced a little jig with her hand over her mouth. She reached out, took my shoulders in both of her hands and sang, "You had sex with the new guy!"

"Shush, Val!" I groaned. "He's irritating, unprofessional, and–"

"And big and handsome! He does have awesome shoulders."

"You don't understand," I whined as she danced around the copy room laughing.

She stopped suddenly and whirled to face me. "That's why you were so crazy during the icebreaker." She gasped. "You lied to me!"

"I'm sorry. We only had a minute, and it was so embarrassing!"

"Forgiven." Val laughed. "And embarrassing, for sure. He saw you in those jammies!"

"Oh, stop, Val," I whined.

"In the meeting, you let me think he'd been mean to you! I was going to beat him up for you after school!"

The printer beeped, declaring itself ready. Shaking my head at her, I grabbed the Welcome to 8th Grade English newsletter I needed to copy. Turning back to the machine, I heard the door to the room open behind me.

Priscilla Henesey breezed in, "Hi all! All done with the printer?" She didn't wait to hear the answer. She put her page into the copier and pressed print. "I need 300 of these for the PTA Open House."

She turned to look at me while papers spit out into the tray. "What are y'all up to?"

Val smirked. "Oh, not much. Audrey just finished feeling up the copier."

I managed to hold it together as Priscilla's gaze switched from me to Val. Eventually, she shrugged and said, "Did y'all hear? I'm looking for nominations for Teacher of the Year!"

Of course she was.

"I nominate my friend, Audrey."

"And I nominate Val."

Pree shook her head, "No, sillies, I am looking for someone to nominate me."

Don't roll your eyes. Don't roll your eyes.

Priscilla was the perfect blend of busybody, brown-noser, political hand shaker, and bully. Winters loved her. She loved giving workshops highlighting her expertise and giving strategies to improve the rest of us. Why did the administration always reward the most annoying people with titles?

I managed to choke out, "Wow! That's exciting," but my tone was flat.

Val poked me and did a much better job faking her enthusiasm. "You deserve it, Pree. I hope you win."

Priscilla nodded graciously to Val before turning her steely gaze back on me. "You looked positively green this morning, Audrey. Are you well?"

She snickered lightly, in an insincere, tinkly way that sounded more like nails on a chalkboard to me.

I tried to keep the irritation from my voice. "I'm fine."

"I certainly hope you aren't having morning sickness or anything." Priscilla cackled as if the thought of me being pregnant was a hilarious joke.

I'm typically a very calm, patient person. But who the hell says that? I debated slamming the stop button on Priscilla's print job and throwing all her papers in her face.

Instead, I laughed like she'd caught me. "Actually, Pree, it's too soon to tell. I'll get back to you."

Priscilla's mouth dropped open, and she struggled to form words. It was extremely satisfying to watch.

"Maybe we can have a joint wedding and baby shower?" I crossed the room to the door and sailed out to Adele, belting out the chorus of *Rumor Has It* in my head.

"Wait!" Val chased me down the hall, her sandals slapping on the gray linoleum floor. "That was epic!"

She lifted her hand for a high-five, and I smacked her palm. The sound was loud in the empty hallway.

"I'm sure Pree is in there right now, texting her evil group chain to watch for my baby bump."

Val laughed. "I can't wait to see who's the first to ask when you're due!"

"I bet it's Dr. Winters. She and Priscilla seem really tight this year."

"I heard they went to a conference together in Colorado this summer and shared a room."

"Ew." I shuddered and started off down the hall toward my room.

"What are you going to do now?" Val asked.

"Is it too early for lunch?"

"It's 10 in the morning, and we have a meeting in half an hour."

"I miss summer," I sighed.

"Same," Val agreed.

"Well, since I can't make my copies, I guess I can't avoid it anymore."

"Avoid what?"

"Dr. Winters made it very clear I needed to apologize to Oz for my unprofessional behavior."

"Sounds like a logical next step."

It seemed so unfair. I'd had an amazing one night stand on the last day of summer. Now, I had to apologize to him, my co-worker, for losing my temper.

"He was the one acting inappropriately," I whined,

"You told him to fuck off. In school. In front of the entire faculty." Val's deadpan description took the wind out of my sails.

"Okay, it's obvious I need to pull up my big girl panties and apologize." I straightened my shoulders.

"That's a solid plan."

"Then I'm going to do what any introvert in this situation would do. I'm going to hide in my classroom and avoid him. Oz is the plague for the rest of the school year."

Val shook her head slowly. "That might be hard to do."

I gave her a questioning look. Thomas Barrandon started singing *Doomsday Clock*, and I knew. I knew whatever Val was going to say was going to be very, very bad.

Val grimaced. "He's on your team."

I opened my mouth to say something extremely uncool for school but snapped my mouth shut so hard, I bit my tongue. Val wasn't finished.

"And he's in the classroom right across the hall from yours."

Chapter 8: Oz

Wicked Game

"Whose idea was it to put bulletin boards in classrooms?" I complained to Bobby as we sat on top of small group tables in my new classroom.

Everything was a disorganized mess. Thirty desks and matching thirty chairs were pushed into corners and stacked haphazardly. Dirty off-white concrete block walls with dried tape and pencil smudges closed in around me. A large dry-erase board dominated the front of the room. Empty bulletin boards filled the other walls, reminding me a little of the training rooms at Fort Leonard Wood.

My previous classroom decorating skills consisted of lining up the desks and slapping a few football and soccer posters on the walls. What the hell was I supposed to do with bulletin boards?

Of course, the anger inside me had nothing to do with decorating the damn things. Being schooled by Red this morning had been bad enough, but being sent to the principal's office had pushed me to the edge. Was I nine? I didn't fucking care about the boards. I was looking for a fight.

Bobby composed her face into a semblance of mock seriousness. "Assholes! How dare they want teachers to have a space to display student work or motivational messages!"

"I'm a math teacher, Bobby. What the hell am I supposed to do with these fucking corkboard monstrosities?"

Bobby laughed harder. "Corkboard monstrosities? That might be a touch excessive."

"I've seen all the lady teacher posts on Insta. Pink paper backgrounds with those matching border things and sparkly letters spelling out shit like Student Spotlight and Reading Rainbow."

Bobby's laugh was more of a witchy cackle this time. "Think of it as a challenge. If we, lady teachers, can do it, you can too."

"Why do I fucking have three of them though? I teach math. I need whiteboards. Not these archaic torture implements." I threw up my hands in exasperation and paced away.

Tears of laughter rolled down Bobby's face. "Archaic torture–" She gasped for breath as her shoulders shook.

"Fuck you, Bobby."

Bobby wiped her eyes with her hands. "Just imagine it... a bunch of stodgy old guys from the Department of Education sitting around a conference table discussing how many bulletin boards will drive a math teacher insane. It's the old lollipop commercial—a one, a two, a three—math teacher screams—three boards it is."

I stared at her stone-faced. I rolled my shoulders, shook my head, and reminded myself that this woman was a sister to me. It didn't stop me from sometimes wishing I could choke her.

"I'll tell you what. I'll put up your bulletin boards if–" She rolled her eyes. "You tell me what happened between you and Audrey in the faculty meeting."

Her words blew the frustration and anger right out of me and left me feeling hollow and anxious. I'd known this was coming.

"It's stupid." I sat back down on a student desk.

"Well. I'm free until noon when I'm going out to lunch with Mel. You aren't invited, by the way, 'cause it's a middle-of-the-school-day date." Bobby beamed. "So spill it, Oz. Tell good old Dr. Roberta what's up?"

Bobby knew just how to push my buttons, but I was a glutton for punishment. I wanted her perspective on Audrey.

"Well, Dr. Roberta, for your information, I did go to happy hour yesterday." Bobby's eyes widened, and I smiled with the satisfaction of surprising her.

"You did? How come I never saw you?" I could see the tiny hamsters racing around the wheels of her mind.

I crossed my arms over my chest. "A certain Ms. Audrey Hot-Pants Freemont met me at the door with an offer I couldn't refuse."

Bobby slapped her hand over her mouth. I would have laughed if I wasn't so irritable. It was damn hard to leave Bobby speechless.

"WHAT?!" was all she could say when she recovered. "Are you sure?"

"Am I sure? What the fuck does that mean?"

Bobby shook her head hard. "Are you *sure* it was Audrey?"

"Fuck, yeah, Bobby."

"So Audrey Freemont—the little redhead with pale skin and freckles—jumped you in the bar?"

"She told me her name in the car, but I called her Red."

"I bet she hated that."

I smiled, remembering the sound of her orgasm. "Not really."

"How did you two meet? I mean, I never even saw you."

"She walked up, rubbed her hot body all over mine, and kissed me. Then she dragged me into the parking lot and did it again."

Bobby coughed harshly, and I clapped her on the back with my palm. This would've been funny if I wasn't so annoyed.

"It's so out of character," she gasped in a breath. "Audrey is a great person, friend, and teacher, but she's kinda wound tight."

"Well, she was tossing back shots before I got there, so maybe they loosened her up. How the hell would I know, Bobby?"

"Okay. Okay. Tell me the rest of it."

"I drove her home in her ugly, green excuse for a car 'cause she'd had a lot to drink. I was gonna jog home–"

"Three miles." We both knew that was practically a walk in the park for me.

"She made me laugh. I'll admit, she turned me on, but she was drunk. I was going to walk her to her door and go, but she wrapped her body around me until I couldn't see straight."

"Holy shit!" Bobby had obviously recovered her usual eloquence. "Audrey?"

Bobby lay back on the desk, her arms and legs dangling off the sides. "I mean, Audrey's hot in a kind of unaware-of-it way. You're absolutely sure it was Audrey?"

My hands fisted. But this was a civilized world, so I reined in my anger. "Did you see any other hot redheads in the bar last night?"

Bobby thought for a second. "Nope."

"So, of course, I'm sure, you idiot." I practically shouted at her, my hands thrown in aggravation. I was regretting ever telling Bobby anything. Kissing and telling was not my usual style.

She sat up with a wild look in her eyes. "But that doesn't explain why she was so angry this morning. Wait... were you premature?"

She cackled wickedly again. I counted to ten while picturing her in a pointy black hat, stirring her witch's cauldron. She had a big green wart on her nose.

"Shut up, Roberta."

"Couldn't get it up? There are pills for that, dude!" She lay back on the tabletop, laughing riotously.

"Damn it, Bobby!" I jumped up and stalked to the door and opened it. "Get out."

"Whoa, cowboy," she said, sitting up fast. "I'm sorry if I insulted your manly ego. Tell me what happened."

"Don't laugh, but I would appreciate your advice." I knew she would laugh her ass off, but I just wanted a few minutes before it happened. I shut the door and sat back down on the table.

She crossed her heart and then held up her left hand. "I swear."

I rolled my eyes. "I fell asleep after."

"Slept over?" she asked.

"Like fell face down in the bed and didn't move for hours."

"Yeah, but you held her after, right?"

"I'll remind you that I moved a house load of boxes and furniture by myself because my friend was too busy to help me. I was basically asleep on my feet when I walked into that bar."

"Holy shit, man! Did you pin her under your huge biceps?" Bobby laughed so hard she almost fell off the table.

I rubbed the pulse points on the sides of my head, a headache brewing from listening to her hysterical peals of laughter.

Bobby hiccupped. Her face was red. "Thank you for moving to Virginia and getting a job at Marchfield. What happened next?"

"You are making me regret my life choices, Bobby." But I knew if I really wanted advice, I should rip the Band-Aid off the rest of this story and get it over with. "That isn't what really pissed her off."

Bobby wiped her eyes again, so she could look at me clearly. "What else could you possibly have done?"

I groaned, imagining punching one of those infernal boards. I imagined crushing it under my fist with a satisfying thud. It would have been so satisfying, but no corkboard was hurt in the making of my humiliation.

"Fuck, Bobby, maybe it was the shock of being introduced to me as her coworker by the damn principal."

"You didn't tell her your name? What is wrong with you?"

I turned to glare at her. "I was a little busy kissing the lady, but yes, we did exchange names."

"I guess you neglected to tell her why you were invited to *faculty* happy hour."

"I was fucking surprised to see her sneaking in the library door too." I shrugged. "Neither one of us really had a lot of time to talk about our professions."

Bobby snickered. "Cause you fell asleep."

"I blame you for it all, Bobby. I wouldn't even have been at that happy hour, but you sent me a hundred texts–"

"Ten! I sent you ten texts."

"And guilted me into going. I shouldn't have even been there."

"Don't blame your sexual frustrations on me, Oz. I'm gay." Bobby smirked.

I rolled my eyes at her. "Just let me tell you the rest of this so I can go hide in the men's room where you can't laugh at me."

Bobby straightened her face. "Okay, I'm ready. Lay it on me."

"After you left, Red got snooty. She set me straight and told me how things were going to be."

"Oh, fuck."

"It put my back up, and I egged her on, and then we got busted by Winters."

And then it hit me. I was a grown-ass man, and I'd been an immature brat because I liked Red. No matter how hard she pushed me away, I wanted to know more.

Bobby snorted, "Damn, Oz, you have such a way with the ladies." She stood up to give me a standing ovation.

"Oz, you're my best friend in the whole world, but you're an idiot." She started to launch into a lesson on how to treat women when, thank God, there was a knock on the door. She jumped up to open it.

"Oh, hey, Bobby."

I heard Audrey's voice float into the room, and I was struck by the sudden image of her moving above me, with her beautiful breasts filling my hands and mouth. I laid my hands in my lap.

She stuck her head into the room. "Can I come in?"

I shrugged, trying to keep my face blank.

The dark-haired woman from the faculty meeting came in behind her. They hovered close to the door. Red probably wanted to say what she needed to and run.

Bobby greeted them. "Hey, Val. Hey, Audrey. We were just talking about–"

"About bulletin boards," I interrupted, shooting Bobby a glare. "I have three too many."

Bobby laughed. "He's being tortured with too much corkboard by the Department of Education."

Audrey didn't seem to have a response to that. She rubbed her temples as if to soothe a headache as I had a few moments ago. She looked at Val and gave an almost imperceptible nod toward Bobby.

Val waved at me cheerfully, but her brown eyes were serious. "Nice to meet you, Oz. I'm Val, Audrey's bestie, so watch yourself."

Something about the way she said it made my balls shrivel a little. I stood, nodding once.

Val turned to my friend. "Hey, Bobby, let's go grab a snack from the cafeteria."

"But," Bobby hesitated. She turned from Audrey to me. Obviously, she wanted to stay for the entertainment. She sighed, following Val out and closing the door behind her.

Red's, *I mean, Audrey's* eyes darted around the room, anywhere but at me. Her back was so straight she could've been shot out of a bow. "Oz, I overreacted today in the library. I'm so sorry. Can we start over as friends?"

She walked over and stuck her hand out. Her eyes were focused somewhere on the wall behind my head. She was probably looking at one of the damn bulletin boards.

I took her hand to shake it. My voice was low when I spoke, and I smiled slowly. "I'd love to be your friend, Audrey. I'll even negotiate the benefits."

The heat of her palm meeting mine was like standing in the desert sun. Her wide eyes jumped to mine, and I dove into the cool green pools. Suddenly, friendship was the last thing on my mind. Squeezing her hand, I ran my thumb across the skin between her thumb and index finger. I felt the shiver travel up her spine and heard her breath hiss in.

This woman brought out the devil in me.

Her eyes flashed to mine, and I could see the battle and then the war inside them. She was attracted to me, but she was going to deny it.

Audrey yanked her hand away. She cleared her throat, speaking quickly. "We work with children, Oz. Impressionable children. We're role models, and that demands that we maintain a professional relationship."

I took a step toward her. "I can be professional, Red," I whispered near her ear. The smell of her skin was warm and flowery, reminding me of the smell of her sheets when I woke up this morning.

For a second, she leaned toward me. I could feel the heat of her breasts, and I wanted to ease forward and pull her in. I waited, wondering what she would do. She bit her lower lip, working it between her white teeth. I thought she might kiss me. I willed her to do it.

Audrey coughed, taking two steps back. She edged closer to the door. "I'm not sure there is a professional bone in your body, but the fact remains that we have to work together. If you can't at least pretend to be a professional educator, I will have to make a complaint to the administration."

I put my hands on my hips. If she wanted to play with fire, so could I. "And I'll be happy to explain how *warmly* you welcomed me at the school's happy hour."

She gasped. Her hand flew to her mouth, covering those soft, pink lips. "You wouldn't dare!"

"Try me, Red." I threw the proverbial gauntlet down.

Color flooded her face, and her eyes sizzled with red-hot anger. I cocked my hip against the damn bulletin board and smirked.

She stood up straight, all five foot five inches of her, and her voice was cold and dismissive. "There's no reasoning with you, so I'll do my best to stay out of your way. I would appreciate it if you would do the same."

Whirling away from me, she yanked open my classroom door. Bobby and Val, who'd been listening at the door, practically fell into the room. Red pushed through them and stormed across the hall. She disappeared into the classroom opposite mine and slammed the door behind her.

Bobby shook her head. "You're hopeless, dude. Absolutely hopeless."

I felt some gratification in slamming the door in her face.

Chapter 9: Audrey

Calm Like a Bomb

The rest of teacher orientation week flew by. I kept my classroom door closed, avoiding Oz and racing through my to-do lists. Before I knew it, Labor Day weekend was over, and students filled the empty desks in my classroom.

Thursday afternoon, after the dismissal bell rang, I slipped off my shoes and sat at my desk with a groan. My body ached, my head hurt, and I had to pee. Most of them were really nice, but the typical ten percent were a handful.

My classroom was already a mess, and I needed to do a thousand things before leaving school. I started to prioritize the list when Val walked in.

"Girl, is wrangling teens and pre-teens harder this year, or is it just me?" Val's dark hair was piled up in a messy bun with a pencil stuck through it. She pulled out a chair from the small group table and sat down, kicking off her fancy brown INEZ heels.

"Stop talking. My head hurts. I'm exhausted." I sounded as whiny as a class of students assigned an essay for homework. Not that I ever did that.

She looked at me critically. "You know what would help relax you? Another night of shoulder action."

I groaned. "Stop."

She'd told me repeatedly throughout teacher orientation that I was blowing this thing with Oz out of proportion. Maybe she was right, but after being chewed out by the principal on the first day of school, I wasn't taking chances. I'd cursed myself for wanting a summer of fun and the excitement of a one night stand. All I really needed was job security, Stevie, and Netflix.

I can't say I never saw Oz. I did. I even might've given myself the tiniest of chances to remember the steely softness of his muscles and skin, but only when I was sure he wasn't looking. Of course, as soon as I realized what I was doing, I'd force myself to look away.

Val shrugged. "I'm just saying, there are studies that show sexually satisfied women experience more success in all areas of their lives."

I rested my forehead in my hands. "You're making that up."

"It's true." She laughed. "Want me to cite sources?"

I grabbed a sticky note, squished it into a ball, and threw it at her. Ignoring her look of shocked innocence, I grabbed a dry-erase marker and started writing tomorrow's goal on the whiteboard.

"Oh! I forgot all about why I came in here in the first place!" Val said. "I wanted to see if you wanted to have your students enter The Art of the Military Child Contest. It's a writing contest, too."

"Sure. That's a great idea." We had a lot of students at our school who were affiliated with the military. Growing up in the military was hard, and I knew firsthand how challenging it was.

As the daughter of a career Navy sailor, I changed towns and schools like lonely, single women change the batteries in their vibrators.

Picking up discarded pencils off the floor and straightening up my classroom, I remembered how Dad and Mom always made moving into an adventure. New places and friends, a fresh start, but I secretly dreamed of a real home—the kind that wasn't in a military housing development and changed every two years. I prayed for a school where everyone had known me since kindergarten and I was part of the gang.

I lived in fear of every new military assignment, every new city, but moving wasn't what I should have been afraid of.

I'd just turned eleven, and I was angry that Dad hadn't been at the party. I sat sullenly in Mrs. Rease's sixth-grade classroom, pretending to concentrate on a word problem when the secretary called for me to report to the office. My mom was there, waiting with my two older brothers, their eyes wet and red.

It was like trying to listen underwater. A horrible explosion. Three other sailors were killed. No bodies recovered. My daddy was dead.

Val was still explaining about the contest, but I wasn't listening.

My mom had never gone to college, never worked outside of the house, and dad's military death benefits didn't make ends meet. I remembered returning to school a few weeks later with no lunch. A week later, Mrs. Rease announced the annual sixth-grade field trip to visit the state capital. Which one? I didn't know or care. We didn't have the money. I balled up the permission slip and never showed it to my mother.

As an adult, I recognized I needed the structure my military upbringing instilled in me. I'd lived in Marchfield for eight years, the longest I'd ever lived in one place. I thrived in the familiarity of the town and the school, and I'd do anything to ensure that I never had to give that up.

Looking out my door and across the hallway, I saw the chaos in Oz's classroom. Even from my room, I could see the desks were scattered and balls of paper littered the floor.

"He's such a mess." I closed my door.

"Who?" Val dropped the contest information on the table and looked at me. "Oz?"

"He's one of those teachers who needs to be friends with the kids. He lets the children sit on the floor, and they talk constantly."

"I heard him bellowing algebraic expressions at the kids yesterday. 2x minus 10 divided by 5 = y. He must have said it five times before they even started working on the problem." Val snickered.

I rolled my eyes. "If he keeps screeching like an overwhelmed papa bird, he's going to lose his voice," I said while writing the agenda on the board.

Val wiggled her eyebrows. "You sound a little worried about poor Oz." Her voice was full of innuendo.

"I'm not worried. It's disruptive. And annoying."

"I'm sure it is."

"Honestly, it's good I came to my senses before the school year really started. We're complete opposites."

Val laughed. "I'll agree his bulletin boards are a disgrace. Bobby went to all that trouble and he only stapled a formula sheet on each one."

I felt a bit of vindication. Oz was not the 'one' for me. His lack of imagination in crafting a bulletin board assured me I'd made the right decision.

I was about to say as much when the classroom phone rang. Putting it to my ear, I heard Rhoda, the principal's administrative assistant, ask me to please come down to meet with Dr. Winters.

Val laughed as I raced back to my desk for my shoes. "Oooooooooooooh, Audrey's in trouble."

Just like when you're a kid, being called to the office is an *Oh shit, what have I done now?* moment. And it was happening after only three days of school? I played scenario after scenario in my head. To say I was nervous was an understatement.

"I'll text you later," Val called as I walked out into the hallway.

And then I saw him. Oz. He must have left his classroom only moments before. His burgundy dress shirt skimmed over his back and shoulders, and his black pants hugged his butt as he walked down the hallway in the same direction I needed to go. My first instinct was to stare. My second was to hide. I settled for tiptoeing down the hall behind him.

At the end of the hall, he turned right. Damn it. He was going to the office too! A sense of dread gathered in my stomach. Had we been summoned together? Did Dr. Winters know I was avoiding him? Or worse, did she know that we'd slept together? Oh God! My brain exploded with a hundred *What Ifs* all set to the beat of Kane Brown's song.

My eyes were glued to his shoulders as I turned down the main hallway behind him.

One minute I was upright and the next I was stumbling. I'd tripped over something. A tiny sixth-grader, carrying an enormous cello case three times her size, dashed in front of me. What was she doing here?

The black case bounced, knocking the little girl's unzipped backpack off her shoulder and up into the air. A stack of library books she was carrying fell to the floor as the instrument ricocheted off the wall and buried itself neck-first in an open locker. Crumpled papers floated down to cover the floor.

"Oh, sweetie, I'm sorry," I said in my most calm, soothing voice while I looked around. Where was my right shoe? Dave Mathews started singing *Crash Into Me* on my mental playlist.

Before I could find my shoe under one of the five open library books on the floor, the girl burst into tears. I started to grab all of her things, stuffing papers and books into her K-Pop backpack.

I glanced a few feet toward the security desk. The security jerk who hadn't helped me on the first day of school scowled at us. "Is there a problem here?"

"Is that a rhetorical question?" I gestured to him to help us pick up the remaining papers, but he sniffed and crossed his arms over his chest.

The 6th grader continued to cry big, wet tears down her red face. Her bottom lip trembled. "It's okay. All we need to do is get your cello."

I walked over to the locker and tugged on the big, awkward black case, expecting it to slide out easily. No such luck. I grabbed onto the handle and pulled hard, actually leaning back, but it didn't budge. It was stuck on the lock mechanism.

I could hear the miniature munchkin sniffling behind me. "Don't worry, sweetie…"

A deep, slightly amused voice interrupted me. "Hey, hey, what's happening here?"

I looked over and followed some impressive legs up the front of that burgundy shirt. Shit! No, no, no. Why did he have to turn around?

The little girl hiccupped softly.

"Is that your cello?" Oz gestured to the locker and the instrument in the locker.

She nodded, and Oz smiled at her. "Let's see if I can help Ms. Freemont get your cello out. Does she have a name?"

She looked at him blankly.

He gestured to the cello case. "I'd call her Cherry. You know Cherry Cello."

The little girl giggled, craning her neck up to look at him.

I melted a little. He was a natural with kids. "Or if you think of it as a he, then Chuck."

Smiling, I lifted the lip of the case off of the lock, freeing the cello.

"It's 3:43 PM, all students should have already vacated the property," the security jerk announced from his desk. Oz and I helped the girl get all of her stuff outside to her mom's car.

We waved goodbye as they drove off and started back inside. Security jerk was nowhere in sight.

"You know what the moral of this story is?"

I braced myself. "Cellos are a nuisance?"

He shook his head. "You gotta always look down. Those 6th graders are mice. I accidentally bump into one every other day. I ran into that exact same one yesterday."

I wanted to laugh, but I swallowed it down with a cough.

Oz rolled his eyes. "It was out at the bus loop. She came sneaking up behind me, and I hip-checked her right into the bushes. I had to fish her and the freaking cello out."

For a second, I forgot all the reasons I didn't like Oz, and I chuckled. I met his crooked smile and had to mentally slap myself.

"I need to go. I was summoned to the office." I tried to speed-walk the final yards down the hall, but Oz matched my pace.

"Me too. Why does it feel as bad as an adult as it did when I got caught starting a food fight in the 6th grade?"

My heart swelled a little. He understood. He knew exactly how I felt, and I wanted to hug him.

This time my mental slap actually hurt. I needed to get it together.

Rhoda looked up from her desk and smiled. That was a good sign, right? If we were in trouble, she wouldn't have smiled. Would she?

"I was wondering if you two were coming."

I almost... almost... laughed. Dirty eighth-grade humor is something I've never outgrown. Sometimes, Val says the word "duty" to me just to crack me up.

Rhoda's voice cut through my amusement. "She's in her office and wants to see both of you together." I felt ice-cold anxiety return.

***

My mind flashed back to the last time I'd been here after the icebreaker, and Dr. Winters had spoken to each of us separately.

"I'm disappointed in what I saw and heard today in the library, Ms. Freemont," she began. "No teacher in my school is allowed to speak in such a way to a colleague, especially a new teacher. I will not tolerate it."

My hands curled into fists as I held myself rigid. I swallowed hard, trying to hold back the tears that stung the corners of my eyes. Following the rules and being a good employee was important to me. How had I lost sight of that?

"I'm so sorry," I started, but she cut me off.

"You have taught in this school for many years. You know I hold my staff to the highest of standards, and yet you arrived tardy and hungover today. I never expected to have to speak with you like this, and if I ever have to again, there will be serious repercussions."

I blinked hard and sniffled. "What type of repercussions?"

"Well, I suppose I might move one of you to a different grade level or possibly initiate our transfer to another school, but we're not at that point."

My stomach clenched, and I wanted to sink through the floor. "Trust me, it will never happen again."

"Since he was in the military, I'm certain Mr. Taylor is used to that sort of language, but I don't want any of the faculty to associate Marchfield Middle with cussing and drinking. I expect you to apologize to Mr. Taylor by the end of the day."

***

Trying not to freak out, I walked past Rhoda.

Dr. Winters looked up and saw us through the open door. "Come in."

Inside the spacious office, Dr. Winters sat behind a large wooden desk. Framed diplomas hung on the wall behind her. She was wearing a beige blazer over a black blouse, and her straight light brown hair was neatly combed. She gestured to the two upholstered chairs. Sitting, I distracted myself by looking at the happy photos of her French bulldogs.

"Thanks for coming down." Dr. Winters smiled. "I trust the two of you have worked things out?"

I nodded and saw Oz do the same out of the corner of my eye.

"Excellent because I need a favor, and since it involves you working together, I thought we should discuss it. We need a girls' soccer coach."

I almost laughed out loud. She wanted me to coach soccer? That was the best joke I'd heard all week. The most I knew about soccer was that David Beckham married Posh Spice, and suddenly I was jamming to *Wannabe*. Not helpful at all.

"Mr. Taylor," Dr. Winters continued, "You played soccer in high school and college, so you were my first choice. However, since you're a new teacher, and it is a girls' team–"

Oh, crap. The pieces were falling into place.

"I thought it would be perfect if Ms. Freemont was your assistant coach."

"But–" So many reasons why this wouldn't work flooded my brain, but Dr. Winters cut me off.

"Oh, I know you don't have any formal soccer experience, Audrey, but I'm sure you'd be very helpful to Oz as his assistant coach. Plus, you're an excellent organizer, and the girls really need to have an adult female as part of the team. It's really a fantastic solution." She folded her hands in front of her and beamed at us.

Fantastic? Not only did I know absolutely nothing about soccer, this was going to force me to spend time with Oz. Every day of school. For weeks. Months.

"Sure," Oz said casually. Of course, he didn't need time to think this over. A dark voice laughed in my mind. Was this his idea of revenge?

I could feel the pressure gathering at the back of my skull. I knew with one hundred percent certainty that Dr. Winters would knock down my next evaluation from Exemplary to Average. I'd always said yes before. Student Council Sponsor, National Junior Honor Society Advisor, Debate Coach—I'd always been a team player before. She would question it if I wasn't now. And then what?

Pain pulsed behind my eye to the beat of *Lonesome Loser* by the Little River Band. There was no way I could get out of this without the whole sordid one-night stand story rearing its ugly head. I'd made one bad choice, and the cosmos was having a huge laugh at my expense. I had no choice but to be Marchfield Middle's new Assistant Girls' Soccer Coach.

"Ms. Freemont?"

Dr. Winters tilted her head, waiting for my answer. Oz quirked his eyebrow.

"Of course, I'll do it," I said, hearing a choral version of *Amazing Grace* in my mind. It was my funeral.

Chapter 10: Oz

The Wheels on the Bus

Our first soccer match on a cool Friday evening in late September was a blowout. We trounced Henderson Middle with a score of 6 -1. The Marchfield Maidens, as I secretly called the team, celebrated the sweet thrill of victory on the bus ride home as only middle school girls could: by singing, loud and off-key.

They sang about SpongeBob SquarePants and Phineas and Ferb's summer vacation but quickly moved on to Beyoncé and Pharrell. They knew all the words, and co-captains Adrienne and Haley belted them out while tinny cell phone speakers provided the music. Their contagious spirit was uplifting but also head-splitting.

"How come they know all the lyrics to these songs but can't memorize the order of operations?" I muttered.

Either she didn't hear me over the din, or she enjoyed ignoring me. Audrey scrolled on her phone in the seat across the aisle. She didn't look at me or speak to me on the ride to the match. Apparently, the ride home included a big helping of the silent treatment.

Status fucking quo.

For two weeks, I'd coached the girls and run them through drills. I'd set up the plays and practiced with them. They were a great group of soccer players and an excellent team. I couldn't say the same for my assistant coach.

I'm not saying Audrey wasn't great with the girls. She was. She handled all the shit I didn't want to—stowing equipment, hauling snacks, and arranging transportation. She laughed with them and worked through their issues. The Maidens fucking loved her, but she wanted nothing to do with me. Our conversations were one-sided. I talked, and she listened. She never disagreed, argued, or laughed with me, and it made me crazy.

I'd start with some polite conversation when she arrived on the field for practice.

"Hi, Audrey, how're you?"

"Fine," she'd say, walking off to talk to Haley and Chris.

I'd cross over after warmups to stand on the sideline next to her. "What do you think of their foot play?"

She'd stare at me for a minute, making me squirm, before answering. "Good."

What the hell did that look mean? Didn't she know the term foot play? Did she think I was propositioning her?

Finally, at the end of practice, I'd try again. "Thanks for everything, Audrey. See you tomorrow."

Of course, she probably didn't even hear me as she speed-walked away to her vomit-green car.

Yup, she definitely hated me. But why did it bother me so much? She acted like a spoiled brat. She and I weren't in a relationship or anything. I hardly knew her. The least she could do was be polite.

And yet, I thought about her all the time. I'd see her in her classroom, in the cafeteria, or during a fire drill, and I'd remember how her body snuggled against mine; the heat of her skin branded me. She would smile at a student, and I'd remember the taste of her lips like fresh cherries warm from the sun, and I'd close my eyes and smell the coconut and almond scent of her skin. I wanted to take down the messy bun she piled on top of her head and tangle my fingers through her silky hair.

My thoughts were not cool for school.

To tell the truth, the whole fiasco with Audrey left me feeling old. It had been a long time since I'd been hung up over a woman who wanted nothing to do with me. The last time was Amie Peterson, a nurse at Camp Bastion Hospital. I was nineteen, and she broke my heart.

And then there was my mom. She constantly asked me when I was going to settle down. She'd say, "Oz, find a girl. Your dad and I were already married and having babies at your age." What she doesn't say is that Dad died when he was only forty, leaving her with two kids and a pile of debt. She doesn't remind me that his heart condition is genetic, and I only have eight years until I'm forty. Two Christmases ago, when we'd both had too much eggnog, I confessed that I worried dying young might be in the cards for me, too. It still kicks me in the heart that she didn't disagree; she just urged me to hurry.

In the back of the bus, Adrienne and Haley started an ear-splitting rendition of Meghan Trainer's *Better When I'm Dancing*.

Looking at my watch, I sighed. We were twenty minutes from the school. I'd been at work since 8:00 AM, and I still had a shit ton left to do for tomorrow. I wanted a beer, a huge burger, and some fries. Maybe I'd text Bobby and see if she and Mel wanted to grab some dinner. There was no point in inviting Audrey. She'd dismiss me with a glance.

The bus gave a little lurch, and the engine sputtered. I turned toward the driver. Smoke poured out of the engine. The girls stopped singing, and silence hung thick with tension in the back of the bus.

Burgers were going to have to wait.

"Everybody, stay seated," Audrey called out.

The driver swerved over to the side of the road and stopped the bus. She picked up her radio, reporting that we'd broken down.

Audrey and I looked at each other for a second. I could practically see the wheels turning in her head. Teachers have to make more than a thousand decisions in a day and very few of them have to do with math or English.

"I'll call Brian," she said as she scrolled through her contacts for the activity coordinator's number.

"What's going on?" Merry, our center fielder, called from her seat near the back. A chorus of voices echoed her question.

"Uh, we broke down." I gestured to the smoking engine at the front of the bus.

"What are we gonna do?" Merry asked.

Haley chimed in, "How're we supposed to get home?"

We were seconds from a full-blown riot. I glanced at Audrey.

Luckily, she'd finished her call. "Ladies, we need you to call your parents. Have them pick you up here on 12th and Elm instead of at the school. Does anyone need to use my cell phone?"

The next thirty minutes were a blur. The sun went down. Audrey and I talked to the girls' parents. We waved goodbye as, one by one, they were picked up.

It was a chaos of chatter, a thousand questions, two thousand reassurances. And then it was done. The last girl pulled away with her dad, and I finally felt myself relax.

A tow truck arrived in the midst of it all and started hooking up the bus. The truck pulled out with the bus as the driver's boyfriend drove up on a motorcycle. He tossed her a helmet, and she jumped on the back. She waved as he peeled out.

Darkness fell around us as the sound of their engine faded away. I walked over to where we'd dropped our coaches' bags in the grass. I glanced over at Red and realized, for the first time in weeks, we were alone together.

Chapter 11: Audrey

Slow Burn

Haley's dad was the last to arrive in a shiny, black Beemer. He rolled down his window and Steely Dan's *Peg* blared through the window.

He shouted over the song. "Thanks for everything. You guys need a ride?"

I glanced around. The bus driver and the tow truck operator were still on the scene.

"No, thanks. We need to stay here a little longer, and I don't want to keep you." He and Haley gave me a wave as they pulled away from the curb.

I looked over at Oz like a teenager with a crush. He waved goodbye to Chris as she drove away. The muscles of his arms and back strained under his shirt, and I almost drooled. I wiped my mouth with my sleeve, just in case. Why couldn't I ignore him?

Seconds later, a motorcycle pulled over with a throaty growl. The bus driver hiked her leg over the seat and drove off with the guy.

The tow truck driver, a huge fleshy man with a plumber butt problem, finished hooking up the bus. "Y'all need a lift?"

He gestured to the small cab of his truck. If I got in there with Oz, I'd have to sit on his lap. And I'd hate myself for enjoying it.

The fall evening was warm, and a full moon rose over the trees. Marchfield was only a few blocks away. I shook my head. "I think I'll walk back to the school. Have a good evening," I waved, hoping Oz would get in the truck.

Oz grabbed our bags and slung them both over one shoulder, and I felt my knees go weak at the sight of those muscles in action. This would not do.

He waved off the tow truck driver and jogged over. "Mind if I come with?"

I wanted to scream, but I shrugged instead. I wasn't going to cause a scene by the side of the road. Maybe we could make it back to our cars without talking. He matched my pace, and we started down the sidewalk side by side.

After a few minutes of silence, I began to feel awkward. I struggled to think of something to say. I finally landed on, "The game was pretty awesome."

I gave myself a mental high five for finding the perfect safe, neutral topic of conversation.

Oz's eyes flew to my face, studying me. Finally, he answered with equal politeness. "Yeah, the girls really came together and worked as a team. If they keep playing like they did tonight, we might make the playoffs."

After Dr. Winters had passive-aggressively forced me into this mess, I'd counted off the days on my calendar. We practiced four days a week and had matches on Fridays—forty-five total days. I'd barely made it through fourteen, and now there might be MORE? My inner voice told me to stay calm. Take deep breaths. Relax.

Fuck that.

"Playoffs? You mean we might have an extended season?" I asked in my most innocent voice.

Oz choked out a laugh. Could he tell I was freaking out? "There's a good possibility of going all the way."

I gave him a sideways glance in the dark. Was he messing with me? Going all the way?

He smiled wide, and he seemed relaxed walking beside me. He wore what I'd dubbed his coaching gear, shorts and a Marchfield Soccer T-shirt that stretched tight across his chest and shoulders.

My hormones revved. Why was he so handsome? Why couldn't I stop looking at him?

Obviously, I was the one with the problem. I could talk all day about maintaining professionalism, but it all melted away when he was around. I spent all my time secretly checking him out, and he never once glanced at me.

I forced myself to turn away, studying the houses along the road.

He cleared his throat. "Thanks for all your help with the Maidens. I couldn't do this all by myself."

Luckily, I was studying the sidewalk four feet in front of me, so I had enough brain cells to respond. "Maidens?"

He laughed. "I think of the girls as the Mighty Marchfield Maidens, but only in my head." Oz shrugged, lifting those hard, strong, drool-worthy shoulders. Apparently, I'd lost all control and couldn't help myself. I tried to look away.

I laughed weakly. He glanced over at me and smiled, and the warm night air turned hot. I started to sweat. Luckily, Iron Maiden's "Invaders" screamed through my mind with heavy bass and drums. I laughed. "Can you imagine them in Viking helmets, charging the ball?"

His bark of laughter boomed out across the dark street. A dog barked in the distance, and lights glowed from the windows of the houses we passed. It wasn't even eight o'clock on a Friday night, but we were completely alone on the street. We crossed the last side street, and the school building came into view in the distance. Our cars were the last two parked in the faculty parking lot.

He cleared his throat. "Audrey, I want to apologize to you."

"Oh, don't, Oz," I said weakly. I didn't want him to apologize. Then I'd have to forgive him. We'd have to be friendly, and I wasn't sure being nice to him was possible without wanting to jump his bones.

He apparently disagreed. "I didn't handle things right that night when we–"

"Stop," I begged. "We don't need to talk about it."

Please don't make me talk about it.

I sped up, walking faster. His long legs matched my pace easily.

He reached out and touched my elbow. "Audrey, stop. I didn't—I shouldn't have fallen asleep in your bed and then snuck out. And I shouldn't have egged you on in the faculty meeting. I was an asshole."

Oh, fuck. Now, what was I supposed to do?

"Well, um–" I couldn't think. And I sure as hell couldn't talk, and you know it's bad when an English teacher is speechless.

"My mother raised me better," Oz grinned sheepishly, "and she'd beat me within an inch of my life if I didn't apologize."

We continued to walk side by side for a minute.

He had a point. I searched my empty brain for something funny to say. I settled on, "Well, *my* mother would ground me for life if she knew I'd picked up a man in a bar after drinking too much."

We both laughed, and I felt better than I had in weeks. Lighter. *Walking on Sunshine* by Katrina and the Waves almost had me dancing down the sidewalk.

"I'd really like it if we could start over," Oz suggested. He stopped under a streetlamp and reached out his hand. "Hi, I'm Oz Taylor. I'm the new algebra teacher at Marchfield Middle."

Suddenly, this drew me into an alternate universe. How would things have been different if I'd bothered to introduce myself before dragging him off to my apartment? Would I have been smart enough to go home alone? For a second, I looked at the crinkles around his eyes. They were totally adorable. My gaze shifted to his hand, and images of all the naughty things he'd done with those fingers flashed before my eyes. Fucking universe! I knew I'd have ended up in this mess anyway. Oz drew me to him like a moth to a flame.

Mentally, I slapped myself. I was an adult. This is what adults did. Just because every time I touched him, I wanted to slide my hands over him didn't mean I had to act on it. I could control my hormones.

I grasped his hand and shook. The warmth of his palm seeped into mine. I tried to ignore the electric sparks that seemed to leap from his skin, zap my palm, and squash the trail of electricity that sent heat to my center.

"I'm Audrey Freemont. I believe your classroom is across the hall from mine."

Did he notice how shaky my voice sounded? I tried to pull my hand away, but he squeezed it tight.

"It's great to meet you, Audrey." His voice was husky and low, and I shivered despite the warm air around us. My senses were on fire. The scent of late summer flowers was thick in the air. His masculine scent mingled with them intoxicatingly.

The dark school building loomed over us like a sentry in front of us, reminding me of Dr. Winters and her expectations. For the 1000th time since I'd woken up hungover and stumbled into the school library, I wished things were different. But the fact that he was a teacher in my school meant he was off-limits. The icebreaker disaster had proven that I couldn't handle sexy extracurricular activities.

I stiffened my spine and dug deep to find my calm center as we walked into the parking lot. We approached our cars, and I pulled away. Stevie Wonder encouraged me to *Go Home.*

The wind turned, and the warm night air chilled. Clicking open the locks on my car, I tried to make myself get in and drive away. Slowly, I turned to scan the area for Oz. He stood by his truck, watching me with his hands in his pockets. His eyes were dark, and I could feel the heat of his stare.

I should have waved goodbye, hopped into Green Lightning, and headed home. I should have taken a cold shower and written in my journal all the reasons why we should *Never Ever, Get Back Together.* Thanks, Taylor Swift. I should woman up.

But there he was, giving me sexy, smoldering eyes as he leaned against his truck. He looked like a modern-day cowboy, all hard and rugged after a day on the ranch. I have always had a thing for cowboys. They were hard, tough, weather and work-worn on the outside but warm and loyal on the inside.

The logical side of my brain warned me to stay away, but he'd lassoed me with an invisible rope. I took a step toward him and watched his eyes widen, and his chest rise as he drew in a deep breath. It was all the encouragement I needed to close the space between us.

I stood inches from him, staring into his eyes, searching for a sign. His mouth hitched up on the right side, and I felt myself rise up on my toes, my hands on his wide shoulders, and kiss him.

Chapter 12: Oz

Burgers and Fries

One minute, Red's about to get into her ugly, green excuse of a car. The next, she pressed her curvy body up against mine and branded me with a smoking hot kiss. I wrapped my arms around her, drawing her close to align her body against mine. Blood pounded in my ears. She tasted sweet as honey, so I drank her in. I deepened the kiss with a groan as her tongue played over mine.

A minute, or maybe ten, I couldn't tell how much time had passed before she took a step back. I let her go even though I needed to pull her back and kiss her again. She searched my eyes for the answer to a question to which I didn't know the answer. Reflexively, I leaned toward Red, breathing in her fresh scent, and ran my fingers down her cheek and along her jawline, trailing them along the line of freckles there. A cool breeze lifted the auburn hair around her face, and Audrey shivered.

I felt the change in her as soon as she leaned toward me. I shifted forward, rubbing my body up against hers, and took her mouth with mine. I kept the kiss gentle, soft, and slow, not wanting to scare Red away. This time, when she broke the kiss, she stayed close, resting her head against my shoulder.

The sounds of the night filtered in. The trees sighed as the wind brushed through the leaves. Frogs croaked high up in the branches. The stars appeared across the indigo sky, and the crescent moon rode low on the horizon. Red felt so good in my arms, so right. I felt my body's reaction to her, aching to push the boundaries. I didn't want to spook her, but forcing myself to keep it light might kill me.

A loud gurgle bubbled up from Audrey's stomach in a loud plea for food. "Hungry, Red?" She inched back from me, but I held her tight.

"Oh gosh, I'm sorry." She pushed lightly on my chest, so I loosened my grip. Her face was pink when she looked up at me. "I'm starving. It was my turn to supervise lunch detention, and then I had back-to-back meetings during planning."

"I was going to get a burger at Barrel before heading home. Wanna go?"

A moment of silence stretched between us, and I held my breath. I fought back the urge to pick her up and deposit her in my truck even though I felt my muscles tense and ready to jump into action.

"Want me to draw you a Pros and Cons chart, Red?"

She stepped back, the cool breeze slid over my heated skin, and I almost cried.

"I'm sorry, Oz. I feel like I'm throwing out so many mixed signals. Can we go as only friends?"

"Friends." Hadn't I just had my tongue in her mouth? I had to bite my lips to not add *with benefits*. Audrey wouldn't think that was funny.

She tossed me a self-conscious smile and walked toward her car. I studied her hips as they swayed. Her tight butt in those dark jeans burned blind spots into my eyes. My mind flashed back to the night she'd led me into her apartment.

I jumped into my truck and turned over the engine. Gary Allan came on the radio singing *The One*, and I hit the off switch hard.

Hell no, Gary. Shut the fuck up. Audrey was sweet and funny, but she was also difficult. Gary needed to keep his damn opinions to himself. Thank you very much.

In silence, I followed her glow-in-the-dark car to the pub. Why would such a beautiful woman choose such a horrible car?

People filled the tables, chatting, eating, and relaxing after a long work week. At the back of the building, the game room rang with the sounds of the arcade games. Pool cues sent balls crashing and ricocheting. The thud of axes hitting targets reverberated through the open space.

We claimed an empty table in the corner. Candles, surrounded by fresh flowers, flickered on each table in the dark room. Audrey sat down in the chair across from me. The glow of the candle created beautiful highlights in her hair. Who'd have thought a sports bar could be romantic?

Not that I cared or would mention it to Red. Thankfully, the waitress came over before I did something stupid like try to hold her hand.

"Hey, Krissy, it's good to see you. How's your little brother?" Audrey smiled at the young blonde who wore a tight t-shirt printed with DON'T BE A PAIN IN THE AX.

"He's really good, Ms. Freemont. Tommy's on the football team this year. I'll tell him you said hi." Krissy beamed at Audrey.

"I'll run by the next home game and cheer him on."

"He'd love that!" Krissy left us with the menus and a promise to be right back for our order.

When I decided to move here, I hoped the small town and school would be a better fit for me. The closeness I'd felt in the military was missing back at home. And the larger schools in Delaware left me feeling cold and empty. In Marchfield, teachers were the heart of the community. Even though I'd only been here a few weeks, I felt like I belonged here.

I looked at the menu for a second, then asked, "One of your former students?"

"Yeah, poor Krissy suffered through my first year. I was a much better teacher for her brother last year." Audrey's wistful smile told me how much she cared for the teens.

I nodded. "The first year is rough. College doesn't teach you how to manage a classroom of kids or make a thousand decisions all in an hour and a half. I'm still figuring it out in year four."

"It's a learning curve, for sure. How do you like it at Marchfield?" She gave me a thoughtful look, tilting her head to the right and exposing the smooth, long line of her neck. I swallowed hard, imagining kissing down that ivory column to the tops of her perfect breasts. I grew hard remembering her pink nipples.

Fuck me!

Mentally, I shook myself. If Red wanted to be friends, she was going to have to start wearing sweaters. Better yet, a parka.

"It's different. Smaller. The kids are great though. Curious, lively." I coughed.

She rolled her eyes. "That's one way to say it. Thirty thirteen-year-olds in one room can be a handful."

Krissy arrived to take our order.

"I'll have a cheddar bacon burger and fries."

There was probably something seriously wrong with me, but Red ordering my favorite item on the menu was hot.

Krissy nodded when I said, "I'll have the same."

The restaurant side of Barrel thinned out around eight as diners left to play games or head home. Randy Travis twanged out the vocals to *Forever and Ever, Amen* on the sound system. I began to feel like Audrey and I were alone together in the darkened room.

Without thinking, I reached across the table and put my hand over hers. "Thanks for coming out to dinner with me, Red, and celebrating our win."

I felt like I'd won the lottery when she didn't pull her hand away.

I rubbed my thumb against hers. "And surviving the bus breakdown. Red, you're a freaking rock star."

Her laugh sent ripples of pleasure through me, and my heart raced. I felt like I was Rocky jogging up those stairs. I shoved that thought away into a locked box in the furthest recesses of my mind.

Red laced her fingers through mine. I considered sliding my chair back and pulling her onto my lap. I wanted to taste the dark warmth of her mouth again. Instead, I settled for running my finger over the inside of her wrist, feeling her pulse leap.

Audrey made a choking sound and pulled her hand away. "Oz, I–" She tucked a strand of her red hair behind her ear. "I'm not sure this is a great idea. Dr. Winters..."

I crossed my arms over my chest to keep from reaching for her again. "Red, you're running hot and cold, but I agreed to be friends, so I'm following your lead."

Audrey sucked her bottom lip into her mouth and worried it between her white teeth. I smiled at her. "So where are we going?"

Her green eyes smoldered. "There's a big part of me that wants to throw caution to the wind and bring you home with me."

I fisted my hands into my sides to keep them from reaching for her and smiled humbly. "Sorry I'm so irresistible."

She sighed and shook her head. Definitely not the reaction I hoped for. "This isn't going to work."

I winked at her. "Red, it doesn't have to be so complicated."

Red burst into song about making things complicated with a smack dab Avril Levine impersonation.

I laughed. "Bravo."

This time, her smile lit up her eyes. "I always have a song stuck in my head. It's been like that since I was little.

Somebody says something, and boom, the lyrics just pop into my brain."

"Happens to me, too." I nodded.

"That's what everyone says, but for me, it's kind of a curse."

I could have asked her a thousand questions, but Krissy arrived with our burgers. We devoured the food in silence for a few minutes. With our hunger appeased, we fell into an easy conversation about school.

"I agree, St. Patrick's Day is bad with kids trying to pinch each other. But the day after Halloween is the one that gives me nightmares. All those kids on sugar highs, eating candy out of their backpacks, and every year one of them barfs." I shuddered dramatically to make her laugh.

"No, Valentine's Day is much worse than that!" Audrey argued. She dipped a French fry in ketchup and popped it in her mouth, chewing. "One year, this poor boy brought balloons and a bouquet of silk roses for a girl he liked. All the boys teased him, egging him on until he gave them to her right outside my room. She brought them into my class and took them out of the plastic. Turned out they weren't flowers."

"Don't leave me hangin', Red." I enjoyed the sparkle of humor in her eyes

"They were thongs," Audrey snorted with laughter. "A half dozen red, lacy thongs. The girl practically died of embarrassment. The poor guy looked like he wanted to cry. All his friends were hooting and hollering."

I winced. "I feel for the guy."

"Me too! Poor kid is probably scarred for life!"

Her eyes twinkled with humor. Her face was practically glowing, and I couldn't look away. "What did you do?"

108

"I took my cue from The Beatles' *You've Got to Hide Your Love Away*. I marched over there, confiscated the panties and the rest of the roses, and threw them in my closet. Then I started class like nothing happened."

I loved the sound of her laugh. It was light and fresh, and it filled the empty cracks I didn't know I had in my soul.

"They're still there. I'm afraid to throw them out. What would the custodians think?" Audrey wiped tears of laughter out of her eyes.

I leaned forward, captivated by her. I wanted to know everything about her. "How did you become a teacher?"

She smiled. "I was a brat in school. Being a teacher was probably the last thing I wanted to be when I was in eighth-grade. I was failing most of my classes. My mom was distracted and not as on the ball as before my dad died. I lied to her about my grades and pretty much everything." She paused to sip her drink.

"I'm sorry to hear about your dad. My dad died when I was seventeen, so I get it." I reached for her hand, but she pulled hers back.

"Thanks. I'm sorry to hear about your dad, too."

"It was a long time ago."

"Yeah, but it never leaves you."

I nodded and waited for her to continue.

"Anyway, Mrs. Rayburn told me that if I wasn't happy with my life, education was the key to change it. It was a lightbulb moment for me. She was my mentor until we moved again. She was a career teacher who'd taught in the same school for twenty years, and I decided I wanted to be just like her. And now I am."

"Did you move around a lot?" I didn't want her to stop talking.

"Before my dad died, we moved like clockwork every two to three years. A couple times, we were stationed overseas, but mostly, we hopped around the US from base to base. After he died in an explosion on the ship, we were left with a lot of debt, and we moved a lot until my mom's art took off. I got a scholarship to go to college.

"What about you, Oz? How did you get into teaching?"

"Three months after my dad died, I ran away and joined the Army. A buddy of mine, Eddy Tilson, died in an IED explosion. One minute, he was there making some dumb joke about a dog, and the next, he was in pieces. After getting discharged, I went to see Eddy's widow and kids. I decided I wanted to teach so I could help children like Eddy's."

We were silent for a few minutes, and I thought about how our lives mirrored one another's. The loss of our fathers had defined us.

She sat back from the table, patting her belly. "That burger was amazing."

Krissy came over to check on us. "Y'all want anything else?"

"Oh, Krissy, I'd explode if I ate anymore."

I watched her hand run that slow circle across her stomach. If Red kept rubbing her belly like that, I might need to excuse myself. I was hungry to touch her there and a few other places to the north and south. What in the fucking hell was wrong with me?

Krissy winked at Audrey. "They had a cancellation for ax throwing if you wanted to work it off."

"That sounds fun, but I should probably–" Audrey met my eyes and blinked.

My heated gaze crashed into hers. I wiggled my eyebrows. "Want to toss some wood? We could bury the hatchet."

She put her head down on the table, her shoulders shaking with laughter. After a minute, she sat back. "Cut it out."

"Come on, let's get axed, Red." I stood holding out my hand.

My confidence felt itchy and hollow. Inside, I flashed back to Christmas and my mom telling me to hurry. I buried the memory in the same box with Eddy Tilson and locked the box. This thing with Audrey was casual. We'd scratched an itch, nothing more. If I could convince my body to agree with my brain, it'd be good.

I opened my mouth to take it back. I should go home, get some rest, and watch an old football game while grading the tests the kids took last week.

And then her soft hand slid into mine, and my heart pounded in my chest. The cardio workout Red was putting me through was enough to make me out of breath.

I needed to get her naked again and get whatever this was out of my system.

Chapter 13: Audrey

Sugar We're Goin' Down

His fingers were calloused and warm as they curved around mine. He tugged me toward the back of the restaurant. There were a lot of people playing pool and foosball. A few waved. I waved back with my other hand, trying not to blush. I was over thirty, for God's sake, much too old to be embarrassed by holding hands in public.

We stopped in front of two wooden targets. A team of four hooted and catcalled as a woman in a white tank top grasped an ax between both hands and studied the target with total concentration. A series of circles labeled 1, 2, 3, and 4 surrounded an even smaller red bullseye on a battered, dented piece of wood. Two small blue numbered circles were in the top right and left corners.

The woman swung her arms up over her head, releasing the ax. The heavy hatchet rotated in an arc and stuck into the three-point ring with a vibrating thunk. She spun around and high-fived her friends as they cheered.

"You ever done this before, Red?" Oz let go of my hand to pick up two of the axes out of a rack by the empty target. I immediately missed the warmth of his palm.

"Nope, but it doesn't look that hard," I said confidently. If I could teach a bunch of thirteen-year-olds subject-verb agreement, I could do anything, right?

Oz handed me an ax. It was heavier than I'd imagined. I fought to keep my shoulder from popping out of its socket and steadied it with my other hand. Oz smirked as he watched me struggle.

I felt my competitive side surge. Growing up with two older brothers taught me to fight hard and dirty.

I batted my eyes at Oz and smiled sweetly. "Can you show me how?"

As I predicted, Oz came up behind me, his arms curling around me, and his hands brushed over mine. He adjusted my grip on the ax, so I had one hand above the other on the handle. "Lift it up behind your head, Red, and whip it forward."

Devo started to play *Whip It* in my mind, but they were drowned out by his deep voice right by the sensitive skin of my ear. "Need me to demonstrate?"

"No." My voice sounded rough and husky. His lips were so close to my ear it was almost a kiss.

He ran his hand down the inside of my arm, and I almost lost my grip on the ax. "Just keep your eye on the bullseye, and release when the ax is just above your forehead." He stepped back, and I yearned for the heat of his body

Using the calm breathing techniques I'd learned in therapy when I was a teen, I lowered my heart rate and focused on the target.

"Why are you holding your breath, Red?"

"I'm focusing," I lied as I tried to block the image of me stepping closer to him. Conflicted was an understatement.

"You should open your eyes before you throw it, Red. Wouldn't want to hurt anyone." The humor in his voice was irritating.

"I'm going to drop this ax on your foot if you don't back off."

His laugh was husky as he stepped away. I immediately missed his heat.

I swallowed hard and took a few more deep breaths. My panties were damp, and part of me wanted to drop the ax and drag Oz out into the alley. Another part of me wanted to whip his ass in ax throwing. I made a mental list of all the reasons pursuing a relationship with Oz was a bad idea.

1. I worked with him.
2. Our names didn't combine well—Audz? OzRy? Bleh.
3. Our boss was not a fan.
4. He was a bed-hogging jerk.

This list was by no means exhaustive or complete, so I resolved to kick his ax and go home. Chuckling to myself, I swung the ax up over my head. As I released it, I whispered a little prayer for luck.

Wings sang *With a Little Luck* in my mind as the ax spun in slow motion toward the target. It hit the target with a thunk. For a second, I tasted sweet euphoria as the ax vibrated. Admittedly, it was in the furthest ring and only worth one point, but victory was mine!

Until the ax slid down the wall, and it clanged like a death knell to my dreams onto the cement floor.

"So close, Red." Oz's eyes twinkled. He grinned wickedly and picked up his ax. He swaggered forward toward the throw line. His red, Marchfield shorts showed off his long, muscular, tan legs, and I felt a magnetic pull between us.

His teasing made me eager for a little payback. I wrapped my arms around his chest and pressed myself against his back. I stood up on tiptoe, kissing his neck lightly. He sucked in a breath with a hiss. I whispered, "Good luck," in his ear and retreated behind the safety line.

He turned to give me an incredulous look. The ax dangled loose in his grip. I felt his hot hazel eyes travel up my body to clash with mine and shivered a little.

"You sure you want to play with fire, Red?"

I winked at him even as the heat burned low in my belly.

Oz growled and turned back to the target. He took a couple of deep breaths, then threw the ax one-handed, sticking it to the board.

"It's outside the target circle. How many points?"

He looked a little irritated. "No points. We're tied, Red."

I laughed at his slack-jawed expression. "All's fair in war and axes."

The group next to us hooted with laughter. The woman in the tank top winked at me and called out, "Amen, Sister!"

Oz pulled the ax out of the target. The material of his t-shirt stretched tight over his shoulders. He turned, smiling at me when he caught me staring. "Game on, Red."

I quickly looked away.

Get it together, Freemont!

I carried my ax to the throwing line. Breathing deeply, I closed my eyes. Opening them, I focused on the target and swung the ax. It struck the wood solidly in the second ring— two points.

I danced in victory, swinging my hips and singing *We Are the Champions* with Queen. The team next to us gave me a standing ovation. I bowed.

Oz rolled his eyes at me, so I stuck my tongue out. He stood to get his ax, brushing past me to the throwing line. His arm made contact with the side of my breast, sending a frizzle of electricity raced through me at the touch.

He turned to face the target. The sultry smile he sent me seemed to say he knew how much that little touch had affected me. Taking his time, he raised the ax and threw. It stuck a hair to the right of the bullseye, earning him four points.

Time to get serious.

Standing in front of the target for my third throw, I looked back at Oz over my shoulder and asked, "What are the blue circles for?"

"They're blue balls." He wiggled his eyebrows at me.

"Are you kidding me?"

Oz winked at me. "I'm always serious about blue balls, Red."

Laughter bubbled up my throat and came out with a snort, which turned into full-body seizures. My shoulders shook, and my eyes watered while Keith Urban began singing *Blue Ain't Your Color* in my head. I'd always had a thing for Keith and his sense of irony.

I put the ax down to wipe the tears of laughter out of my eyes. "Of course you are."

He sauntered over like a jock, cocky and full of himself. I wanted to hate how good-looking he was, but my mouth watered despite myself. Leaning over, he whispered in my ear, "Red, if you can stick your ax there, it's called a blue ball bust."

I doubled over laughing again, giving him a view of my butt in tight jeans. He took my hand and pulled me to the bench by the scoreboard. One minute, I was laughing; the next, I was sitting on his lap with his arms wrapped around my waist.

"What are you doing?"

I squirmed, trying to get up, but he held me firmly. I tickled him lightly. He laughed but still didn't let go. "You trying to give me blue balls?"

That husky chuckle was my undoing. I forgot where we were. The sounds of the games and people—all of it faded. My eyes were glued to his mouth as it moved closer. I felt him shift beneath me and his hard cock pressed up against my butt.

A thousand conflicting ideas flew through my head.

I shouldn't want this. *Oh yeah, big boy, bring it on!*

I should go home. *Bring Oz home, too!*

I should definitely go home alone. *Kiss me! Kiss me! Kiss me!*

Get up! Put a stop to this. *Just a few more minutes, please.*

Oz pulled me closer. His hands slid down my back. I groaned softly as his lips brushed mine. His tongue made a very persuasive argument, and my conflict melted away as I pressed closer, threading my fingers through his soft blond hair. I couldn't get close enough.

A soft cough came from behind us. Oz eased back. My heels lowered to the floor.

A familiar voice said, "You two done playing? We've got a 9:30 reservation."

Bobby's voice worked, as did the Ice Bucket Challenge. My sexual energy went from 100—*Do me now, big man!*—to zero—*Get away from me, sir!*—quicker than a race car braking into the pit. I jumped off Oz's lap, my face burning with embarrassment.

Val, Bobby, and Mel stood there staring at me. Bobby's face was a meld of confusion and dry amusement. Mel smirked knowingly, and Val bounced on her toes, trying to fight down her laughter.

The universe was toying with me. It was like some sick standardized test created by the most ironic of deities, and the questions all boiled down to this:

Audrey Freemont fucked up the worst by:

A.making out in public.

B.devouring a man she'd vowed to stay away from.

C.getting caught by her friends while sucking face with her co-worker.

D.ALL OF THE FUCKING ABOVE

Chapter 14: Oz

22

Finally, I had Red right where I wanted her. Well almost. We needed to find someplace more private and away from this bunch of clowns. My balls tightened, turning as blue as the ones on the damn target. I shifted, feeling uncomfortable but reluctant to let Audrey go.

"Grinding the ol' ax, Sarg?" Bobby's grin was so wide it made me wonder if her face would crack. I sort of hoped it would. Her eyes danced with mischief.

"Fuck off, Sergeant Major," I growled back while giving Audrey a side glance. I didn't want this interruption to embarrass her.

"Now, now, Oz," Bobby chided playfully. "I outrank you. Don't make me bust your balls for PDA and inappropriate language."

Mel snickered. "This evening is way more ax-citing than I expected." She smirked at me. Under other circumstances, I'd be happy with how cute they were together. Tonight, I wanted them to disappear.

On my lap, Audrey groaned, not in a good way. She buried her face in my shoulder. My arms tightened in response. All my protective instincts roared. I wanted to pick up Audrey and carry her away from the noise and laughter.

My instinct was to throw her over my shoulder and carry Audrey out *before* this got any worse. But Keith arrived with a tray of glasses. Setting the tray down, his eyes bounced between us like a kid on a trampoline. "What did I miss?"

Val giggled. "Audrey and Oz were trading tongues."

"Stop it!" Audrey jumped off my lap. I missed her soft, warm body immediately.

"Damn," Keith whistled. "You do know, Audrey, he uses that tongue to teach math."

Bobby high-fived Keith and then bent over laughing. When Bobby stood back up, her face was red, and she was gasping for breath between chuckles. Mel patted her back.

I stood up, brushing past my not-so-well-meaning friends to stand by Red.

"Audrey likes big axes," Val rapped while the others laughed. Audrey's lips twitched and then straightened as she seemed to choke down the urge to join in.

"Sir Mix-A-Lot should sue your ass for butchering his song," I joked.

And of course, Bobby jumped in. "And when Oz walks in with his big hard ax–"

"Are you buffoons drunk?" I interrupted her, crossing my arms over my chest.

Audrey turned away and let out a soft sound beside me. I heard her take a deep, shaky breath. If these idiots made her cry, they would regret it. I hated it when women cried.

I followed her, reaching over to pat her shoulder. What should I say? When she looked up at me, I braced myself for a look of wet humiliation. But Audrey's green eyes sparkled as she burst out in laughter.

"Big, hard ax," she gasped between giggles.

My own lips quivered, and I let out a chuckle. "My ax is pretty impressive." Red laughed harder until she stepped away to wipe her eyes on some paper napkins from a nearby table.

Mel asked, "You guys out celebrating a soccer victory?"

"Something like that," I agreed, watching Red walk over to stand near Val.

Keith coughed. "Speaking of celebrating, I heard through the grapevine you have a lot to be happy about, Audrey."

Red stared at him with confusion. "Huh?"

Keith winced like he was ready to eat his foot. "Rumor has it you're expecting."

WHAT THE HELL? My head turned toward Audrey so fast I almost got whiplash.

Val burst out laughing. "I had ten bucks on Keith bringing it up first."

Audrey made a choked, embarrassed sound, and I searched her face for clues. I wanted to drag her off like a fucking caveman and demand answers.

"Priscilla Henesey asked Audrey if she was pregnant on day one of school. It made Audrey mad, so she didn't deny it," Val explained.

Who the hell was this Priscilla Henesey? What a bitch!

I took a step toward Audrey, ready to stand between her and any danger.

Red shrugged. She seemed to be taking it all in stride. "I wondered how long it would take to get around school."

"I knew it wasn't true. The Ice Queen wouldn't get knocked up."

"Ice Queen?" Red arched her brow and gave Keith an angry glare.

My eyes narrowed. I wasn't sure who I wanted to take out first—this Priscilla monster or Keith. I leaned toward Keith only because he was standing right in front of me.

Keith laughed like a fool. Couldn't he feel his closeness to death? "No offense. In the last few years, you've shut down a lot of guys."

"That's not true," Audrey spluttered. Her eyes flew to mine, her face pink.

Keith lifted his hands in a shrug. "Remember Mike? How about Vern?"

"Oooh," Bobby jumped in. "I remember you slapped someone at the eighth-grade dance a few years ago."

"Oh, come on," Audrey protested. "Those guys were never serious, and Carlos was an asshole to everyone." She huffed, rubbing her forehead. "He totally deserved it. And none of this matters. Not a single one of those guys asked me out!"

Keith smirked. "You froze them all before they could."

Audrey's eyes drew Keith's blood. "I'd like to see your evidence."

Bobby put herself between Keith and Audrey. "Let it go."

Bobby, Mel, and Keith picked up singing the song from that Disney movie about the Ice Princess. What was her name? Elvira, no, Elsa.

Audrey groaned deeply, looking irritated. But she'd joined them before they finished the first chorus.

Why did I find that sexy? She twirled around like a princess, and I wanted to eat her pussy. She sang off-key, and I imagined her sucking my cock. I shifted uncomfortably in my jeans and wondered how soon we could leave and explore some of my fantasies.

They finished the song, and Val asked, "How did you guys end up throwing axes?"

"Our bus broke down on the way back to school. We had to get all the parents to pick up the girls at the scene. After that, we walked to our cars and came here before we perished from hunger. Oz wanted to throw axes, so we came back here."

"It makes perfect sense. Team victory plus a stressful situation equals a freakin' powerful aphrodisiac," Val agreed.

"Turns enemies into lovers," Mel added.

"Sounds like Stockholm Syndrome to me." Keith tested the weight of the axes on the rack.

Mel laughed, "More like sexual tension."

"I don't need to live through a stressful situation to be in the mood." Bobby winked at Mel.

Mel patted Bobby's butt. "Good to know, sweetie."

Keith finally chose an ax and stepped up to the throwing line. "Yeah. Yeah. Yeah. All this sexual attraction is ruining my ax-pectations. Let's toss some wood."

We spent an hour throwing axes. Then we spent another around the fire pit outside. I loved the sense of community and bond of friendships I'd found in Marchfield. I'd missed Bobby and her eternal laugh track. But all I wanted was for them to go away. Audrey and I had unfinished business. I'd caught her staring at me a few times when the others were distracted. I knew because I'd been checking her out, too.

Her red hair glowed in the light of the fire like red hot coals. She relaxed in a chair across from me between Val and Keith, her shoes off and her feet tucked up under her. She sang bits of songs that related to the context of the conversation. Audrey was sassy, funny, and cute, and I couldn't deny that I wanted her.

I was debating the best way to get Red home and naked when Bobby threw a curveball. "Audrey, can you give Val a ride? I should take Mel home."

Mel snored softly, her head on Bobby's shoulder. Where was my wing-gal? Bobby should be stepping up to help me out, not throwing complications in my way. Bobby blatantly shrugged off my stare with a wicked grin, and with her arm around Mel, she left without a backward glance. Times had changed since Afghanistan.

"Can I give you a ride, too, Keith?" Audrey asked as she put on her shoes.

Keith winked at Audrey. "I'll stay. I've got my eye on those women." He raised his glass and toasted two brunettes standing by the outside bar. They waved and giggled. "Anyone want to shut this place down?"

We all declined Keith's invitation. Val and Audrey headed out to the parking lot. I needed to get the sex train back on track fast, or I'd miss my opportunity.

I wrapped my arm around Red's shoulders as we walked out together.

I noticed a man by the side entrance to the bar just as he called Val's name. She smiled tightly. In the harsh glow of the streetlamp, Val seemed pale and my instincts told me something was off.

"I know him," Val said. "I'll just go say hi." She walked over to the man. The two of them stood close together, talking in low voices.

"Do you know that guy?"

Audrey looked up at me. "No, but Val's very popular. You don't need to wait."

Hold on...

I assumed we were going to pick up where we left off in the restaurant, but she was sending me home? Frustration welled up from deep inside me, but I choked it down. It was probably just a miscommunication.

I tugged on a lock of Red's hair, twisting it around my finger. "I could meet you at your apartment after you drop Val off."

She chewed on her lip. "It's better if I take Val home and then head back to my apartment alone. I'm tired, and it's been a long day."

Irritated, I let go of her hair. "Are you sure that's what you want, Darlin'?"

Her eyes narrowed into slits. "Are you insinuating I don't know what I want? Am I supposed to be flattered that you want sex?"

I shook my head, but my hands rolled into fists that planted themselves on my hips. Anger rolled through me. "Audrey, you've sent me so many mixed signals tonight, I can't see straight anymore. It's a valid question, and I stand by it."

"If you'd kept your hands to yourself, there wouldn't be any mixed signals."

"You kissed me, Red. Hell, you climbed me like a tree."

"You need to give me some time and space. You take up all the oxygen in the room. I need to figure this out without you hovering over me with all that testosterone."

"We're outside."

She growled low in her throat like a lion about to go in for the kill. "You're not listening."

"All I do is listen. All you talk about is your feelings, your career, your students."

"Oh, I see. I'm supposed to care more about your feelings. Well, this isn't the 1950s, Oz. Women are allowed to put themselves first now."

"Maybe Keith had a point."

Red's eyes were like a frozen pond. "What the hell does that mean?"

"You turned on the heat, and now you freeze me out."

"Are you actually saying, to my face, that I'm an Ice Queen?"

I shoved my hands into my pockets. Society frowned upon shaking sense into people. "If the shoe fits, Darlin."

"I've told you, don't Darlin' me, you asshole." Her gaze was scathing. "I wouldn't have sex with you if you gave me a million dollars," she hissed.

Audrey stared at me in silence, her eyes full of hurt and confusion. All the anger and frustration drained out of me, and exhaustion seeped into its place. She was right. It had been a long ass day.

"Okay, Red."

"Okay? What the hell does that mean?"

"It means you win. I'm not fighting anymore."

"What gives you the right to decide the argument is over? I may have more to say."

He shrugged. "I'm listening."

Across the parking lot, I heard Val say goodbye to the guy. She hummed a tune that sounded familiar as she walked toward us.

An engine roared to life and a car shot out of the other side of the lot, its bright lights flashing.

Val jumped, and my instincts flared back to life. "Everything ok?"

Val nodded. "Oh, sure, he's just being dramatic."

Audrey gave me one last angry scowl before saying, "Oz and I just finished saying good night. Ready to go home, Val?"

Audrey stomped off to her car, and Val followed.

Sighing, I got in my truck and watched as Red's taillights disappeared around the corner. The tune Val had been humming was stuck in my head, and now I realized it was *Hit the Road, Jack* by Ray Charles.

I started the truck, the engine roaring. She'd told me time and again to stay away, and I should listen. I should hit the road, like the song said.

But Red burned like a bright light, and I was the moth dancing around her. I was drawn to her.

And I pondered why all the way home.

Chapter 15: Audrey

I Can't Make Up My Mind

Drizzle fell from the sky late Saturday morning, and I burrowed deep under the covers and let my mind drift. At first, I relaxed in my cozy nest, but then my thoughts turned to school and from school to Oz. I replayed our argument and had to admit I might have handled it better. Then I remembered his lips on mine and the heat of his strong body, so I chose the coward's way and threw back the covers to get up.

Bleary-eyed, I stumbled into the kitchen for coffee. I tripped over Stevie's wiry body, and he let out a howl of indignation.

Muttering to myself about cats running out of their nine lives, I fed him while my coffee brewed.

My mug was the size of a small country—thank you, Timmy or Susie, or whoever gave it to me. I collapsed on the sofa, pulling a throw blanket over my Llama Reading Mama pajamas, and flipped on the TV. Stevie, who had forgiven me, jumped into my lap and curled up.

I relaxed back onto the cushions. The world was my oyster on the weekends. I could pee and eat whenever I wanted. I didn't have to hurry anywhere or talk to anyone. I might read a novel or watch a movie. Sitting all day and cuddling Stevie was also an option. He'd love it, and so would I.

I sat there, stroking my cat. I should have been happy, but I felt off. My mind flipped around like someone switching channels. I picked up a romance novel, read a sentence, and put it down, my concentration busted.

Closing my eyes, Britney Spears performed *Gimme More* in my head. I imagined the warm, hard skin over his shoulders and chest. Thoughts of Oz throwing an ax naked whirled in and out of my head. I smelled the spicy, outdoorsy scent of his skin. I followed the blond hair on his chest as it trailed down to—

My eyes flew open.

The fact that I seemed fixated on Oz annoyed me. He wanted sex, and I—Well, honestly, I wanted him, too. When I was alone with him, I forgot why we couldn't.

But we couldn't.

I needed a distraction, so I decided to try to get some work done. I moved Stevie off my lap and onto a pillow. I hauled my school bag over with a groan. Essays exploded out of the heavy satchel. If anything could stop me from thinking about Oz Hunky-Shoulders, it was these essays.

I pulled out a stack of thirty-five essays by my first class. It was always peachy-keen to teach students who thought they knew everything. Especially when their hobbies involved asking me why English was mandatory because they'd been speaking it since birth? Hardee-Har-Har, kids.

I grabbed my purple felt-tip pen and a stack of rubrics and settled into a rhythm. Grading a class set of essays sometimes took all day. I had grading down to a science, and I shouldn't spend more than ten minutes on each one if I wanted to finish before sunset. But Ainsley's paper took twenty minutes, and Brad's took almost thirty.

Grading in my moody mindset would be unfair. I put them back into my school bag, but I felt them mocking me. I hid the whole thing in my front closet. I'd get to them tomorrow. I walked down the hall and into my bedroom to shower.

In my bedroom, a million fractured memories of Oz in my bed flooded my senses. Blurred and hazed by a mixture of shots and beers, they overwhelmed me. I could still smell him even though I'd washed the sheets. He'd imprinted himself on my bed.

Grabbing an old University of San Joaquin sweatshirt and some mostly clean jeans from my closet, I went into the bathroom. I turned up the 80s playlist on my phone and sang *Billie Jean* at the top of my lungs with MJ. The song changed to Salt-N-Peppa's *Push It* as I shampooed my hair. I danced until I almost killed myself on the wet tile.

When the song changed to Boston's *More than a Feeling*, I wanted to cry. Even Spotify had turned against me! Wrapping up my shower quicker than usual, I skipped to the next song. *Kiss* by Prince filled my tiny bathroom. I'd angered the gods of popular music. I switched off the tunes.

By the time I dressed, it was noon, and my stomach growled like a rabid bear. My fridge taunted me, empty and neglected. The inside of the grocery store was a stranger to me. Who had time? A stale Pop-Tart in my pantry and a box of health cereal mocked me. I did have twenty cans of cat food in the cupboard. Stevie ate far better than I did!

I debated eating a cold can of green beans when someone knocked on my door. For a moment, I let myself hope it was Oz. I scolded myself sternly as I hurried through my apartment.

Val waited with a big, reusable grocery bag over her shoulder. "Please say there's food in that bag," I begged.

"Girl, I don't come over here on a Saturday at noon without food. I know you." She set down the bag on my kitchen counter, pulling out a carton of eggs, milk, an onion, red pepper, and cheese.

"Are we having omelets?" My stomach growled, reminding me of last night with Oz.

"Omelets and–" Val pulled the last two things out of the bag with a flourish. Orange juice and a bottle of sparkling wine. "Mimosas!"

"You're the best bestie ever!" I hugged her hard.

Val patted me on the back. "You'd say that to anyone who showed up at your door with food."

I let her go with a grin. "Probably. But you are my true ride-or-die."

Val knew how to cook. I respected that because I couldn't. After chopping up the onion and red pepper, I poured our mimosas into big wine glasses and set them on the table.

Minutes later, she slid a mouthwatering Western omelet in front of me and sat down across from me with her own. Taking a sip of her mimosa, she waited, watching me scarf down a few bites. "Want to talk about last night?"

"Nope." I swallowed another deliciously spicy bite of egg.

"Okay." She drew out the word and gave me a patient smile.

I didn't want to talk about Oz. Turnabout was a good distraction and also fair play. "Do you want to talk about the man skulking about in the parking lot?"

She glanced up quickly. "Who? Logan?"

"Oh, is that his name?"

She stuck her tongue out at me. "He's the son of my parents' best friends. We've known each other since birth. I was being polite. That's all."

"Mmmph." Her story was logical, but I wasn't buying it.

"Don't mmmph me. You had a hot guy ready to go, but you let him get away."

"I chose to decline. Semantics."

"I heard your semantics last night. You expressed them very loudly." Val winked.

"Nothing is going on between us."

"And pigs can fly." Val flashed me a grin and poured me a second mimosa. "Spill."

"I did a great job ignoring him. Then the bus broke down, and everyone left. And we were alone together."

"Mmmph." Val raised her eyebrows. "Go on."

"He stood there, leaning against his truck under the streetlamp. Like he's in freakin' *Casablanca* or something. I just lost it."

"Wait. How did you lose it? By going to Barrel together?"

"Yes, but first I wrapped myself around him in the school parking lot and used him like a stripper pole."

"Go big or go home."

"I'm so weak." I lowered my head to my chest and moaned.

"A good man will do that to you." Val's sad eyes met mine.

How long had it been since she'd seriously dated someone? A year? More? How much more of a story was there with Logan? I filed this away for later.

"We were making out, and my stomach growled. Oz laughed and invited me to Barrel. There were candles on the table."

"Damn sexy candles."

"Right?!" I demanded. "The atmosphere distracted me. He was sweet and funny. We talked about school, and then he held my hand."

"Ugh." Val crossed her arms over her chest. "Don't you hate that?"

I nodded. "Next thing I know, I'm flirting with him! I asked him to show me how to throw an ax. Then he's all pressed up behind me with his hands over mine."

"Oh, man, he pulled all the tricks out of his hat."

I shook my head, determined not to laugh. "And he's all Darlin' this and blue balls, that–"

Val sputtered, her mimosa going down her throat wrong. She coughed. "What?! Blue balls?!"

"You know those blue circles on the target." I laughed despite myself. "He's all talking in innuendo, whispering and kissing my neck. Whoever makes those pine and wood scents for men's products should be shot! One smell of Mr. Deep Woods by the Sea and all the reasons why Oz is off limits fly out of my mind."

"I just don't get it." Val looked at me skeptically. "How is this thing with you and Oz different from Bobby and Mel? They're buying a house and moving in together, maybe even getting married. You know it started with sexual attraction. At school. Where they work. Together."

I ticked reasons off on my fingers. "Bobby and Mel aren't in the same grade level. They don't teach across the hall from one another. They aren't coaching soccer together. They didn't piss off the principal on the first day of school. And most importantly, they didn't start their relationship with a failed one-night stand."

Val gave me a look that said she wasn't buying it. "The man gave you an orgasm, and then you used him like a stripper pole."

"Okay, maybe not failed," I admitted begrudgingly. "The sex rocked my world. And then he became my co-worker, and it turned weird." My brain switched into a slow-mo fantasy of shirtless Oz dancing to Hall and Oats singing *You Make My Dreams Come True.*

"Earth to Audrey. Come in, Audrey." Val snapped her fingers in front of my face.

"I'm here." I shook my head to dispel the delightful images.

"I think you should embrace it. A sexy-as-hell man wants you. Take advantage of it and him. Especially since the rumor is, you've got a bun in the oven."

I laughed. "I'd forgotten all about that until Keith brought it up last night."

"Everybody is looking for your baby bump, girl."

"Oh God," I moaned. "Could this year get any worse?"

"Relax, Keith and I are on Operation Dispel Rumors. We're telling everyone it was a false positive."

Did I want to laugh or cry?

Val rubbed my arm soothingly. "Honestly, Audrey, Dr. Winters can't fire you for exploring your sexual feelings with Oz."

"Maybe not, but she can make my life miserable."

I knew I wouldn't get fired for having sex with Oz, but Dr. Winters might split us up, move us to different grade levels, or initiate our transfer to a different school. Her power over my happy little life terrified me. It felt like I'd built my life on sand and it was in danger of crumbling into the sea.

"Maybe."

Time to turn the tables. I nudged Val with my elbow. "What does Logan smell like?"

"Boiled cabbage."

"Ewwww! He doesn't."

She crossed a finger over her heart in an X. "I swear it."

I snorted. Liar. I'd drop it. For now, anyway.

We cleaned up the dishes, settled in front of the TV, and caught up on a few *Yellowstone* and *House of the Dragon* episodes.

"I love Saturdays," Val yawned after we finished watching. "I wish there was time to take a nap."

"Why can't we?" A snooze sounded fantastic. I stretched and settled back with my eyes closed, my brain wimowehing to *The Lion Sleeps Tonight*.

Val picked up Stevie and put him on the floor. She stood up and glanced at her watch. "We signed up for the fundraiser game. It starts in an hour."

My eyes popped open, and I sat up straight. "No, no, no, no, no."

"Unfortunately, yes. Marchfield's Tenth Relay for Life Tricycle Basketball game, teachers vs. students, starts in an hour and a half. We should also stretch 'cause we're playing in the first half of the game, and those trikes are brutal."

I collapsed back on the sofa and whined. "I couldn't walk for three days last year. Why did I agree to do it again?"

"It's for a good cause, and the kids love it."

"Ok, but–"

"Plus, the halftime show is always hilarious. The male teachers do that cheer routine. Keith is always hysterical, and he said…" Val stopped talking abruptly.

"What?"

"It doesn't matter." Val practically flew toward the bathroom.

I had a bad feeling. I hurriedly followed her down the hall. "What did Keith say?"

Val stopped with one hand on the bathroom door.

"He said…" she paused dramatically and winked at me, "Oz has a special part in the show."

She disappeared into the bathroom, closing the door behind her.

I should've been able to come up with a thousand excuses why I needed to stay home tonight, but I was already jumping up to get ready. What did it say about me that my heart pounded with excitement at seeing Oz? It frustrated me to no end that the emotional side of me easily silenced my logical side, but I was elementally attracted to Oz. He'd burrowed under my skin. Perhaps tonight would be my moment of truth.

Chapter 16: Audrey

LoveGame

The school's parking lot was full to capacity. Packs of tweens and teens shrieked, laughed, and yelled as they entered the building, their families trailing behind. They roamed like caged animals, never sitting but pacing back and forth.

In the lobby, teachers manned the concession stand, and Val and I scurried over to the ticket booth, where a long line of people was waiting for us. Music pumped through the sound system in the gym, still loud but muffled and distorted in the hallway. It felt like the entire town squeezed into the school tonight to see the game.

After selling every ticket, Val and I made our way past the bags of popcorn, boxes of candy, and hot dogs and moved into the chaos of the gym. We joined the faculty team of teachers, staring at a circle of tiny tricycles.

A good-looking journalist from the local paper took pictures and interviewed fans. Priscilla smiled wide enough to swallow a shark as she answered questions. Behind her, the Marchfield mascot, an unidentifiable bird in a red shirt, danced with the cheerleaders. Little ones got their faces painted by students in the National Junior Honor Society, and the party music made me want to dance despite my problems.

Keith stood amid ten tiny, toddler-sized trikes donated for the game. He wore a blinding pink T-shirt that encouraged us to "Punch Cancer in the Face."

"We're riding these?" I asked. The bike's hard metal seat barely reached the top of my calf.

"Only the best for you, Audrey." Keith laughed as he checked each bike, tightening bolts.

"At least you aren't a giant like me." Val snorted. "My glutes are going to be on fire tomorrow."

"I'm pretty sure five feet, ten inches doesn't make you a giant." I smirked. "And I know my five feet and five inches are going to be screaming tomorrow."

Keith tightened the bolts on the handlebars of a Teenage Mutant Ninja Turtles trike. "Y'all need to find your t-shirts and pick out your trikes."

He gestured to where Priscilla was now picking through a pile of obnoxiously pink shirts.

"I asked for an extra small, but all I see are medium and large shirts." Priscilla threw them back into the box.

"Just take a medium and tie it at your waist." I took a shirt out of the mess.

"That might work for you, but I don't work out six days a week to wear a medium."

Val nudged me with her elbow. "Do you think a medium will work for you, Audrey? Is your baby belly too big?"

My mouth fell open. Val's narrowed eyes shot daggers at Pree, and I flashed back to that first day in the copy room.

"Oh, I thought I told you, Val. It was a false positive. But why is everyone gossiping about it at school? I never told anyone."

Priscilla flushed pink and then stalked away.

Val shook her head. "It's a shame all that working out and running doesn't make her nicer."

Val and I changed into matching pink t-shirts and returned to the trikes with the rest of the fools who had signed up to play.

Dee waved to us from the stands, and her actual baby bump was starting to show.

My instincts flared, and a fierce desire to be pregnant washed over me. It was ridiculous. My maternal clock should not be ticking!

I blamed Priscilla.

Scanning the crowd, my eyes collided with Oz's. In his Marchfield coach's jacket, he leaned against the boys' locker room door next to Bobby. I hadn't been watching for him, I assured myself, but I felt like I'd been caught red-handed. My face flushed with heat, and I averted my eyes, praying he hadn't seen me gawking.

I forced my brain to clear. Don't think about sex or babies! Oz talked to a group of students. My uterus clenched. His babies would be so cute. Damn it! Stop thinking about sex and babies. I tried to focus on Keith, who explained the rules, but my eyes had a will of their own and zeroed in on Oz again. He laughed at something Bobby said, and I squirmed, feeling my panties grow damp.

Val nudged me. "Looking for something? Or someone?"

I shook my head. "No, nope, uh-uh."

"Then what are the rules of the game?" Val asked.

I shrugged.

"If you'd been listening, you'd know the rules are to stay on the bike and dribble twice before shooting."

When the buzzer sounded, I scooted out onto the court on my pink trike with glittery silver tassels. I basically held a deep squat, perched on a hard metal seat the size of a mango. My thighs banged against my chest, and my knees threatened to break my jaw as I dragged myself along with my feet on the floor.

Val scrambled past, riding a bright red trike with stickers of dragons on the fenders. She yelled over the music and crowd. "If this wasn't for charity, I'd take this bike outside and run it over with my car."

I laughed and almost fell off my bike. Righting myself, I finally made it to my spot on the court.

Priscilla rolled to a stop near me. She'd refused to change into the team shirt and had it flung over her right shoulder instead. How she managed to make sitting on a child's trike look graceful, I'd never know. I nodded to her, hoping she wouldn't speak to me.

Priscilla grumbled, "I want to get this over with. Ned and I are leaving for New York right after this. I'm out on Monday."

I struggled for something appropriate to say but settled for a tight smile. Luckily, our student competitors glided out onto the floor. Some of them were even pedaling their trikes, knees spread out. They all wore white shirts that read "Marchfield Trikes to Defeat Cancer" in pink print.

Fifteen minutes were on the clock. Dr. Winters, acting as the referee, tipped the ball up. Keith tapped it over the head of a seventh grader, and the game began.

I glanced over at the locker room. Bobby was there, cheering us on, but Oz was gone.

The adults moved like crabs, scrabbling back and forth across the court. The kids were quick and limber. They could move the ball to the net but had a hard time throwing it high enough to score a goal. The teachers were clumsy and awkward. Our one advantage was we were taller than the students. The competition quickly grew fierce between the two sides.

"Ms. Freemont, you look tired." Zavier, a rascal from one of my classes, smiled as I puffed, red-faced, down the court with the ball squeezed between my chest and thighs.

I swatted at his hands as he tried to steal the ball. "Thanks for worrying about me, Z."

He shrugged. "Just hand over the ball."

When he tried again, I kept my grip on the ball. "In your dreams, young'un."

Finally positioned under the hoop, I bounced the ball twice on the floor. I took aim at the net.

Zavier shot in front of me, his hands up, getting between me and the basket. Instead of taking the shot, I passed the ball to Keith. He passed it to Val. When Zavier moved to intercept, she passed it back to me.

I leaned back and hurled the ball as hard as possible at the goal. It hit the rim with a clang and bounced. A mad hustle began to regain the ball, and I managed to pull it away from a seventh grader.

"Dribble," Val and Keith yelled. I bounced the ball twice and hurled the ball into the air again.

It hit the rim again, then bounced straight up. It bounced once, twice, and fell through the net. The adults cheered, and the kids booed.

The game continued while I scooted around the outside of the court. I glanced toward the crowd and waved at Dee when she gave me a standing ovation. I checked the time remaining on the scoreboard. Four minutes.

And then I saw Oz by the locker room. Instantly, I forgot all about the game. Desire lit a fire under me. I wanted to limp over to him. Laugh with him. Kiss him.

Pree called my name. I glanced away from Oz toward her voice and got hit square between the eyes with the ball. I fell off my trike, hitting the floor with a thud. Teachers and kids jumped off their trikes, surrounding me in a blur of sneakers and sweat socks.

Priscilla jumped off her trike. "You need to keep your head in the game, Audrey! We could've scored!"

Keith called a time-out, and Oz pushed through the gawking crowd. He picked me up off the floor like a baby or maybe a bride. It made me dizzy, so I wrapped my arms around his neck, breathing in the smell of the warm cedar of his soap. I held on like a koala even as he lowered me to the bench. The school nurse pushed past him and started checking me out.

Val hovered by my shoulder, pressing ice to my forehead. "I'm so sorry, Aud. Are you okay?"

"Yeah," I said, wiggling my nose with my fingers. Not broken.

The nurse checked my eyes with her penlight. Oz hovered nearby, and I saw Priscilla pat him on the shoulder. Telling him lies like the snake in the grass she was.

"Oh, *you're* Priscilla," Oz said, and I smiled when he took a step away from her.

The nurse finished poking and prodding me and declared, "You're not concussed."

She left me sitting on the bench as time ran out. Keith put Margie Denwith, a plump sixth-grade social studies teacher, in to replace me. The game continued while I held the ice to my nose and forehead. I wanted to see myself in a mirror to fix the damage.

The nurse returned with two ibuprofen and a cup of water. I took them gratefully. "Go freshen up in the girl's locker room."

I stood, my legs jiggling, and wound my way through the crowd.

Lionel, the brat from the 4th block, pointed and laughed. I frowned at him, and he melted back into the crowd.

"You all right, honey?" Mrs. Romeo, the art teacher, patted me on the shoulder and I nodded.

"Ms. Freemont, will we have a substitute on Monday?" Ashley, a sweet advanced student from my first block, asked.

"Definitely," I promised.

All the attention made me want to disappear into the locker room even more. Head down, I pushed through the crowd, putting one foot in front of the other and singing about walking five hundred miles with the Proclaimers under my breath.

I ignored Bobby when she laughed. "You look like you have three eyes."

I should have kept my head up because I slammed into a wall. A very warm and familiar wall.

"Oof," I bounced back, and rough hands closed around my upper arms.

A streak of fire ran down my arms and settled in the pit of my belly. How did this man smell like a mocha latte with extra whipped cream? I peeked up slightly, taking in his tight black t-shirt that did nothing to hide his muscular chest.

Where were the best make-out spots in the school? Under the bleachers? Definitely close by, but noisy and full of people at the moment. Perhaps my car would be better.

"Audrey? You okay, Darlin'?"

"Umm," I stared, drinking in the sight of him. I'd never noticed the little dent on the bridge of his nose. My fingers itched to trace it and ask how he'd broken it. I doubted the nurse. I must have a concussion.

"Red?" He shook me a little.

"Oh, yeah, sure. I'm fine." I blinked, remembering where I was and the hoopla going on around us.

His eyes sparkled with humor. His blonde hair was messy, and I fisted my hands to stop my fingers from running through his hair. "Okay, good."

His smile turned into a scowl. I must have looked more of a mess than I thought. I reached up and touched my hair, smoothing it.

"I'm fine," I repeated with a little more force.

He nodded, still smiling. "Can I get a favor, then?"

A favor? Maybe a little skin-on-skin action? I'd help him out. A little moan escaped from the back of my throat.

He stepped closer, his voice a low growl in my ear. "What are you thinking about?"

A shiver ran down my spine, and I swallowed hard, faking a little cough. Somebody should slap me! I was in the freakin' school! There wouldn't be sexual favors on the copier or anywhere else. I took a step back and then another, hoping the distance would help.

I cleared my throat and used my most professional tone. "What can I help you with, Oz?"

He blinked. Could he read my mind? We stood staring at each other while Modern English reached a crescendo about stopping the world in my head. Would it be so bad to have a second-night stand with Oz? No one would know, and we could get this lust out of our systems.

The buzzer sounded, and I jumped. My heart stopped. Were people watching?

Dr. Winters spoke over the loudspeaker. "Our students are leading at the half with a score of 4-2. Concessions are on sale in the lobby. I'd like to remind you all that the proceeds are going to cancer research. The halftime show starts in 10 minutes. Trust me, you don't want to miss it."

People around stood and began moving toward the bathrooms and concessions. Oz grabbed my hand and pulled me toward the boy's locker room door. When I realized he was going to take me in there with him, I dragged my heels.

"Wait! I can't go in there!" I said, trying to pull away.

Oz held my hand tighter, pulling me into the dim room that smelled like a thousand damp, dirty socks. I squeezed my eyes shut, but when I didn't hear boys yelling at me to get out, I slanted them open. We were alone.

Peeking up at Oz's face, I saw a wry smile. "I need your help. I go on in 10 minutes, and this costume is a menace."

Chapter 17: Oz

The Greatest Show

The locker room stank. How did cement walls and floors
absorb years of the essence of teenage boys? Dumb question.
Lockers full of dirty sweat socks and muddy sneakers.

The pungent adolescent miasma acted like a bucket of ice
water, dousing the heat Audrey had ignited in me. I pulled her
into the dressing area and slammed the door behind us. Rows of
lockers surrounded us, and benches wrapped around the room.
A tattered pair of Nikes, a few red Marchfield gym uniforms,

and some old gray socks littered the floor. My outfit hung on a nearby hook.

Why had I agreed to do the halftime show? When Bobby told me about it, she left out that I'd be doing a drag routine. *It'll be fun*, she said. *You should support the other male teachers in the school while raising money for cancer research.*

In other words, she played me.

I picked up the extra-large red dress that Marnie McQuistion, the teen living teacher, created for me. It was a red and white tent with a long zipper going up the back. I'd tried it on exactly once in Marnie's classroom a few Wednesdays back after school.

Marnie'd taught at Marchfield for almost forty years. She was as tiny as a pixie and old enough to have been my middle school teacher. Keith had warned me she had a bit of a dirty mind.

"My knees aren't what they used to be," she'd said as she gathered her box of silver pins.

"I can stand on the table," I volunteered.

Marnie blushed. "Honey, that's so sweet of you."

She hemmed up the fabric, chatting about the students and the year so far.

It wasn't until I jumped off the table that she let out a cackle. "You're lucky, Oz." Her grin was wide.

I grinned back. "How so?"

She snickered. "No one from the yearbook caught us in that compromising position."

What can you do but laugh? And be thankful Yearbook Club only met on Mondays.

Back in the locker room, I shoved the dress at Audrey. "Hold this a second while I put on my shorts."

Her eyes widened as I pulled the clothes out of my bag. Her cheeks turned red, and she turned her face away. Did she expect me to strip in front of her? I would in a heartbeat, but the clock ticked down. I ducked into a nearby stall, yanked off my t-shirt, and changed out of my jeans and into the black shorts I'd brought with me. No way would I go out in front of the whole school in a dress with only my boxers underneath.

"Where are the other guys?" she asked as I came back into the room.

"They're taking turns changing in the faculty bathroom, but I'm too big to get into this costume in that tiny stall."

Audrey nodded and hopped on a bench, gathering the dress in her hands when I returned. She swallowed hard as she stared hard at my chest. I gave my pecs a little flex and heard her sigh. I winced at the bruise blooming in the center of her forehead. Half an inch lower, and the ball might've broken her nose. Dragging her off like a caveman hadn't been my best move. Smooth, Taylor, real smooth.

"How's the head?" I reached out and rubbed my thumb over the bruise.

"Ouch."

"Keep icing it, Red, or you might end up with a black eye."

"Yes, Doctor." Was that a wink? "Now stop wasting time, and put your dress on."

I stepped toward her, and she lifted her arms. Her breasts strained toward my bare chest. She nudged my shoulder, and I held my arms up. I leaned toward her while mentally telling my cock to stand down. I breathed in deeply, but even the stench of the locker room couldn't make my hard-on disappear.

She slipped the dress over my head and smoothed it down over my shoulders and biceps. The fabric swooshed down to my bare knees. She smelled of sunshine and hot as hell woman, and suddenly I was standing in the boy's locker room dressed like a drag queen with a boner. I needed to get back under control fast.

"Turn around," Red ordered, and I spun away gratefully. My heart pounded like I'd run a marathon. I took a deep breath and released it slowly.

And then Audrey's hands danced across the base of my spine. Her warm fingers played over my skin, and I froze, holding my breath. She fumbled with the zipper pull and then tugged it up an inch at a time. Every muscle in my body tensed as breathed in.

Thankful for the protection of the sack-like dress from her prying eyes, I sat on a bench next to Audrey and rolled up a pair of red knee socks.

"I didn't know you were Scottish." Audrey laughed, "What's under that kilt?"

"Laugh all you want, but a Scot never tells," I spoke in my best Shrek impression.

Audrey hopped down off the bench, groaning a little as she bent her legs.

"You should stretch."

"Put ice on my face. Stretch my legs. Got it, Doctor Oz," she teased.

"Ugh. Don't associate me with that controversial TV guy, Darlin'. I've got more class."

She snorted and then clapped her hand over her mouth. "Don't make me laugh. It hurts."

"Sorry." I gestured for her to bring over the big black shoe box on the bench.

Audrey lifted off the lid. "Holy shit, Oz. Where did you get these heels?"

"My sister, Stella, works in backstage design with Opera Delaware. I told her Bobby roped me into this. She sent me these red sequined heels and a wig. She has a terrible sense of humor."

She ran a finger over the satiny sparkles, "I love them. I'd wear these every day." Her eyes glittered. "Dorothy, your stripper-slippers are ready."

"Will you drive me to the hospital when I break my leg?" I stood up like a wobbly baby giraffe, taking its first steps. Audrey howled with laughter as I slapped my right hand onto the lockers to keep from falling.

"Oh my God!" She wiped tears from her eyes. "I need to take a picture!"

She fumbled for her phone, but I put out a hand to stop her. "You might as well wait for the wig, Red."

With a flourish, I pulled the long platinum blond wig out of another box. I tried to pull it over my short hair, but it tangled and caught on my fingers. "I feel like Miss Piggy from *The Muppets*."

"This is real hair." She fished a brush out of the box and smoothed out the tangles. She rummaged through the box. "Wig cap and bobby pins. Somebody is watching out for you."

She slid the tight beige cap over my hair. Red put her hands on my shoulders, turning me around so she was behind me on the bench.

I closed my eyes and spoke between gritted teeth. "My sister, Stella, stole it from the fat lady while she sang."

She giggled. Her breasts rubbed across my back as she reached around me. Suddenly, hair was everywhere, brushing my face, tickling my ears, streaming down my back. My eyes popped open as she jabbed my scalp with the bobby pins, fixing the wig in place before finally brushing the tendrils away from my eyes.

"You're done." She hopped off the bench, walking around to survey the front

"It's heavy." I reached up to touch it, holding it away from the sides of my face. "How do women see out of the corners of their eyes?"

"Evolution," she snickered before slapping at my hands. "You're messing it up."

"It's loose," I muttered as it slid into my eyes.

She zipped behind me. "I can tighten these elastic things. How's that?"

"Better."

She turned me around again with her hands on my shoulders. Through the fringe of platinum blond bangs, I watched as she brushed the long hair behind my shoulders. She bit her lip in concentration, and my blood boiled over. I closed my eyes and breathed in her scent, a mixture of flowers and vanilla. Her fingers tugged the wig around my ears, and I opened my eyes. Her breasts were so close I could almost feel her nipples, fresh berries in my mouth. I swallowed hard and tried to picture myself a world away in a desert bunker.

Audrey clapped, snapping my mind back into focus. "Dang, girl! You are hot!"

I choked down my desire and laughed despite myself. I mentally thanked Marnie again for the loose cut of the skirt. Channeling my inner RuPaul, I put a hand on my hip and bent my knee. "Thanks, girl."

Audrey clapped. "I keep hearing *This is Me* in my mind. You know that song from *The Greatest Showman?*"

"The one where the bearded lady sings?"

She nodded, singing something about drums and having confidence in yourself. She raised her arms over her head with a flourish as she finished singing. She was Venus, standing on the bench, red hair shining, creamy skin glowing. I gazed up at her, soaking in her light and energy. She made my knees fucking weak.

She also made my ankles weak because I wobbled off balance in the damn shoes. I grabbed Audrey's shoulders for balance, but she didn't have time to brace for impact. She fell backward off the bench. I held her waist tighter and pulled her towards me.

Her head collided with my shoulder with a thud. I pivoted in my heels without breaking either of my ankles. My legs collapsed, and I sat on the bench with Audrey on my lap. We sat there together for a solid minute, catching our breath.

"Are you okay?"

"I'm fine."

I felt electricity jump between us. I reached up to cup her jaw with my palm. She was impossible to resist. Her eyes slanted closed, and her lips parted slightly. I lowered my mouth to hers, thirsty to drink from her lips. Time slowed. I leaned toward her, the long wig hair swinging around my shoulders.

I tilted my head, aligning her mouth to mine. The position sent the platinum locks swinging into our mouths and eyes. Sputtering, Audrey jerked away from me. I groaned and hung my head, white hair flying everywhere.

Audrey giggled, brushing the hair away from her face. She stood and straightened my wig again. "All fixed. You're ready to go."

Out in the gym, Dr. Winters's voice boomed over the loudspeaker. "Everyone, please take your seats. The halftime show will be starting in one minute."

Oh shit. I had to go! I stood up fast and turned toward the door. My ankles teetered. Preparing for the worst, I stood with my arms out to the side for balance.

Audrey reached out and brushed a stray lock of hair out of my face. She pushed the hair over my shoulder. She lifted up onto her toes and kissed me on the lips. "Break a leg, Oz."

I rolled my eyes and walked like a baby stork on stilts, taking tiny steps out of the locker room and into the gym. I met up with the other volunteers for this crazy stunt on the sidelines. Keith, Brad, and Frank wore dresses like mine, but the bastards were in flats.

"How did I get conned into this mess?" Brad, a seventh-grade math teacher, groused. He smoothed the red fabric of his dress down.

Frank, the school's guidance director, laughed. "I kinda like it. Very free and airy." He did a spin, his dress floating out.

"I hate the shoes," Keith complained, lifting a foot in a large ballet-style shoe. "No arch support at all."

"I'll switch with you," I offered.

"No chance, stilts," Keith laughed.

Dr. Winters spoke on the microphone. "Put your hands together for the faculty spirit halftime show!" Parents and students stood, cheering and laughing. Their feet pounded on the metal bleachers, making a loud roar.

HandClap by Fitz and the Tantrums pumped through the gymnasium. The four of us took careful steps out onto the basketball court. When we formed a line in the center of the court, the audience exploded. Students screamed and laughed, pointing at us with their mouths open. We began to dance.

We should have practiced in costume. What seemed so simple in jeans and sneakers was a lot harder in a dress. Frank had zero rhythm and sense of direction. He stepped left instead of right. I stomped on his foot, and he howled in pain. I turned my ankle but recovered.

Keith shouted out the steps and direction, "Right, right, spin, left, left, shake it."

Audrey and Val watched on the sidelines, jumping up and down and cheering for us. Audrey blew me a kiss. I had a new motivation to get through this dance.

We danced for an hour. Okay, it was only a minute. My pulse raced. I breathed hard like I'd run a marathon. By the time the Marchfield cheerleaders joined us to finish the dance, a blister formed on my heel. By the end of the three-minute song, my legs shook in the effort to not die by stiletto. These shoes had been made in hell.

When the song finally finished, I flipped my long hair and struck a pose. It felt like the whole school erupted into thunderous cheers. Bobby lowered her phone and gave me a salute. A little embarrassed to have my awkwardness on film, I had to refrain from flipping her the bird.

I kicked the monstrous shoes off, picked them up, and waved to the crowd. The four of us curtsied and then shuffled off the court with the cheerleaders.

I longed for my jeans and Nikes. I never wanted to see the dress and demonic heels again.

Red met me at the locker room door. Her bruised forehead now sported a red swollen knot. I should take her home and get her a cold compress and some pain pills.

But déjà vu slapped me hard. The sassy smile with the wicked gleam in her eyes reminded me of the night I first met her. I sucked in my breath, my heart kick-starting. My gut tightened. I was ready for action. The ice and Tylenol would have to wait. She grabbed my hand and pulled me out the gym door, leaving me no choice but to follow her.

Chapter 18: Audrey

Leave the Door Open

After the heat of the gymnasium, the cool evening air gave me goosebumps, and I shivered. The door clicked shut behind us. The muffled noise continued from inside the gym as I led Oz around the corner of the building. In the shadows of the tiny courtyard, the darkness was almost complete. We stood for a minute as our eyes adjusted.

The Earth Club had planted a small garden against the south-facing wall last spring. Late-blooming milkweed and asters added a sweet aroma to the air as *Butterfly* by Crazy

Town cranked up in my head. I turned to face Oz. His eyes darkened, and his gaze made my heart race. I wanted to fan myself in reaction.

Oz dropped his red heels to the ground with a thump. The light of a distant streetlamp reflected in their glittery surface like jewels. He pulled the wig off, and it landed on top of the pile of shoes. My eyes made the long trip past his yummy shoulders, neck, and chin to his hooded eyes. They burned across my skin and traveled over my breasts, up to my neck and face.

He pressed my back up against the rough bricks of the building and sealed his mouth to mine. I breathed in his warm, masculine scent, hot salt and sweat. Stretching up to meet him, I slid my hands across his wide shoulders. I lowered the zipper part way down his back and slipped my fingers inside the soft fabric to stroke his smooth skin.

His hands found the edge of my t-shirt, and his palms slid up the bare skin of my back. I held my breath as fingertips brushed the sides of my breasts, then arched into him with a soft gasp.

We should stop. We were outside the school. Hundreds of parents, teachers, and students were inside. I should step back and take him home. But the danger excited me. I led him deeper into the shadows. A bench was half-hidden behind a large flowering bush. In the dark, I pushed him down onto the seat. His hands wrapped around my waist and drew me onto his lap.

Oz groaned deep in his throat. My butt brushed across his erection. His mouth and tongue demanded more, and I surrendered. His urgency delighted me. I clung to his hard body as the kiss became more passionate, encouraging me to rub myself against him. I dragged my fingers through the soft, blonde hair at the base of his neck.

Oz's hands slid lower. His fingers teased at the edge of the elastic waistband of my leggings. The world around me faded. I wanted this feeling, this moment, to go on and on.

"Oz," I breathed his name.

"What, Red?" His fingers disappeared between my legs, touching me through the thin fabric. My hips tipped toward him as he teased around the spot I most wanted him to touch.

"Please," I moaned and rolled my hips, hoping he'd understand.

His lips curved against my neck. "So polite, Red. Tell me what you want, dirty girl."

"Touch me." I didn't recognize my husky, breathless voice. I snuggled closer, wrapping my arms around his neck and snuggling closer.

"I am, Red," he spoke lightly, playfully. His fingers softened their touch, shifting away from my pleasure point.

I cracked my eyes open. "Are you toying with me?"

"No. I just want to make you feel good."

"Good, because ever since the night we met, I haven't been able to stop thinking about fucking you."

He sucked in a hissing breath. His hands gripped me harder, and I smiled, relishing his reaction.

His fingers drifted beneath the stretchy fabric, finding their way inside my panties. The roughness of his skin skimmed over my lower belly and shifted toward him like a moth to a flame.

"I told myself I didn't want you, Oz, but I lied to myself."

He sank one finger and then two into me. "You're so wet. So good."

I gasped as he shifted inside me and over my clit. The pleasure inflamed as I unraveled in his embrace.

"Make me come," I whispered into his ear. I kissed him hard, clutching his shoulders. I felt my insides coil tight. I leaned into it, moaning and panting.

"Take what you need, Red." He played my body like an instrument. His other hand moved to my breast and flicked my nipple. Energy flashed from the sensitive peak to my core. I gulped back a moan. His lips found mine, and his tongue urged me on, sending me spiraling.

My heart pounded. My head spun. I closed my eyes. Music, a clashing orchestra of sound, roared in my ears. It swelled louder and matched his rhythm. Building to a crescendo, my body coiled around him. I felt, rather than heard, the song reach its climax as I exploded. A million tiny lights and sounds swirled above me, through me.

Oz broke the kiss. Dipping his head down, he nuzzled his lips against the soft skin behind my ear. "You're so beautiful, Red."

My head flew high in the clouds. Lullabies and sweet chords of relaxation hummed through my body. I sat heavy in his arms.

"Wanna carry me home?"

"It's five miles, Red."

I ran my fingers lazily down his shirt and over his nipple. "I'd strip you down and have my way with you."

"Probably wouldn't have the energy to enjoy it after running with you on my back."

"I'd let you rest first. How much time would you need?"

He was about to answer when the gym door abruptly opened. Both of us froze as the sounds of the game and the crowd intruded into our quiet night. Pink's *Get This Party Started* washed over me like a cold shower. I shivered, arranging my clothes. The second half must be underway. I sat up with a jerk, and my feet hit the ground. Cool air filtered into the space between us.

The door closed with a bang, cutting off the noise. Nothing moved around us except the breeze. We listened for footsteps or sounds of people coming closer. A minute ticked by. Nothing.

My body hummed, loose and heavy, but the few inches of space between us allowed a sense of responsibility to flood in. What was I doing out here? I was a freaking chaperone! I cleared my throat, not meeting his eyes.

Sensing my emotional retreat, Oz gathered me close, touching his forehead to mine.

"Ouch." I jerked away, my head throbbing.

Oz's lips soothed the spot. "Sorry."

I met his eyes, the pain forgotten. Even in the dark, I knew he was throwing down the gauntlet. Could I finish what I'd started? Was I brave enough?

"I should find Val and finish the event," I whispered.

He winked and gave me a smile. "And after?"

"Maybe we could continue... this...whatever this is..." A rendezvous? A hook-up? I didn't know.

His white teeth flashed. "I need to change anyway. I'm not walking out of here in a dress."

I rolled the hem of the dress between my fingers. "Maybe you should. It's easy to take off and get my hands under it."

"It's drafty, though. You better zip me up before we go back in."

Tugging up the zipper, his warm skin made my fingers itch to explore his body.

Oz turned back to meet my eyes in the dark. "Will you come home with me, Red?"

A few days ago, hell, a few hours ago, I'd have stormed off at the invitation, but the more I got to know him, the more I liked him. He made me laugh and cared about the people around him. He was a good teacher and an excellent coach. And I couldn't ignore that I'd come in his lap. But no matter how damp he made my panties, friends don't bail on friends for booty calls.

"I need to take Val home."

"That's not a no." He kissed my cheek. Butterflies took flight in my stomach.

"It's not." As I said it, I wondered if a mild concussion might result in loose morals. I'd research it. Later. Much later.

"Is it a yes?" His low voice sent shivers down my spine.

I thought of my long list of logical reasons I shouldn't. But here, at this moment, nothing on that list mattered. I wanted this man. Fuck everything else.

My tongue tripped over itself as I spoke. "Can I come over after I drop Val off?"

"Red, are you propositioning me? Again?"

"Yes. I mean, if you want–"

He kissed me. "I think it's pretty obvious. You can persuade me to do almost anything."

"Anything?"

"Almost." He smiled sheepishly. "But do me a platonic favor first."

I blinked. Did he say platonic?

"Unzip me again in the locker room, so I can get out of this costume."

I laughed all the way back into the gym.

Chapter 19: Audrey

The Spy

The teachers lost fourteen to two.

Despite his smirk, Zavier reached out his hand. "Good game."

I smiled back with all my teeth. "Don't forget to finish that assignment for Monday."

He rubbed his neck. "Aww, man!"

I laughed and patted his shoulder. "Since y'all won, I'll postpone it till Wednesday. I'll change it on the website."

His smile was like sunshine. "You're the best, Ms. Freemont." He ran off to tell the others.

I caught Oz staring from the other side of the gym. He winked, and I blushed. He and Bobby were folding tables and carrying them to storage. Watching his muscles bulge for the last half hour fanned the bonfire in the pit of my belly. I checked my watch for the hundredth time. The minutes inched by like a tortoise on a cold day, and my frustration mounted.

Trying to distract myself, I volunteered to drag tricycles out to Keith's truck. Wrestling with the handlebars as the metal bikes whacked against my shin.

"Shit." I kicked a tiny tire. I hoped this fundraiser raised a ton of money because I'd paid for it in aches and pains!

Of course, I'd also had a pretty awesome orgasm. Just thinking about it, my body relaxed. I needed to get these trikes into this truck and get out of here. I wanted more.

"Stay focused, Freemont," I muttered out loud, lifting the red tricycle up and over the tailgate. It clattered into the truck bed, metal grating against metal.

Humming Queen's *Bicycle Race* to myself, I didn't hear Priscilla approach in the darkness. She coughed, and I jumped. I caught a whiff of her citrus and apple perfume as I turned toward her. Her smile was wide and feral. She'd changed into a blue pantsuit a la Hillary Clinton.

"Trying to give me a heart attack, Pree?" Ignoring the spike of anxiety she gave me, I leaned down to lift another trike into the bed of Keith's truck. The handlebars swung toward Priscilla, and the tire whacked the side of her head.

Her mouth opened in a scream, nightmarish and hostile. "You did that on purpose!"

I dropped the trike. "I'm so sorry, Pree. These trikes are a menace."

"I don't believe you!" she screeched. She spun away from me, stomping to her car.

"Have a good weekend, Pree," I called, trying not to sound snarky. When I reached down for the trike, I heard her coming back.

Priscilla's ponytail whirled in an angry arc behind her as she marched back, her shoes slapping the pavement like gunshots. She loomed over me, hands on her hips, a sour expression. "I'd wish you the same, but I'm afraid of what it would encourage you to do."

I let the second trike drop into the bed of the truck and stepped back to face her.

Priscilla's face was blotchy and red. Her right eye twitched. "Oh, don't play innocent. We both know you're far from that."

I reeled back as if she hit me. Was she going to accuse me of being pregnant again? I struggled to respond, but Priscilla steamrolled on.

"You do realize this is a school, right? There are impressionable children everywhere." She gestured to the deserted parking lot as if teens lurked in the shadows.

Cold dread slid down my spine to my stomach. The bonfire Oz created turned into ice. Did Priscilla know?

"What?" I blurted out, feeling stupid.

"You are always trying to one-up me, but you aren't going to do it this time. I promise you that."

I gaped at her, speechless.

"Pree," I started, but she interrupted me.

"I don't have time for you. I've got to go."

She powerwalked to her white Audi and started the engine while I stood there dumbly gawking until her taillights disappeared into the night.

The darkness closed around me. I tried to swallow my panic. If Priscilla knew about Oz and me, what kind of rumors would she spread? What if she complained to the administration?

I'm not sure how I got through the next fifteen minutes. Rockwell's *Somebody's Watching Me* pounded through my head. I stowed the rest of the trikes in Keith's truck and picked up trash around the concession stand. I could feel Oz's eyes on me, but I turned away. I needed time.

On the way out, Oz squeezed my hand and whispered, "See you soon." Nodding, I choked on unshed tears and hurried toward my car with Val.

What was the etiquette for canceling a hook-up?

Go with direct? *Peeping Pree saw us. I'm never having sex again.*

Casual? *Hey. Something's come up, and I'm not going to make it.*

Vague? *It's not you, it's me.*

Val bounced on the passenger seat. "You and Oz disappeared after halftime."

My stomach knotted, but she had me cornered. I backed out of the parking space and headed toward Val's house. "He needed help with his costume."

"Oh, girrrll, please, I saw your rosy cheeks and well-kissed lips. You got down on the school grounds." Val laughed.

I swerved and over-corrected. "You spied on us!?"

Val grabbed onto the dashboard. "No. Don't be gross. I just kept watch, so no one would interrupt whatever you two were doing."

A bitter laugh in my throat almost choked me. "You're a terrible lookout. You missed Pree stepping out for a cigarette or something."

"What?" Val gasped. "No, I—Shit! I only walked away for a minute. I grabbed a Band-Aid. I scraped my leg on my trike and realized I was bleeding."

"It only took a minute." I sighed.

"It had to be pitch black out there. How could Pree see anything?"

"I don't know. I was a little busy coming in his lap!"

"Whoa!" Val slapped her hand over her mouth.

Gripping the wheel hard, I wanted to pound my head on the horn. "What the fuck am I going to do?"

"If you murder Pree, I'll help hide the body. I'm your ride or die."

I rolled my eyes at her suggestion. Neither of us could watch The Red Wedding in *Game of Thrones* without looking away. Murdering Priscilla was inconceivable.

"I need to call Oz. I can't go over there tonight and pick up where we left off."

"No!" Val leaned over and smacked the dashboard. "Do not call him, Aud. Priscilla is jealous. She only gets off if she's run a marathon."

I laughed despite myself. "I don't know, Val. I thought I wanted to take this further with Oz, but now..." I shrugged.

"Was it at least as good as the first time?"

The light turned green, and I drove on humming Foreigner's *Feels Like the First Time*. Val sang along as I sorted out my emotions. "I can't say it was good.

"It was mind-blowing. I forgot we were at school and there was a game going on."

Val sighed and relaxed back into the seat. "I knew he had stamina. I'm glad the first time wasn't a fluke."

"I'm supposed to meet him at his place to pick up where we left off. But I don't know."

"Stop that!"

"What?"

"You *have* to go!"

"I don't know." I shook my head. "Priscilla will be in my head the whole time."

"Do not let Priscilla Henesey ruin your booty call. What is she going to do? Pin a giant, red A on your back?"

I pulled up in front of her apartment, parked, and turned off the engine.

"I'm not committing adultery, Val. Poor Hester Prynne." I could think of several traits I recently had in common with the character.

Val rolled her eyes. "You know what I mean."

"It's a poor analogy."

She groaned in exasperation. "How's this—Don't let Priscilla brand you with a giant, pink penis? Does that meet with your approval?"

Was it the imagery, the stress of the situation, or my aching head? That picture broke the dam inside me. "Where would she put it? On my butt? It could double as the new JUICY logo."

Val's giggles joined mine until we resembled teenage girls at a sleepover. Or middle school teachers.

Val pulled two tissues from the box in my glove compartment. She handed one to me and dabbed her eyes with the other. "You can't let Priscilla win, Aud."

I felt tugged in two directions. The sane, logical side of me insisted that I should head home. It whispered, *Call Oz and tell him something came up. Rub tiger balm all over your legs and go to bed early.*

The sex-starved emotional side of me shouted. *Drive over to his and dare him to make you come at least two more times!*

Val met my eyes. I knew she silently cheered for Team Orgasm.

Logical Audrey had a point, but sex-starved Red was an elemental force to reckon with. Oz made me feel beautiful. He encouraged me, took care of me, and got me off. But I hadn't reciprocated.

Damn, but I love sexual reciprocation. My naughty voice whispered, *You can't leave him rejected and alone with blue balls.*

I turned the engine over. "Get out before I change my mind."

She squealed and clapped her hands. "Call me tomorrow! I'm living vicariously through you, so I need lots of details." She ran to her door, turning after she'd unlocked it. In the headlights, she did a little dance, ending with giving me two thumbs up.

I waved and put the car in reverse.

My apartment was between Val's place and Oz's house, so I swung in to feed Stevie his bedtime snack.

Inside, I caught my reflection in the mirror. My face was flushed, the bruise on my forehead was purple, and my hair was wild. Logical Audrey suggested I stay home and call Oz for a raincheck, but Red decided to go all out.

I rooted through my underwear drawer. Logical Audrey whispered, "Granny panties are comfortable."

Red dismissed that with a shrug and jumped in the shower.

Half an hour later, Logical Audrey gave in and helped Red by going through the hook-up checklist:

Mouthwash and deodorant? Check!

Red matching bra and panties? Check!

Sexy, low-cut top and skinny jeans? Check! Check!

I played with my hair in the mirror, putting it up and then taking it down. I smoothed on Passion Pink lipstick and spritzed my pulse points with Night Garden perfume.

Logical Audrey whispered, "Will Oz initiate a sleepover?" Red stuffed supplies into a duffle just in case.

Stevie wandered in to inspect the bag. He clawed my spare undies out and began to knead the small pile of clothes.

I picked him up, rubbing his ears. "I'm not taking you with me." Stevie purred contentedly.

"I'll be back soon, big man." I carried him into the kitchen and set out food and water. Before self-doubts snuck in, I grabbed my bag and keys.

Checking my phone, Oz had texted me his address. He lived in a residential area a little farther from the school.

Driving along Bradbury Street, I admired the small single-family houses. Tidy front yards stretched down to the street, and tall shade trees started to turn red and orange. Oz's blue truck sat in the driveway in front of a ranch in the middle of the block.

I parked my car behind his and hopped out. The red brick ranch had big front windows and a cheerful red door. Following the sloped sidewalk to the small front porch, I smiled at the sight of two rocking chairs. They begged to be sat in on this cool autumn evening. Taking a deep breath, I knocked.

The door swung open, and Oz stood on the threshold, barefoot and shirtless. His jeans slung low over his hips, and his hair dark from a recent shower. From behind him, Chris Stapleton crooned *Tennessee Whiskey* through his Bluetooth speaker.

My mouth watered, and I wondered what to say. Should I mention the problem with Priscilla? Or throw myself into his arms and beg him to take me to bed?

I went with, "Hi."

Oz reached out and tugged me close. I wrapped myself around him and trailed my fingers through the cool drops of water on his shoulders. The clean smell of cedar and nutmeg tantalized my senses.

Kicking the door shut, he crushed my lips with his. I chuckled despite myself. Oz enjoyed pinning me to any vertical surface. My back pressed into the smooth wood of the door as he leaned into me. Running his hands up my sides from my hips to the sides of my breasts, he reignited the fire inside me.

"Took you long enough. A man could die waitin' on you, Red."

"Perfection takes time." I surrendered to his kiss.

My arms wound around his neck. His lips and his tongue tasted of peppermint and chocolate. I wanted to breathe him in. The feel of his mouth on mine awakened all my senses.

"Red, you're so beautiful. Definitely worth the wait." His hands played with my breasts through the fabric of my thin shirt and bra, stroking and pinching. The blood pounded through my veins. The hair on my arms stood up in response to Oz's electrifying touch.

His words made me feel powerful.

"I want to taste you, Red."

He started behind my ear, and I sucked in a breath as his soft tongue prepared the way for his teeth on my earlobe. Shivers ran down my spine, and I moaned as he continued to my collarbone. His hands found the hem of my shirt warm and rough against my skin as he traced the neckline with his mouth.

His playlist rolled over me. Dierks Bently sang *Come a Little Closer*, and I felt myself sway to the rhythm. I urged him on, arching toward him, moaning. I wanted to feel his rough hands on my bare skin, but Oz refused to hurry. His teeth and lips trailed across my neck and then back to my mouth. I moaned, grinding my hips against his body.

He took a step back, took my hand, and tugged me through the small living room and down the hallway.

"I'm enjoying the caveman tour." I snickered.

Oz turned, picking me up. I screamed as he threw me over his shoulder.

"You asked for it, Red."

"Did I?"

"Sounded like it to me."

My first view of his room was his bed. A huge wooden frame and mattress dominated almost all of the space. It was a bed straight out of a castle in some romance novel. Covered in a rich brown and gold-colored comforter, it inspired sensual dreams.

"Wow."

"In the Army, I slept in a lot of tiny cots. Life's too short to sleep in an inferior bed."

"I need you to take me shopping."

Oz lowered me down the front of him, kissing my breasts as they slid past. When my toes touched the floor, he took my face in his hands and kissed me. I locked my arms around his neck, losing myself in him.

His hands were everywhere. He pulled my shirt up and over my head. His breath caught at the sight of the ladies in red lace. Grateful for having taken the extra time to get ready, I held my arms over my head, lifting them up to his gaze.

"You're incredibly sexy, Red," Oz whispered. His hands slid into the waistband of my jeans. "You're like a gift I need to unwrap."

He unhooked my bra, and my breasts tumbled into his hands. His rough fingers loved my nipples, pinching and rolling them. My head spun. I panted. They felt heavy, and when he took them into his mouth, sucking and bathing them with his tongue, I clutched at his hair, sailing out onto a wave of wanting.

"Hurry," I urged him. I wound myself around him. Urging him closer, encouraging him to take me. But he was an unmovable mountain.

"Our first time was too fast. I've wanted you slow and hot ever since." The huskiness of his voice sent shivers over my skin.

Breathless, I reached up for him, intent on changing his mind.

Oz evaded. "Trust me."

He knelt, taking off my shoes and running his palms over my instep and then up my legs. He kissed my belly, making me shiver as his tongue traveled along the edge of my jeans. Slowly, he drew my jeans and panties down. Wet and hungry for him, I stepped out of them. He nudged me against the edge of the bed, and I sat.

"Oz, please." I tried scooting closer, but he held me with one hand against my belly. His mouth trailed up my leg, pausing to kiss behind my knee. I squirmed wildly.

Lying back on the bed, I arched up, giving him greater access to the places that most wanted his attention. His head dipped between my legs, and I stopped breathing. Stopped thinking. My legs fell to the side as his lips and fingers opened me. He filled me, tasted me. There was only his tongue and his mouth.

I cried out, feeling my body tighten, my heart pounding as sensations flooded through me.

"That's it." His mouth burned me, branded me. His tongue was water, teasing, and playful. I arched up toward him, totally out of control. Then the tightness in me burst, and I was flying.

Oz moved, sliding up my body. He kissed me softly. "So fucking hot."

Pulses of energy zipped through me as I lay back, watching through sultry eyes. He unzipped his jeans and pulled them off.

Lying beside me, his muscular body stretched out. I reached between us and stroked him. I wrapped my hand around his hard cock and teased him with my fingers.

"I never thought I'd touch you again," I whispered. "But I wished for it."

His hips pumped under my hand. "A hundred times, a thousand, I dreamt of you."

I bent, taking his length in my mouth. I shivered at the feel of him—solid, warm, and alive under my tongue. He tasted of salt and sea, and I wanted him.

"Audrey." I relished the sound of my name as he moaned.

I rose up onto my knees, studying the pile of condoms on his bedside table.

"Optimistic. I like that in a man."

"Realistic. I want the hell out of you, Red." Oz quirked an eyebrow, and I melted while he slipped the protection on.

Chris Young's *Getting You Home* played in the background, reminding me of our first time together. His hands gripped my hips, lifting me until I straddled him.

"Slow and easy, Red."

But I was past that. I sank down on his cock, driving him into me until there was no more to take. I leaned over and kissed him, running my hands over his shoulders and chest. My hips set the rhythm.

Oz's hands burned hot on my breasts. His mouth nipped and licked, making me wild with need. Rearing up, his mouth plundered mine while he pumped deep. His fingers found my clit, and my body rocked harder as he touched me.

Breathing raggedly, I cried out as another orgasm ripped through me. Oz threw his head back as my pussy pulsed around him. He groaned, and I felt him come hot inside me. I wrapped myself around him and stopped thinking for a long, long time.

Chapter 20: Oz

I Won't Let Go

Red curled up, her head on my shoulder. Her fingers caressed the skin on my chest, playing with the hair. I held her, letting my thoughts wander as my fingers made invisible patterns on the skin of her back. I smiled and nuzzled my nose into her hair. The fresh smell of flowers and vanilla washed over my senses and soothed all my rough edges. Holding her was a balm to my soul. Audrey filled me up in a way I didn't want to dwell on but also couldn't ignore.

For the first time in years, I relaxed completely, but I fought against the waves of exhaustion that rolled over me, threatening to drag me under. What if the ghosts of war came back to haunt me? In addition, I didn't want to be a caveman and fall asleep on her again. None of this stopped me from wanting my cake and eating it, too.

Wrapping her up in my arms, I hugged her close. "Wanna stay over, Red?"

"Do you want me to?"

Instead of answering, I brushed my hand down her back and pinched her butt.

Audrey jumped and punched my arm playfully. "Is that a yes?"

Wide awake, I shifted and rolled on top of her. "Stay."

I sealed her mouth with mine and let my hands play over her. I loved her body. She tightened and arched as I stroked. I'd memorized the secret places that made her moan and beg. The space behind her knee and the soft spot on the back of her neck called like sirens. I lavished them with attention and then slipped my fingers inside her.

"I want to fuck you again, Red."

Her arms wound around me, guiding my mouth to her breast. Her skin was smooth, creamy, and sweet as honey. I lavished each nipple with attention, making them hard and ready.

I reached between her legs. "You're dripping for me, Red.

She rose up to meet my fingers. The perfume of her body danced over my senses, spicy and sweet. I trailed my lips across her chest and up her neck, breathing her in.

She hummed low in the back of her throat with the Black Eyed Peas on my playlist.

Smiling, I nuzzled my lips against her throat and sang along. *Boom, Boom, Pow.*

Music was her magic aphrodisiac. She arched up, clawing at my back with her nails, trying to get closer. I lost myself in her body and feasted on her.

Her hand slid down and squeezed my balls. I held onto my control by the skin of my teeth. Her fingers wrapped firmly around my cock, and my brain almost shut down. I yearned to flip over on top of her and make her mine. Instead, I grabbed her hands, pulling them up to my shoulders. I wanted to slow things down and draw out our pleasure.

Red wriggled free. She rolled over the bed, thrusting her hips and beautiful butt back. "Fuck me from behind."

Her sultry voice pushed me to the edge. I grabbed a condom, rolled it on, and thrust into her. She cried out, taking me deep. Reaching around, I cupped her breasts. I rolled her nipples between my fingers as I kissed the back of her neck.

"Please," Red begged.

I found the spot between her legs. She moaned low and long. I closed my eyes and pounded into her. Her pussy tightened around me, so close. And then her muscles clenched and squeezed my cock hard. Her orgasm roared through her. Unable to stop myself, I followed her over the edge.

When I pulled her close and wrapped my arms around her, she relaxed into sleep, her breathing slow and even. And I followed her into the abyss.

***

When I woke Sunday morning, I puzzled my way through a thick fog of sleep. I dreamed I was back in the sandbox, on patrol in the dark, tense and scared. The dream shifted into a nightmare when a bomb exploded. My entire body jerked as I woke, my senses reeling out of control. Breathing deeply, I sat up, instinctively reaching for a weapon that wasn't there.

Audrey's red hair splayed across my pillow. She snuggled up under my blanket. Her hands tucked up under her chin, her soft face innocent.

My palms itched to touch her. The nightmarish hyper-awareness subsided as my morning erection strained toward her. My first instinct was to unwrap her and continue where we left off. I rolled onto my side and reached for her, but the bruise on her forehead stopped me. Its purple and green hues made my stomach clench as images of my nightmare resurfaced.

Audrey inched closer in her sleep, her soft body warm against mine, but with my heart still pounding from the dream, I needed space. I eased to the edge of the bed and slowly stood, careful to keep the blankets around her. I pulled on my jeans and left her snoozing.

In the kitchen, I started coffee. My stomach growled. I could make the two of us breakfast in bed. I had eggs and bacon. Red needed protein for better healing. Of course, she also needed sleep.

Setting that idea aside, I fried a couple of eggs and shoveled them down along with some sourdough toast. I picked up a paperback copy of *American Gods* by Neil Gaiman and settled into my favorite chair.

My sister and Mom would point out it was my only chair, but how many chairs did a guy need? If I wanted more chairs, I'd buy them. What did it matter if I didn't feel like lugging a bunch of furniture with me every time I moved?

Of course, Mom and Stella didn't stop there. They sent me pictures of shelter dogs all the time. Their obsession with chairs and dogs was unhealthy. What would I do with a dog anyway? Walk it? Play with it? Who had time for that?

I lost myself in the hard-core fantasy of my novel for about an hour before I heard Red stirring.

"No," I heard her moan. Was she dreaming? I tip-toed back to the bedroom.

Stretched out under the sheet, Red's eyes opened as I came in. She lifted her arm toward me, and my body reacted instantly. *Let's go!*

But when she yelped, I froze in my tracks. Her arms fell limply onto the bed.

"I'm dying!"

Had I been that rough? Had I hurt her?

"What's up, Red?"

"My muscles are frozen. It hurts to move." She blinked. "It even hurts to close my eyes."

Changing gears, I set aside all ideas of ravishment. Retreating to the kitchen, I got her a glass of ice water and some pain pills. Back in the bedroom, I gave her the pills and helped her sit up.

"Ow, ow, ow." Every muscle from her calves to her neck was rigid with agony. "Fucking tricycles!"

A basketball had hit her in the head. I knew she should have stretched and hydrated. But what had I done? Kept her up late so I could get off. I shuffled my feet and met her eyes, ready to grovel.

"Red, I'm so sorry."

"I'm too sore to even guess why you are apologizing." She rolled over onto her back and groaned with pain.

"I took advantage."

She snorted. "I think that was me."

"You were hurt, and–"

Red tried to sit up, but her muscles protested. "Shit, Oz, stop. Can we debate this later? I can't move. I'm dying."

"Let's sit you up." I propped some pillows behind her. I brushed the hair out of her face and held her hand.

When her phone chirped in her bag, I got it for her. If I adopted one of those dogs Mom suggested for me, he could've retrieved it. Perhaps I needed to give it some more consideration.

"It's Val," Audrey said, reading the text. "She's dying. Even my fingers hurt! Can you text her back? Tell her *me too.*"

"Sure." I kept my chuckle silent as I responded.

"This isn't how I envisioned waking up in your bed."

Only an asshole would agree with that. I winked at her. "I've got a beautiful naked lady in my bed. Seems like a pretty good morning to me."

She leaned toward me and moaned.

Not in a good way.

"I need you to help me get up. I've gotta go home."

"Let's get you in the shower, Red. The hot water will loosen up your stiff muscles." I supported her as she stood. Every movement precipitated an *ow* until it became a mantra.

She'd been awake a half an hour, and I'd already tallied thirty-three. Am I a jerk or a math teacher? Both?

She stood in my shower—alone—for another half an hour. I sat on the bed, imagining her lathering my shampoo in her hair. Rubbing my soap over her breasts and down her belly to the little nest of curls between her legs. I heard her muttering and cursing off and on. The water stopped, and she came out wrapped in my towel.

I tried hard to focus on the colorful bruise on her forehead. "How do you feel?"

"Like I'm going to sit on the sofa all day, taking pain meds every four hours while smothering myself in Tiger Balm." She laughed awkwardly. "On the plus side, I'm too sore to hold a pen or grade papers."

I wanted to make a joke about how an orgasm might loosen her up. Again, only an asshole would say that out loud. "You should stretch. Take a walk, keep your muscles engaged."

She moved to sit on the edge of my bed, wincing as her legs bent to sit. "I hear you, and I hate you."

"I'd be happy to give you a massage."

She rolled her eyes. "We both know that means sex. Hand me my leggings."

I handed over the soft, stretchy pants and watched Audrey struggle to bend down to put her feet into them. "Ow. God damn it, ow."

"Let me help you." I knelt in front of her and slipped her feet into her leggings.

"It will help if I stand up."

She and I groaned at the same time. Red's sound was rooted in pain. Mine too, but because I was now eye level with her pussy.

I focused on yanking the fabric up over her freshly showered legs. "These things are a menace."

She gave me a small smile. "But my butt looks great in them."

I stood and walked around her to check it out. "You aren't lying. Now sit down, and I'll put on your shoes."

"How can I feel sexy and broken at the same time?"

"I have that effect on women," I teased.

When her shoes were on, I winked at her. "There you go, Cinderella."

"Thanks, Oz. You went above and beyond."

She seemed so little and fragile. I wanted to scoop her up and hug her, but I was afraid to hurt her. "How about some breakfast?"

Her white teeth close over her pink bottom lip. "I think I should go."

"Okay," I said, trying not to feel disappointed. I helped her gather her things, walked her out to her ugly car, and kissed her gently.

"I'll see you at school tomorrow," she whispered as our lips parted.

"Sure will, Red."

A few minutes later, I watched her drive away.

Restlessness consumed my mind and body. Like on a rainy day when you want to soak up rays at the beach, but you can't. And the weight of the rain gets almost unbearable, and you feel like you might scream.

Heavy silence filled the house. Turning on the speaker, *Dead or Alive* started singing about spinning like a record.

This song always made me think of sitting in the mess with Bobby and the others. The Radio in a Box DJ loved *You Spin Me Round* and played to several times a day. Sometimes it haunted my dreams.

When I let myself think about my time in Afghanistan, I remember how abysmally hot it was day after day. The sand gets in every part of your body until you're sweating rocks. Every single second, you're on edge even when you think you tell yourself you're relaxed. But when you sleep, it's like falling into the dark depths of the ocean.

The physical and emotional toll of Army life builds up like an invisible wall. I locked away my emotions and fear behind the gate and tossed away the key so I could live. But when I got out, the dam burst. I relived missions, the loss of friends, and a thousand bad decisions. The nightmares and insomnia plagued me even all these years after being discharged. The stress and anxiety after military life seems harder than actually living it.

I made the bed and started a load of laundry. I picked up the brown leather satchel off my coffee table but didn't feel like grading inequalities test papers. I considered working out but wasn't in the mood. I picked up my novel but couldn't get back into the story.

An hour later, I figured it out. I missed Red. And it confused the Hell out of me. Sure, I liked Red. And the sex was fucking amazing. But pining for her? The last time I'd brooded over a woman had been in high school.

I wandered into the kitchen and checked my phone. Not that I expected anything. I mean, why would she text me? I shook my head, disgusted with my inner mopey hound dog.

There were three other texts, though. The first from my Mom:

10:00 AM Mom: I'm driving into Dover for Stella's opera. No need to call today. I'll talk to you tomorrow.

Ten years ago, when I left my mom and Stella to join the Army, months would go by between conversations and emails. The guilt over leaving so soon after my dad passed drove a deep wedge between us.

When I got discharged, I called to tell her I accepted the invitation to attend Fordham University in New York. I assumed she'd be proud, but Mom raged at me. She demanded that I come home to Delaware, so I got in my truck and drove the five-hour drive home.

Mom hugged me at the door, leaned back, and stared into my eyes. Then she grabbed my ear and pulled me into the kitchen. She whacked me on the head with her wooden spoon and yelled at me. Lamenting all the nights she worried, and all the years she'd waited for me to grow up.

Sometime during that night, I aged twenty years. And since I valued my life, I called Mom every Sunday. Except today.

The second text came from Bobby.

10:32 AM Bobby: You are the G.O.A.T., dude, freaking hilarious.

I snorted. *Greatest of all Time, my ass.*

She sent five pictures from halftime with the caption The Giant Red Yeti in Drag. I refrained from responding FUCK YOU.

The final text was from my little sister.

10:35 AM Stella: Spam me with drag pics!

Wincing, I sent my sister two of Bobby's pictures. She'd get a huge laugh over them with Mom.

I set the phone down. Now what? It wasn't even eleven AM, but I decided to start some chili. The family recipe was red hot, full of spices and meat. My dad and grandad perfected it together and won the Dover Chili Cook-Off four years in a row. It was all I had left of them.

My dad and grandad loved to cook and play baseball. They'd been huge Yankees fans. I could remember Fourth of July barbecues with them bickering over the grill and the game on TV. Mom got so sick of them arguing that she'd sprayed them both with the hose, and Dad chased her around until he caught her, tickling her until she screamed.

Both men died young. Grandad had been fifty-six when he passed, but my dad died at forty. His massive heart attack caught us all by surprise exactly fourteen years ago tomorrow. Heart disease ran in the family. My doctor did echocardiograms yearly. She said I was in excellent physical health, but sometimes I could hear the sands of time slipping away.

I channeled my emotions into the food. Letting the chili simmer on the stove, I forced myself to grade the tests.

Afterward, I put the students into groups for re-teaching, added grades on the computer, and made some notes about who needed tutoring.

Several hours had dragged by. The chili bubbled in the pot, hot and ready. I boxed it up into two containers and put one in the fridge for later.

Tapping the second box with my forefinger, I wrestled with indecision. I wanted to take it over to Audrey's and check on her. I pictured her lying on her couch, unable to move without saying "Ouch." I wouldn't leave a fellow soldier alone like that, and I sure as hell wouldn't let Audrey suffer the rest of the day by herself. I grabbed my jacket and keys and jumped in my truck.

Seven minutes later, I knocked on her door and heard her yell, "I can't get up."

I wiped the smile off my face and tried the doorknob. The unlocked door swung open. Audrey lay flat on her back on the sofa. Her cat stretched out like a furry gray pillow across her chest.

I cleared my throat, letting her know I'd come in. "Hi."

She didn't open her eyes. "Didn't I tell you to go away?"

I froze. Had I crossed a line by stopping by? Pushing my doubts away, I said, "You said you couldn't move. That's different."

She cracked her eyes open, glaring at me. "Why are you here?"

Shit. She wanted me gone. "I brought you chili. I can fix some for you now or put it in the fridge for later."

Her expression softened. "Chili sounds good."

"Give me a second." I hastily took four steps into the apartment's tiny kitchen and found a bowl and spoon.

By the time I came back, she'd struggled up to a sitting position and shifted the cat to the sofa. She took the bowl and began eating. "I'm starving, but couldn't make myself move."

I eased down next to her on the sofa. My weight shifted her enough to make her say, "Ow," but she smiled. After finishing the chili, I gently massaged her sore muscles, starting at her shoulders and moving down her arms. She moaned and closed her eyes.

"Is it helping?" I asked.

"It hurts, but it also feels amazing." She sighed, relaxing against me.

I moved to her legs, massaging her thighs and calves. "Ow, ow, don't stop," she groaned. I tried not to laugh. Or get turned on.

When I finished, she was a bit looser. I gave her more pain meds, and she lay back next to me on the sofa. We streamed two seasons of *Abbott Elementary*, laughing at the school comedy.

"How come they get to leave and go out to lunch every day? I can barely eat before my class is back, rowdier than ever."

"It's a TV comedy," Audrey yawned. "If they told it like it is, it wouldn't be funny."

"It'd be a documentary about how teachers aren't doing enough to solve all the world's problems."

Glancing at my watch, I was shocked to see it was already nine PM. Plus it was a school night.

I smoothed her hair back and kissed her cheek. "You ready for bed?"

"I'm not sure I can get down the hall without dying," Audrey admitted.

Standing, I pulled her up, listening to her chant, "Ow, ouch, damn it, OW!"

Leaning on me, Audrey limped down the hallway to her bedroom. Her cat jumped up on the bed as I tucked the covers around her. He curled up on the pillow next to hers.

"I'll see you at school tomorrow, Red. Sleep well and feel better."

I hoped she'd ask me to stay, but her eyes fluttered closed. I let myself out, locking her door behind me and ignoring the temptation to stay.

***

At school on Monday, I found an appointment slip in my mailbox. Dr. Winters wanted me to stop by the office at the end of the day. Ignoring the feeling I was somehow in trouble, I went to my classroom, where I turned on my computer and organized materials.

I heard Audrey and Val arrive long before I saw them. Their loud exclamations of pain announced their arrival.

"Ow, damn it," Val moaned. "I am never doing another fundraiser again."

"It'd be fun, Keith said. It'd raise a lot of money." Audrey winced. "He didn't say anything about bodily harm."

"I would punch him, but it's not worth the pain."

They stopped in front of Audrey's classroom, so I stepped into the hallway. "Good morning, ladies. Enjoy your weekend?"

"Shut up, Oz," Audrey growled. "I can't even reach down to unlock my door."

I took her key and opened the door. Chivalry wasn't dead, and I'd punch anyone who said otherwise.

"I'd sit down," Val complained, "But I can't bend my knees. How am I going to teach today?"

"Your muscles will hurt less the more you move them." I ducked as Audrey threw an eraser at me.

"Ow," she moaned, rubbing her upper arm. "Easier said than done," she grumbled. "It's ridiculous how sore I am!"

"How could twenty-five minutes on a tricycle cause so much agony?" Val whined. "I gotta go find Keith and kill him."

"I'd help you bury his body, but again, I still can't lift my arms," Audrey moaned.

Hiding my laugh behind a cough, I rolled my eyes.

Val hobbled out the door. "I'll meet you at lunch if I can walk that far."

She walked down the hallway, bellowing, "Keith! Keith, I know you're here somewhere. I saw your car! My name is Valentine Dellia Bellini. You have killed my muscles, prepare to die."

"Oh God, Keith's toast! Val's quoting from *The Princess Bride*."

Red smiled, and I felt the floor drop out from under me. I wanted to wrap her in my arms and kiss the smile on her lips, but because I knew she wouldn't want me to do it at school, I closed and locked her classroom door.

"I missed you, Red. I can't get you out of my mind." I bent to kiss her. She wrapped her stiff arms around my neck with a soft "ouch" and kissed me back.

"Want to go out to dinner with me after practice?" I asked, easing back a little.

"If I can walk," she laughed, and I felt like the sun rose after a long storm.

Chapter 21: Oz

Your Own Way

For the second time since school started, I was in the principal's office. I shifted awkwardly in my seat. I'd fought in a war, for God's sake. I could handle a meeting with a middle school principal. Dr. Winters shuffled papers on her desk, making me wait. I started to sweat. Being put in my place made me ill at ease.

The knock on the office door surprised me. When Audrey entered, my stomach flipped dangerously. Her eyes widened in shock when she spotted me. This was an ambush. Every instinct screamed a warning as Red sat down next to me.

Dr. Winters sat stiffly, unsmiling, her hands clasped on the desk. "It's come to my attention that the two of you are..." She coughed lightly and focused her eyes on the stack of files on her desk. "Seeing each other."

I glanced at Audrey. Her face turned a shade darker than her hair. Her eyes met mine, and I could feel her discomfort.

My heart started to pound. The hackles raised on my neck, and I felt my anxiety kick in. My heart pounded in my chest while snakes of tension coiled in my belly. I wanted to stand and flip the desk, but common sense and a few years of therapy told me to stay seated.

I gripped the arms of the chair hard and cleared my throat. Grown men didn't get scolded like ten-year-olds. "I'm not sure that's any of your business."

Dr. Winters narrowed her eyes. I felt a stabbing pain at the back of my neck. Maybe she'd stuck pins in my voodoo doll. "When an incident occurs on school grounds, during a school event, it becomes my business."

Audrey sank into her chair with a gasp.

Dr. Winters nodded. "It's come to my attention that you and Ms. Freemont made a scene outside the gym on Saturday night during the second half of the basketball game."

It was like a winter wind had swept through, chilling me. But a moment later, anger took its place, and I prepared for a fight. My body tensed as my eyes narrowed.

A small squeak drew my attention. Red hands covered her mouth. "Oh, my God."

Icy dread washed over me at the sight of her distress. I stiffened my spine. "I don't understand how kissing in a dark garden constitutes a scene."

"Regardless of how you see it, there has been a complaint. It was pointed out it might even be inappropriate for you to continue working together after school. In light of this, I've decided it would be best for everyone if I found new soccer coaches for the rest of the season."

I reeled back. What the fuck? Why?

"You're going to punish the team because Audrey and I kissed?"

"Whether you admit it or not, your behavior went beyond a simple kiss. It is important to protect young, impressionable children after school hours." Dr. Winters sat back in her chair and folded her hands together.

It took all my determination not to leap up and loom over her. "Our consensual actions do not pertain to the girls' soccer team. Teachers begin and end relationships all the time."

A tear slid down Audrey's cheek. Her hands covered her mouth as if physically holding back sobs. My hands clenched at the sight of her misery, but I couldn't fight my way out of this mess. I let out a deep breath, forcing myself to relax. Losing my cool wouldn't help the situation.

"Audrey and I would never behave inappropriately in front of the girls."

"I'm afraid my hands are tied," Dr. Winters said.

"If you realize it's illogical, then why do it?" Audrey's quiet voice wavered a little, and I fought my desire to pick her up and run away.

"Luckily, the witness was an adult and not a child. If a child had been involved, charges would be filed, and you would be forced to take a leave of absence, pending an investigation. Although she is of age, your behavior shocked and upset her. She made it clear that if I don't reprimand you, she will go above my head to the superintendent."

I shook my head. Sure, we got a little carried away, but what the hell? We'd been behind that big bush. The darkness back there was like a cave.

Frustration leaked into my voice. "Why would someone do that?"

Audrey turned away, her fingers clamped onto the arms of the chair. Her right leg tapped out a rapid rhythm.

Realization hit me with a punch to the gut. She knew the witness!

Dr. Winters waited a moment, and I got the sense she was counting to ten. "One might ask you both the same thing."

I stared at Red. If she knew something, why didn't she stop this fucking witch hunt? I coughed and cut my eyes between her and Dr. Winters.

Almost imperceptibly, Audrey shook her head at me.

Could she be protecting someone? If so, why didn't she warn me this might happen? I had a million questions and no answers.

The silence stretched uncomfortably until I couldn't stand it anymore. "This entire thing is being blown out of proportion."

The principal frowned. "Mr. Taylor, would you care to view the camera footage from outside the school on Saturday night? I'll admit it isn't crystal clear, but the night vision recording doesn't leave a lot to the imagination."

Fuck. I sat back in my chair. Cameras.

Audrey sat frozen and mute. Her pale face made her wet eyes huge and tortured. She wrenched her hands together in her lap. But when she finally spoke, my heart broke.

"I cannot apologize enough. You've always trusted me to have the best interests of the school and the children." Her voice cracked with emotion.

Dr. Winters nodded. "I'm certainly disappointed."

"I understand. They've tied your hands." Audrey's voice sounded flat and devoid of emotion.

It pissed me off. "All you have is a shadowy recording and a witness who couldn't see anything in the dark. This is ridiculous."

Dr. Winters steamrolled right over me. "It's your actions that give me no choice in the matter. In fact, if you and Ms. Freemont continue your romantic relationship, I may have to take further actions."

"Other people in this school are in relationships, yet you're singling us out," I sputtered.

She raised her eyebrows. "Other couples were not caught on camera outside the school behaving inappropriately."

I sat back angrily and crossed my arms over my chest. Her tone made me feel like a petulant schoolboy.

Audrey sniffled. "I take full responsibility."

Fuck. I couldn't let her take the fall. "Audrey, no. This is my fault."

She shook her head, not meeting my eyes. "I started this back in August."

I reached out to touch her hand. "We're in this together."

Dr. Winters continued as if we hadn't spoken. "The Office of Human Resources may recommend I move one or both of you to another grade level or school next year. This is not in any of our best interests. However, it may already be out of my control."

"Human Resources? Why would they be involved in the first place?"

This meeting had spiraled out of control. My vision grew hazy around the edges, and I sucked in air. Fucking panic attack.

Dr. Winters tapped her fingers on her desk with a little tap—a tap of irritation. Did she have somewhere else to be? Or was someone else waiting to have their lives ruined? I reined in my thoughts. I inhaled and exhaled, controlling my breaths and centering myself.

Driving the final nail in the coffin, Dr. Winters said, "Since there's camera footage of you during a school function, I'm required to put a letter of reprimand into your personnel files."

No one said a word. I breathed in and out and ignored the part of my mind which screamed for me to react.

Audrey cleared her throat. "What if Oz and I stopped dating? How would that change the situation?"

What the fuck? I stared at Audrey, not comprehending her words. Then I heard the beep, beep as the dump truck of reality backed over me.

Winters nodded at Audrey. "If you assured me you would end your relationship, I could give you both a second chance. You would have to give me your word that nothing..." she paused, "...untoward would ever happen again on school grounds."

A cold mask covered Audrey's face. She took a deep breath, squared her shoulders, and then leaned forward to shake Dr. Winters's hand. "I promise."

I stared from one woman to the other, sucking in air like I was breathing underwater. Wave after wave of disbelief and confusion washed over me. Raw, angry, and betrayed emotions flooded through me. My gut hurt like a festering open wound.

Dr. Winters said something. Her lips moved, but I didn't hear her. The silence in the room felt like a ticking time bomb.

"Mr. Taylor?" Dr. Winters said again.

Why did this matter to me? Audrey and I hooked up. Nothing more. It shouldn't bother me. Whatever, this was ended before it even started. I didn't love her or anything. If Audrey wanted to end it this way, that was her fucking prerogative.

I nodded. "Okay."

Dr. Winters gave us a pinched smile and stood. "Now that we've reached an understanding, I believe soccer practice begins in a few minutes." She turned away from us and began to read her email, dismissing us like fucking children.

Audrey dashed out before I could blink. She flew through the door, disappearing into the outer office.

I followed her out, slamming the door behind me. My mind whirled, and I wanted to punch something over and over until my knuckles shredded and the pressure in my chest subsided.

By the time I made it to the main hallway, Audrey was gone. My head throbbed, and I wanted to go home. How was I going to make it through practice?

On the field, the Maidens were dressed out and ready. Stalling for time, I unlocked the fieldhouse and got the soccer balls. I pasted on a smile, suppressing my irritation at picking up Audrey's slack.

While co-captains Adrienne and Haley ran the team through the warm-ups and drills, I got out my phone to text her.

I deleted: *If the team meant so much to you, why aren't you here?* Too hostile.

I also deleted: *Are you throwing the Maidens away like you did me?* Too hurt.

I settled for—

4:12 PM Me: Are you coming to practice?

Looking up from my phone, I noticed all the girls watching me. Perceptive, kids.

I split the girls into two squads to practice offensive and defensive plays. I watched them and gave directions while checking my phone every few minutes. Audrey didn't reply. Where was she?

Time passed in slow motion. Finally, practice ended, and I reminded the girls when to meet the bus for our upcoming match with Everfield Middle. They all gave me high fives and went into the locker room to get their stuff before heading home.

I checked my phone again. Nothing. I fired off another text.

5:36 PM Me: We need to talk.

As I locked the equipment in the field house, frustration overwhelmed me. What the fuck had I done wrong? Accepted a desirable woman's offer? We hadn't even gone on an actual date. Hell, she'd fucking ignored me almost the whole time I'd known her!

Of course, I'd considered taking it further and asked her out to dinner. I'd hoped to have a repeat of Saturday night if she wasn't too sore, but we hadn't even gotten there! I hadn't even considered a future with Audrey before Winters had shot it down. But now, it ran willy-nilly through my mind.

As I walked across the field to my truck, Priscilla Henesey came out of the school. She wore a suit that buttoned right up to her chin that practically screamed: I'm fussy, uptight, and rigid. She smiled and waved forcefully and came toward me like a bulldozer.

"Oz, hi." Priscilla laughed, showing all her teeth. "I just spoke to Dr. Winters. You and Audrey made the right decision."

My left eye twitched. "What do you mean?"

Priscilla faltered, flinching away at my tone. "Oh, um..."

I waited with my arms crossed over my chest. She met my gaze, and I let my glare speak for me.

She tugged a little on her collar. "Female teachers must maintain an impeccable reputation."

Had I time-traveled or something? What year was it? 1723? My temper boiled, but I bit it back. "You should let Audrey worry about her own reputation."

Priscilla's eyes hardened. The smile vanished, and her voice turned cold. "Easy for you to say. You're a man."

"What's that supposed to mean?" I growled angrily. "I'm not sure what you hoped to gain from threatening us, but it's not going to work."

"I'm trying to protect you both. Society hates educators. Any negative publicity affects us all."

Fuck this.

"Audrey and I kissed. People do that all the time without any publicity at all. You're engaged, right? I assume you and your fiancé kiss from time to time."

"Well, of course, yes. But..."

I couldn't stand here another minute with this crazy woman. Definitely not in the same place I'd kissed Audrey the night the bus broke down. "No buts. Stay out of my business, Priscilla. And stay away from Audrey."

I got in my truck and backed out, driving home on automatic, my brain basically shut down. Ten minutes later, I sat in my driveway but didn't want to go inside. Pissed off and restless, I checked my phone.

The radio silence from Audrey deafened me. Before I could throw my phone through the windshield, I dialed Bobby.

When she answered, I didn't know what to say.

I could hear her brain generating questions, but to her credit, she held back. "Mel's hosting book club tonight. If you give me fifteen, I can meet you at Barrel."

Twenty minutes later, Bobby sat down next to me at the bar. She gave me the once over and raised her eyebrow.

"I need to tell you something, and I need you to be cool."

Bobby nodded, but a minute later, it was obvious that Bobby couldn't be cool. "Wait a minute! You did what? Where?" She wiggled her eyebrows. "You're a dirty dog, Oz."

"Shut up, Bobby." I rubbed my hand over my face. "I know you and Mel have made out in your classroom."

"Well, yeah." Bobby rolled her eyes. "But that's alone in a classroom behind a locked door. Not outside during tricycle basketball, you damn heathen."

She laughed while Krissy brought us our food and beers.

I continued the story while we ate, wrapping up with Audrey rushing out of the office and skipping practice.

"Ouch." Bobby shook her head. "So, to recap, Audrey broke up with you in the principal's office, and you're all butt hurt."

"I'm not butt hurt," I snarled.

She waved her hand in my general direction. "You're the definition of butt hurt."

I glared at her. Why was I friends with her? I ate my burger and drank my beer in silence while Dylan Schnieder sang *Ain't Missing You* through the speakers.

Bobby sighed. "Seriously though, are you okay?"

I chewed slowly and swallowed before answering. "I don't know. I almost tore up the office."

"Hulked out, huh?"

"Yeah. If I'd stayed there two more minutes, I'd have lost it."

"And then you had practice?" Bobby's eyes were sympathetic.

"None of them said it, but the girls knew something was up."

"They always know. They can smell drama like bomb-sniffing dogs."

She laughed, and I could feel the tension in my body unwind. The knots loosened, and for the first time since school ended, I breathed naturally. "I over-reacted."

Bobby chewed her fries thoughtfully. "Winters backed you into a corner, and then Audrey broke your heart."

I snorted. "Broke my heart? We hardly know one another."

"I beg to differ."

I shook my head at her snooty tone. "Beg all you want, but you're wrong. Red and I had casual, no-commitment sex. A one-night stand with zero plans."

Bobby finished the last bite of her burger and rolled her eyes. "Alright, listen up, dude. I'm gonna help you out. You spent the night with her in your house. You made her chili and took it to her. You asked her out to dinner before everything went to fuck. You, sir, most certainly were in a relationship."

I heard the bang as the hammer finally hit me over the head. Red and I had been in a relationship? My whole body tensed as I thought it through.

"I can see from your face, you've realized I'm right," Bobby laughed. "Took you long enough, dude."

I finished the rest of my beer in a long swallow. "Fuck, Bobby, I'm not cut out for this shit. How did I get myself into this mess?"

"Basic Birds and Bees 101. You feel a spark, and all the blood leaves your head, and then you do dumb shit." Bobby slapped me on the back with a laugh. "Welcome to the club."

"I had a full-blown, fuck all panic attack in front of her. No wonder she was so eager to agree with Winters and run away from me."

She sobered. "I doubt she even knew you were freaking out. She was tits up in her own shit. Give her some time. She'll come around."

I leaned back in my chair and closed my eyes. The sounds of the restaurant soothed me. Normal noises of people playing games, eating, and talking acted like a balm to my soul. Exhaustion washed over me.

Bobby's hand landed gently on my shoulder. "I realized earlier it's the anniversary of your dad's heart attack."

A well of pain rose up in my heart. A deep, dark black hole of pain. I'd been trying to ignore it, but it hurt like a bitch. I rubbed my eyes, trying to ease the headache that brewed behind them.

"You told me a long time ago you felt like you had a ticking time bomb inside you. Counting down to your own fortieth birthday and similar death. Do any of these obviously misguided, irrational feelings have anything to do with how you're reacting to this situation with Audrey?"

"Fuck all, Bobby, I honestly don't know."

"Do yourself a favor and take the time to think about it." She reached out and patted my shoulder.

I pulled her into a hug. Bobby talked a lot of shit, but she was my best friend. "There's more."

I relayed the conversation I'd had with Priscilla Henesey.

"Well, shit." Bobby slapped her palms on the table. "Pree's always been a tight ass, but I never thought she'd turn on another teacher."

I picked up the full beer Krissy had brought and drained it. "Tight ass or not, she threw Audrey and me under the fucking bus."

"Let me talk to Mel about it. She's known her longer than I have. Maybe she has some intel we could use."

I shrugged. "It's been a shitty day, so I'll take all the help I can get."

"We'll figure it out."

I nodded. I should head home. I was wiped out but also wired. The adrenaline of the panic attack was still humming in my system. I'd never be able to relax without working off this excess energy.

Bobby slid off the stool. "Let's toss some axes, bro. You need a little ax-tion to take your mind off things."

Dr. Roberta was right again.

Chapter 22: Audrey

Terrified

On my sofa, buried under a blanket and a cat, my phone's speaker blasted Spotify's breakup playlist. Adele set fire to the rain, and I cried buckets. I replayed the humiliation of the meeting over and over in my head and the look of surprise on Oz's face as I ran away. Anxiety chewed away at my stomach. I felt like a fool.

My phone chirped beside me. I dreaded reading the notification. What if Oz was texting me again? And yet, I needed to know if he'd messaged me. Why couldn't he leave me alone? I lifted the soft blanket off of my head and peeked at my phone.

6:31 PM **Val: Hey. Bobby wanted me to check on you.**
6:31 PM **Val: You okay?**

News travels fast in small towns and even faster in small schools. Oz had told Bobby. Bobby had told Val. I wished everyone just minded their own business. But no, tomorrow, everyone will have heard a version of what happened. People would choose sides. There'd be pitying looks or snickers behind cupped hands. I threw my phone on the coffee table as the song changed, and Lizzo reminded me that the truth hurts. Amen, Lizzo.

My phone chirped again, and I ignored it. A minute of silence passed, and then a rapid fuselage of notifications came in.

I picked up my phone.

6:32 PM **Val: Audrey?**
6:33 PM **Val: Are you ignoring me?**
6:33 PM **Val: Are you getting my texts?**
6:34 PM **Val: Is your phone dead?**
6:35 PM **Val: Audrey?**
6:36 PM **Val: Audrey?**
6:38 PM **Val: ?**

There were two choices: text her back or turn off my phone. I ran my finger over the phone's off switch when it buzzed again.

6:45 PM Val: I'm getting worried.

Val didn't deserve my pouty baby routine. She was my best friend. Of course she would worry if I ghosted her.

6:37 PM Me: I'm fine. I just need to process.

There. I smiled at my very adult and mature response. Val would absolutely take the hint and give me time to process my feelings.

6:37 PM Val: I'm coming over.

Or not.

I didn't even bother to tell her not to come. When Val made up her mind, a horde of middle school debaters couldn't change it. Plus, there was an itty bitty part of me who wanted to know what Bobby had told Val. Was Oz okay?

Thirty minutes later, I was still curled up on the couch, hiding from the world, when Val knocked on my door. I dragged myself out from under my blanket, dumping Stevie off in the process. The strap of my teacher bag tangled with my toes, tripping me. Essays shot out of the pockets, sliding across the floor.

When I finally opened the door, Val held up a pink bag from Pat's Bakery, and I could smell warm sugar and chocolate. She took one glance at me, gave me a big hug, and shoved a cookie into my hand. "Tell me what happened!"

She stepped over the papers, ignoring the mess, and pulled me over to the sofa. Val kicked off her shoes and sat down next to me cross-legged. I ate my double dark chocolate cookie in silence and licked the crumbs off of my fingers, before I told her everything. How Dr. Winters mortified me and wanted to remove Oz and me as coaches, and how I had to choose between fooling around with Oz or my job.

"Well, that's stupid!" Val exclaimed. "For seeing each other?"

I nodded. "I sat there and watched Oz argue and fight back, but I didn't do anything. He tried, but I couldn't see any way out, so I ran away. I'm a coward."

"It was a surprise attack. Anybody would have reacted that way." Val's instant, unwavering support soothed the raw emptiness inside me.

I blew my nose. "We're better off this way. Hooking up with another teacher is bad news."

Val leaned forward and held my hand. "What about Bobby and Mel? And remember Carl and Melissa? There've been plenty of teacher relationships in our school. No one's ever been banned from working together."

My eyes stung with tears and my lower lip quivered. "Did any of them get caught on camera having an orgasm outside the school?"

Val's mouth dropped open. She sat completely still for a minute. Eventually, she said, "Well, fuck."

I made a face at Val, flipped my hair, and wiggled my ring finger at her, imitating my nemesis. "Of course, no one would have checked the cameras if someone hadn't complained."

"Priscilla? That bitch!"

"What the heck did I do to Pree?" Eminem and Rhianna sang *Love the Way You Lie* in my head while I thought about it. Priscilla might not be lying, but why report it and threaten to go to the superintendent?

"Pree's always been a rule follower. Remember when we wanted to skip the fire drill during our planning time?" Val settled back against the couch.

I nodded. "It was raining and cold."

"She made a huge stink about it and made us go out."

"We all got soaked, and you and I came down with colds right after that."

We sat in silence for a few minutes. I racked my brain for ideas but kept coming up empty. I sighed, leaning back into the cushions. "She's never liked either of us much."

"She's a narcissist. She doesn't like to share the limelight."

"Like when you and Pree sponsored the Student Council together?"

I rolled my eyes. During my first year at Marchfield, I'd set up a teacher appreciation initiative with the group. We'd sponsored a dance to raise money for it, and when it was a huge success, Pree took all the credit.

"You also have higher test scores, and she hates it."

Shaking my head, I shifted uncomfortably. "That's a horrible reason to sabotage Oz and me."

"You know how Winters tries to pit us against one another."

"Pree and Dr. Winters go way back. They both started at Danvers Middle."

I started to feel sick to my stomach. Could this all come down to something so silly? I took in a deep breath, fending off the nerves that swirled in the pit of my stomach.

Val snickered. "Or she's jealous of your chemistry with Oz. From what we've pieced together, Ned, the sustainable architect, is a terrible lover."

I smiled. "Exercise drove her insane. I ate a donut in front of her on Monday, and now she's getting even."

Val giggled. "She's a monster."

It felt better to pretend that everything was alright, and I embraced it. "Perhaps she's super sexually frustrated because she's waiting for marriage and taking her puritanical ideals out on me."

"And she won't stop until you are as miserable and deprived as she is." Val fell back against the sofa, her long legs out in front of her. Stevie lifted his head to look at her from his spot on a nearby chair. A second later, he was snuggled in her lap.

"I love how you think." My shoulders shook with laughter.

"We should attack the problem like Sherlock Holmes," Val suggested after our laughter died out.

"Lay out the case for us, Watson."

She stroked Stevie like the villain, Goldfinger, with long, sweeping strokes down his back. He loved it and rolled over for a belly rub. "These are the facts. Winters knows about the hanky-panky, and Priscilla Henesey is a bitch. And Oz is in the doghouse."

My eyes bulged. "He's not in the doghouse. We just agreed to not see each other."

Val scratched Stevie behind the ears. "So why are you hiding here? Why aren't we making picket signs and raging against the injustice of society?"

"I needed some time."

"To figure out how to apologize?"

"I don't need to apologize. I am not sacrificing my career for good sex." My voice cracked. "Winters threatened to move us to different grade levels or transfer us to different schools."

Val threw her hands up, and Stevie flew off her lap. His tail swished violently as he stalked off into the kitchen. "We could fight that."

"But then it would all come out. Everyone would look at me differently, and I couldn't let the girls down. Their season is going so well. "

Val jumped up and began to pace angrily. "You always do that! You compromise your own happiness and put everyone else's above your own. You are more than a teacher and a coach. You're a living, breathing woman with the right to have love."

Tearing up again, I threw the blanket over my head. Logically, I knew Val nailed it, but I couldn't handle anything else right now.

Val sighed. She pulled my hand out from under the cover and held it tightly, "It's your coping mechanism, Audrey."

I peeked out from under the fleece. "When my dad died, it destroyed my mom. I was only eleven, but my brothers and I closed ranks around her. I would jump through any hoop or do any trick to make her smile. Since then, I guess I've always been a people pleaser."

Val hugged me. "That kind of trauma leaves an indelible mark on your soul."

Cry Me A River by Justin Timberlake played on the speaker as we sat together.

Val eased back. "Did you at least talk about it with Oz after?"

I hung my head. "I couldn't. I ran out and came here."

Val quietly shook her head. "You should talk to him and figure out your next move together."

I blew my nose, feeling frustration well up inside me. She made the most complicated things sound so easy. "It's not like Oz and I are serious. We barely know one another."

Val barked out a laugh and wiggled her eyebrows. "Except for his body. You know that real well."

"Shut up." I tossed a sofa cushion at her. "I risked my whole career, and for what? A booty call?"

"You're being a little dramatic. Your career is far from ruined."

I threw another tear-soaked tissue into the trash can, which was full of white, wet, fluffy things. A teetering pile of sad clouds. "Dr. Winters is putting a letter of reprimand in my file."

"So what?"

"So what?!" I slapped my fists against my thighs. "She's putting it in my file. Anyone can see it. Human Resources will know I got off outside the gym."

Val pursed her lips. "I repeat, so what?"

"I could get transferred or fired. What if I wanted another job? A prospective boss would know all about it." I blew my nose with a loud honk.

"Know what? You're a good time in the garden?" Val snickered. "If she's a woman, she'll probably be jealous. I know I am."

"Ugh." I cried, covering my face with my hands. "You're not helping, Val."

"Audrey, I'm going to tell you a secret. Guess how many letters of reprimand are in Keith's file?"

My mouth dropped open. "What?"

"Guess!"

Pursing my lips, I said, "Well, we're talking about Keith, so two?"

"Four!" She waggled her fingers at me.

My mouth dropped open. How could it be possible to have four reprimands and keep your job? "That can't be right!"

Val nodded. "He told me once after a few beers. His first years of teaching were a total cluster."

I made a watery snort. "You're lying to make me feel better!"

"Cross my heart," she promised.

I pondered this new information to the beat of *I Got Trouble* by Christina Aguilera.

When the song ended, Val nudged me with her foot. "What's the real reason you're here, hiding out and crying in your apartment? Not answering even when your bestie texts you?"

I stared at the painting I'd hung on the wall beside my TV. One of my students, Francis Hill, painted it for me a few years ago. On the canvas, I rode a cow amongst a herd of others. The sky in the background glowed in a vibrant orange sunset. Looking at it made me happy. But now, I wondered about a darker symbolism. Was I stuck in a groove, heading in the same direction as everyone else? Never brave enough to go against the crowd?

I lowered my head to my hands, my voice shaky. "Dr. Winters watched us on the security camera. She questioned my ability as a role model."

"If you were mortified, I bet Oz was pretty embarrassed, too."

I glanced up at her, dumbstruck. Was Oz ashamed? Angry? Yes. He'd argued with Dr. Winters and rushed to my defense.

And what had I done? Taken the first excuse offered to me. I'd pinky sworn the principal that I'd never have sex with Oz again. Then ran away like a coward! All because I feared losing my cozy safety net!

"Has he reached out? Tried to talk to you?" Val asked.

Unable to speak past the lump in my throat, I tossed her my phone. She scanned the texts while a growing sense of guilt settled on my shoulders.

Val glanced up from the screen. "I love you, Audrey. I get why you reacted the way you did."

I met her eyes. "But?"

"You've been an insensitive jerk. Oz is laying his emotions on the line, and you've stomped all over them. "

"Emotions?" I babbled. "He doesn't love me. I don't even like him. Nobody's invested any feelings."

"Women don't cry after casual sex unless it sucked. From what you've told me, the only sucking going on was the great kind. Oz likes you, and you think he's the best thing since sliced bread. Do I need to draw you a damn Venn diagram?"

I scoffed. "You're making it seem more than it is."

She ignored me, ticking off her points on her fingers. "Didn't you text me that he brought you chili and massaged your stiff muscles? He has feelings. When you bring a bag to sleep over at his house, you have expectations. If you cry over the mess you made with him, it was a relationship. If you're honest with yourself, you'll see that you like him."

Val's words were a slap in my face. Had I been lying to myself? Saying sex with Oz didn't mean anything? Why? So I could stay safe in my bubble? To convince myself I was fine on my own when I was anything but? To once again avoid the fact that Dad's death had fucked me up?

Reality rushed forward with a clarity that I'd been missing for a long time. I hid away in my comfortable hermit's cave because I hated getting hurt. I pretended I liked security and safety because I was too terrified of laying my heart bare. Over the years, I'd built walls around my heart and guarded them with a fire-breathing dragon.

Oz broke down my fortress. He'd snuck in through some open door or window I'd absently left open. I'd thought I wanted a one night stand. A summer fling. A man who was fun, but dispensable, someone who didn't tangle up my emotions and tie them into a heart-shaped bow.

I groaned. "Why couldn't he have just been some guy at the bar? Why did he have to be a teacher?"

"Life throws you curveballs," she said. "Oz is great. He'll understand."

"How can he understand when *I* don't even get it myself?"

"He'll help you figure it out." Val shrugged before adding, "Like in a sexy, naked way."

I threw a tissue at her, but Stevie intercepted it, batting it away and chasing it to the floor.

Val stood and brushed the cat hair from her pants. "Go clean up. I'm starving. Let's go get something to eat."

As much as I wanted to keep hiding, my stomach growled at the thought of food.

An hour later, Val approved my make-up, hair, and outfit. I felt calmer and more together than I'd felt in days, but I still stuffed my purse with tissues in case the dam burst again. We walked into Barrel, and Krissy showed us to a table.

"How's school going?" I asked.

Krissy did a little dance. "I was hoping I'd see you, Ms. Freemont. I have great news! I've got all my credits to graduate! I just need to do my student teaching." Krissy's grin spread from ear to ear.

"Wow! That's so exciting," Val said as we hugged her.

"Have you gotten your assignment yet?"

"I should get it soon."

"I'm so proud of you." My eyes teared up. It seemed like Krissy only just left my eighth-grade class, and now she was going to be a teacher herself. "Let me know if you need a recommendation or anything."

Krissy hurried away to put in our order. Green Day started singing about having the time of your life in my head, a song that always made me feel bittersweet.

"I love how Marchfield is small, and we can see our students after they leave our classes, but it makes also me feel old."

Val nodded. "I feel positively ancient!"

"They grow up, and I stay frozen in time in the eighth-grade."

"Remember Tommy Kilnin? I saw him at the gas station. He's driving now. Can you believe it?"

"Oh my God, I need to up my insurance coverage. I can't imagine him behind the wheel!" I laughed.

Loud cheers erupted from the back of the restaurant. We could hear the sound of axes splitting wood and people chanting, "Bullseye!" When our food arrived, we fell on it like starving women. The hot, crispy fries and the seared meat of the burger did little to soothe my soul. I was an open wound, still bleeding around the edges.

More cheers and chanting started in the back of the restaurant. Krissy arrived with a water pitcher to refill our glasses.

"Sounds like a good time back there." Val smiled.

Krissy giggled. "The cute guy you were with the other day is really swinging tonight, Ms. Freemont."

I swallowed a French fry wrong and coughed. "Excuse me?"

"The cute guy you dined with the other day? He's having a perfect game—all bullseyes." She moved on to another table.

Val threw cash down on the table. "This is it! Your chance to talk to Oz."

"Wait!" I threw my hands up to fend her off, but Val grabbed my wrist and pulled me toward the back of the restaurant. "What if he's throwing axes at my picture?"

She ignored my protest stand kept tugging. "You gotta apologize and get on the horse again!"

I dragged my heels. "I don't want to ride him, Val."

She laughed without releasing her grip. "Yes, you do."

A crowd of mostly women surrounded the ax-throwing area, jostling to get a better view. Three very pretty girls in their early twenties blocked my view. They jumped and squealed with every thud of an ax, giggling at one another. I turned back to Val, but she spun me back around.

"Go!" she hissed.

"Surprising Oz in the middle of throwing an ax is a good way to get killed." Trying to be funny only earned me a scowl.

"You can't just hang back here."

"Why not? He isn't crushed. In fact, he doesn't care at all." Saying it out loud cemented it in my heart. Oz was fine without me. He wasn't sitting at home crying or planning some big, showy, grand gesture to win me back. He wasn't mortified or worried about me. "We should go."

Val put her hand on my back and pushed me forward. "Not until you see him."

The three girls frowned with pouty lips as I jostled them. I gave them a sheepish smile and gestured toward Val, still shoving me ahead. They stepped aside, and I saw Oz.

The ax was high over his head. His blonde hair shone under the lights, and his red t-shirt stretched tight across his shoulders and chest. I swallowed hard, taking in his long legs and tight butt. His biceps bulged as he swung his arm forward and let the ax go.

The blade split the soft wood of the bullseye with a thud. A few men shouted his name and clapped. But the women shrieked his name until it became a chant. They'd probably start throwing their panties at him in another minute.

Oz strode forward and yanked the ax from the target. Lifting his arms over his head in victory, he turned to acknowledge the crowd.

Jealousy by Liz Phair rose up inside me. I wanted to scream. How dare he egg on his harem of ax-throwing groupies! I'd run out of tissues from crying, and the whole time, he'd been out partying.

A thin, athletic woman sauntered up to him. "Congratulations. That was some ax-ceptional throwing." She curved her body toward him, reaching out to touch his arm. "Wanna get a drink?"

Oz shook his head and murmured something. She turned away from him, pouting. His eyes lifted away, and he scanned the crowd.

It felt like a lightning strike when his eyes collided with mine. Time stopped. A frisson of energy shot down my spine, but I was too irritated with all the women to enjoy it. I crossed my arms over my chest and gave him my best poker face.

He locked his gaze on me, and the sullen woman's gaze ricocheted between us. Taking the hint, she disappeared in the direction of the bar. The crowd broke up, and I hung back while people congratulated him.

Oz said something to Bobby. Her face serious, she spoke with him before turning her gaze on me. Her worried eyes spoke loud and clear.

Don't hurt him.

I shrugged. *He better watch his step.*

Bobby nodded and followed Val to the bar.

He swaggered up to me, his arms swinging and making his shirt bunch and pull across his chest. I swallowed hard as he stopped in front of me. "We need to talk."

He nodded, and we made our way through the restaurant in silence. He opened the door, and we walked outside. The sky darkened to a deep purple. A scattering of stars lit up the sky. The breeze turned chilly, and I rubbed my arms to warm them.

I stared at Oz, trying to read his expression in the darkness. His eyes were shadowed. His mouth turned down, and he looked unspeakably tired. Taking a deep breath, I plunged in before I chickened out. "I'm sorry, Oz. I behaved really badly, and I apologize."

Every one of my nerve endings fired at once. He nodded coolly, his expression blank. "Did you see any of my texts?"

The words I'd hastily planned flew out of my head. I shuffled my feet. "I got them. I know I bailed on practice. I needed some time."

"Understandable, but hurt and embarrassment didn't stop me from showing up for those girls."

I hung my head. "I was mortified, and I overreacted. But then I discovered you, playing like an ax-ass, surrounded by women."

"Jealous, Darlin'?"

"Hell no," I said louder than intended. I searched the shadows for a hint of his reaction. "You're free to do whatever you want."

Oz rubbed his hand over his face. "Bobby suggested we throw axes to ease my frustration over the whole damn situation. Your rejection hit me hard..."

His words were quiet, but I felt them like a slap. "But the women..."

His frustration exploded in rapid-fire words. "I don't know any of them, Red. I can't control who watches us play."

"You didn't have to enjoy it so much," I spit out, knowing I sounded foolish.

"The whole time, I wished you were there, Red."

All the anger and the fight drained out of me as mental exhaustion seeped in. Oz's quiet and honestly brutal tone cut through me. I needed to talk to him. None of this was his fault. My past had left me broken and scarred.

"I'm scared of losing the home I've built for myself here. It means everything to me." I swallowed the lump in my throat and reached out to touch him. He took a step back, and my hand swung back to my side. My stomach clenched. "I should've been more careful with your feelings, Oz. I shouldn't have ignored your texts."

I struggled for the words to express my emotions. My desire for a fling had backfired from night one. I deserved to be lonely for the rest of my life.

The silence stretched between us. Even the music in my mind was silent. It made my skin crawl, and I desperately wanted to escape again. We could talk this out later or possibly never.

I clenched my hands into fists, my nails digging into my palms. "I, um, could've done things differently."

In exasperation, I kicked a rock with my shoe. It skidded across the pavement and dropped into the storm drain. I wished I could dive in after it. Why wasn't he saying anything?

"Okay, then," I whispered. "I guess I'll go unless you have something to say."

I stepped back, ready to flee, but Oz reached out. His hand slid across my cheek and tucked a strand of hair behind my ear. His deep voice cut across my senses. "Are you sure you want to know how I feel?"

I stared at him as my heart pounded in my ears. Did I want to know? My chest ached, and I rubbed the place over my heart with my palm.

His finger ran down my cheek, continuing to my collarbone. My pulse increased from a mixture of anxiety and unexpected pleasure. His smile twisted when he spoke. "I'll tell you, and you can explain all the reasons I'm wrong."

I took a step back to break the contact and immediately missed his warmth. My mind, which had been on a momentary hiatus, kicked into overdrive. "Are you making fun of me?"

He shook his head, his eyes weary. "No, Red. It's obvious the joke's on me."

Oz's flat, humorless tone shocked me. He rubbed his face with his hand, dragging it up over his eyes into his hair. I wanted to beg Oz to explain, but terror filled my heart at what he might say.

He smiled, but without the twinkle in his eyes, it was cold. "I thought we were having fun, Red. A meaningless good time."

I'd said this to Val only a few hours ago, but hearing him say it made me want to cry. "Oz, I–"

"No, Audrey, let me finish." His dark eyes sliced through me, and I almost covered my ears. "You tried pretty damn hard to crush my emotions under your boot heel. You've led me around like a bull with a nose ring. I've tasted your pussy, but

I've never seen into your heart. But despite that, I like you, Red. Given some time and TLC, I might even fall in love with you." His harsh laugh washed over me like a wave of sadness.

Thunder crashed violently in my ears. Since the stars stared down from the cloudless sky, my imagination supplied the sound effects. I'd been focused on my career and my pain, and the whole time, Oz thought of me. I'd driven him crazy—hot one minute and freezing him out the next.

And still, he liked me? Enough it might bloom into love?

Oz's eyes glittered under the streetlamp. "Your turn, Darlin'. Tell me all the reasons I'm wrong for wanting you. Cause I know it's true, but I can't stop myself."

Headlights from a parking car blinded me as I struggled to find words. A tiny bubble of emotion fluttered in the vicinity of my heart and worked its way up my throat. I'd only known him a few weeks, but ninety percent of that time, I'd refused to acknowledge him. Of course, the other ten percent, we'd eaten burgers, thrown axes, and had wild monkey sex.

The bubble expanded, working its way down toward my heart and warming me from the inside. This man had gone to the carpet for me. He'd brought me chili and massaged my sore muscles. He'd given me the best orgasms of my life and made me laugh. I liked him.

"Nothing, Red?" He leaned away from me.

I liked Oz. My heart raced. Dizziness rocked me back on my heels. Where was my soundtrack?

Oz spoke again, his jaw tight. "We should take some time. Figure out how to proceed."

His voice echoed as if inside a tunnel. I wondered if I would pass out. My stomach clenched. Shit.

I liked him!

Oz's lips moved, but static in my ears prevented me from understanding more than snippets. I heard "Fall Break," "Home," and "Delaware." None of it made sense.

Did I love him?

I shook my head. Oz continued speaking, and I needed to focus hard on his words.

"...Get through the next two days at school and reassess how we feel after Fall Break."

I opened my mouth to speak but froze. My mind spun dizzyingly like NASCAR racers flying around a track. With the music gone, it seemed any means of communication had gone with it.

I watched him walk to his truck. The unconscious swagger and tightness of his butt called to me, but I froze in place.

When he reached the cab, he spoke again. "We'll talk when I get back."

I let him go, unable to verbalize all the conflicting emotions inside me.

Numbly, I watched him drive away, and I stood in the dark for a long time after his truck turned the corner and disappeared out of sight.

Chapter 23: Audrey

Something's Got a Hold on Me

The next two days inched by. The mid-October temperatures finally dipped toward fall. The sun set earlier every day. As darkness swallowed the Northern Hemisphere, its shadow marched across my soul. I spotted Oz in the hallway with his students. In the cafeteria, I met his eyes while eating a burrito. I don't know how long our eyes clung together, but Oz looked away first.

At soccer practice, we were strictly professional at all times. Scratch that; we barely spoke.

On Wednesday, the last day before Fall Break, I sat on the bus heading to our soccer match, staring blindly at my phone. Around me, the girls laughed and talked. They buzzed with constant energy like a swarm of bees. Their carefree spirit surrounded me, and I hoped it would lift me up. All I had so far was a headache.

Oz plugged his headphones in, effectively tuning the girls and me out. I tried hard not to stare at him from my seat across the aisle, but my eyes clung to him. The stubble of blond whiskers. The slightly darker shade of his eyelashes. His full lower lip, soft yet strong. I dragged my eyes away, scolding myself. Not long ago, I successfully ignored him. Now, his presence loomed bigger, brighter until it was impossible to dismiss.

Plus, new emotions tightened around my heart. Raw and visible like an open book anyone could read, how I was falling in love with Oz. Tearing my gaze away, I peered around the bus. The girls seemed oblivious.

As we filed off the bus, Priscilla pulled in with a squeal of tires. She'd taken spying on us to a whole new level: hiding around corners, sitting in her car before and after school, and now coming to the soccer match. She wanted to be the first to catch us screwing up.

When Dr. Winters arrived at the end of the first half, she joined Pree in the stands. I imagined their hard eyes watching for signs of impropriety or scandal. As regulation time ticked down, a scream bubbled in the base of my throat. I glanced at Oz out of the corner of my eye, but he focused solely on the game.

Marchfield easily beat Glen River Middle three to one. The girls fell into a pile of joy on the field, and I had to smile. Only one more home game after Fall Break, and we'd know if the season would be extended into the playoffs. I searched for Oz in the crowd, wanting to share the moment with him, but he never turned toward me.

Later, as Oz and I herded the girls toward the bus, Dr. Winters approached.

"Great game." The flat, insincere tone belied her words. The force of my will not to roll my eyes tortured already hurting brain.

The principal's smile reminded me of a shark. "The level of professionalism I'm noticing is very encouraging."

"Thanks," I answered automatically.

I shivered as the wind whipped around me. For eight years, I'd worked hard to please my boss and be a model employee. I'd guarded my reputation like a dragon, and for what? Dr. Winters didn't support me. Nothing I'd done had made her care about me.

Oz nodded, and we escaped onto the bus.

The girls babbled and sang in a happy cacophony of teen spirit on the ride home. Oz and I continued to role-play the Cold War from opposite sides of the bus. When we arrived back at the school without incident, I sighed as I exited the bus. Part of me wished it had broken down so Oz and I would have to hike back to our cars, alone.

Oz was a blur of movement, stowing equipment and laughing with the parents and girls. I hung back. Had I really believed he was a bad teacher? What I'd interpreted to be lack of control was really a way of fostering independence. He built relationships with students differently than I did, but it didn't make his way wrong.

I wanted to get in my car and leave but felt obligated to help. So I stayed, listening to his laugh boom out across the field and wishing I could join in.

When the last girl drove off with her parents, Oz turned to me. The clouds parted, and the sun shone down on us like a spotlight. His skin glowed honey tan, and I twisted my fingers together to stop from touching him. When he gave me a tight smile, I held my breath. In a matter-of-fact tone, he said. "I'm heading out in the morning."

My throat closed up, and my eyes stung with unshed tears. My heart lurched. He was leaving.

"I'll be back on Sunday after visiting my mom."

A rush of relief swamped me, and I managed to squeak out, "Okay."

I was a strong, capable woman. I earned my living and paid my bills. I could do anything I set my heart on except talk to Oz. My emotions were too ragged, too on the surface, and I didn't even have my mental playlist to pump me up anymore.

Oz took a step toward his truck. His strong back and shoulders filled my gaze, and I soaked him in. When he turned back, I jerked my gaze away from his butt. I lifted my eyes to the sky like a birdwatcher. Was that a tundra swan flying over? Or a great horny owl? Horned! Great horned owl!

He followed my gaze up to the empty sky. Then quirked that damn eyebrow at me. His lips twitched. "Take some time to consider what you want, Red. I will, too. We'll talk when I get back."

I didn't trust my voice or the words I might say if I opened my mouth. I waved limply instead, half Queen Elizabeth, half Tele-Tubby. He jumped into his truck, agile and handsome.

My heart stuttered in my chest. I felt lightheaded. Did my left arm hurt? Was this a heart attack or simply my heart breaking?

Clutching my chest, I stood there, a caricature of a heartbroken woman: a pencil sketch with a huge nose and giant, misty eyes. The picture would emphasize my long, droopy face. I was more basset hound than a woman at this point. I wanted to howl.

Oz pulled out of the lot and drove away. After he left, I sat in my car, whimpering and alone. I felt hollow and fragile, like a chocolate bunny in a toddler's Easter basket. Where were the chubby fingers ready to rip off my head and put me out of my misery?

Tears welled up and then fell. My emotions jumbled into a confusing knot in my stomach. Automatically, I pushed them away, afraid to take them out and look at them.

My head bowed to the steering wheel. I closed my eyes and relived the last few minutes over and over, punishing myself for the sorrow on Oz's face. Hating myself for putting it there.

Eventually, my tears dried up, and I drove home in painful silence. Bracing for a long, lonely weekend, and I knew I had no one to blame but myself.

****

On Thursday, I woke up at five thirty with an insane desire to clean my apartment. A whirlwind of inefficiency, I started half a dozen projects with no hope of finishing any of them. I threw open my closet and piled all my clothes and shoes on the bed, only to get distracted by the bathroom. How did I live with those toothpaste stains in the sink? Stepping around the mess on my bed, I hurried into the kitchen for an all-purpose cleaner and a rag and ran into another problem. My pantry was impossibly unorganized! Cans and boxes were everywhere. Why had I bought three cans of lima beans? I hated them. This needed an immediate solution.

By noon, my apartment resembled a disaster area. Hurricane Audrey swept in with winds of 140 miles an hour. Seriously, there was probably a meteorologist camped outside my door right now, waiting to use my apartment for a segment on the Weather Channel.

Exhausted, I threw a pile of books off my couch and flopped down on the cushion with a blanket over my head. For once, my inner playlist echoed with silence, deafening in its emptiness.

Mental pictures of Oz filled my head: playing with axes surrounded by beautiful women, saying he liked me, then leaving me alone. My mind replayed Oz's truck driving away over and over until I felt sick.

I forced myself off the sofa and wandered back to the bedroom to organize my shoes. Not even my red cowboy boots or my pink Jimmy Choo's, both gifts from Val's mom, inspired joy. If beautiful shoes couldn't pull me out of the doldrums, I needed therapy.

I pinged my phone and found it under a pile of throw pillows. Stevie crept out from his hiding place under the bed and explored the empty cavern of my closet.

1:23 PM **Me: Help**

1:25 PM **Val: What's up?**

1:26 PM **Me: I've fallen, and I'm trapped under a pile of shoes.**

1:29 **PM Val: Be there in 30. Try digging yourself out with a pump.**

Val knocked on my door and let herself in, calling out, "It's me!"

Val appeared at my bedroom door. "Holy shit!"

I hunched in the middle of teetering piles of sweaters, shoes, and coats and began to cry.

Val blazed a trail toward me, kicking piles of clothes out of the way. "What happened, Aud?"

She handed me a box of tissues and wrapped her arms around me as I wept. Finally, I gave a shuddering sigh and blew my nose.

"Wanna talk about it?"

"I'm old. I forgot how good a man could feel. My vagina was dusty."

Val burst out laughing. "What?"

"Okay, not dusty, but certainly rusty," I griped. "And now, somehow, I'm back in the 8th grade, crying over a boy."

"Boys suck." She hugged me hard and handed me a tissue.

I blew my nose. "They do," I said, taking a deep, shuddering breath. "He left, and now I don't know what to do—which is ridiculous!"

"I have faith that you'll figure this out."

"Just tell me what to do, Val," I whined.

"I can't tell you what to do. Let's try the old Socratic method. I'll ask some guiding questions."

I sniffed. "I'm too tired to play games."

"Humor me. First question: did you have sex with Oz?"

"You know I did."

Val gazed down at me sternly. "Yes or no?"

I sighed. "Yes."

Her next question came in a sing-song voice. "Did you enjoy it?"

It irritated me, but I answered honestly. "Yes."

"Does it honestly matter that he's a teacher?"

"Yes."

Did it? Hadn't I gotten past that?

Val's next question echoed my thoughts. "Really? Does it really?"

I started to nod but stopped. I couldn't say yes again.

"Forget I asked that. Do you like him?"

I blew my nose again. "No." Val raised her eyebrows.

"Okay, yes, I like him."

"Do you love him?"

"Fuck."

Val smirked. "I know you did that. But that doesn't answer the question."

"Ugh," I groaned and buried my face in my hands even as my heart leaped. What kind of joke was the cosmos playing? I'd broken Oz's heart. I'd trampled on his ego. I insisted I only wanted sex. And NOW I realize I love him?

"Still not an acceptable answer."

My heart wanted to shout, to sing and dance to all my falling in love songs. My head cautioned me to slow down and think about the consequences.

"Maybe?"

Val clapped her hands. "Close enough. You love him! You love Oz."

"How can I love him?" I fought against the overwhelming emotions. "I hardly know Oz. Where did he grow up? What's his favorite color? What was his life like in Afghanistan? How did he become friends with Bobby? I have a thousand questions and no answers."

"You've got time. Right now, you need to focus on the big picture. How do you feel when you're with him?"

"He makes my heart race. All I want to do is take his clothes off. He kisses me, and I can't think. I'm overwhelmed by sensations and emotion," I admitted.

Val fanned herself with her hand. "Sounds pretty good to me. I'll take it."

"It's like a nuclear reaction. An explosive, singeing heat. But that's lust."

"What does Oz say?"

"He likes me. Possibly even loves me."

"He's a strong maybe, too!" Val clapped and then started to taunt, "Oz and Audrey sitting in a tree! K.I.S.S.I.N.G."

I threw a sweater at her. "Stop it."

Questions flew like arrows through my mind. Why would he love me? I'd been awful to him. Would he be able to forgive me?

"He's probably thinking with his–" I broke off to blow my nose again.

"Wiener?" Val wiggled her eyebrows. "One-eyed snake?"

"Exactly. His other head," I laughed despite myself but sobered quickly. "Lovers need things in common. You have to want the same things."

Val shifted to look me in the eye. "Why can't you just relax? Have a good time. See where it goes?"

"When he dropped the L-bomb, we zipped past exploring our options."

"He said he *might* love you? Did he say that he absolutely, definitively loved you for now and forever? Maybe I'm missing something."

I shook my head. "It muddied the water. His possible feelings complicate everything."

Val laughed, leaning back against a pile of jackets. "And yours don't? How about we talk about how you're possibly in love, too?"

"I don't want to." I crossed my arms over my chest.

"Just admit you're overthinking this whole thing. Stop worrying. Oz is coming back, and you'll talk. Until then, you need to let it go."

I sighed and slumped back. A boot heel jabbed me in the side. I wrestled it out, throwing it across the room; I considered what Val had said. I had over-thought the whole thing.

Val smirked. "I can tell you agree with me."

I looked around at the mess I'd made. It seemed symbolic. I'd trashed my apartment just as I'd destroyed my relationship with Oz. Now, I needed to pick up the pieces.

Stevie jumped off the closet shelf into a pile of pants. Holding his long, fluffy tail high, he began to knead the pile.

Val rose and held out her hand to me. "How about we clean up your apartment? Then we can watch some shows."

With Val directing, the two of us had an easy time righting the chaos I'd made. Val was my Mary Poppins. giving me a spoonful of sugar to make the medicine go down. She put on music, and we sang and danced.

Two hours later, we sat down at the little dining table I'd set up in front of a pair of wide windows. The sun was setting in a blaze of orange, red, and gold. I ordered pizza while Val ran home to get her jammies and an overnight bag. Together, we ate the cheesy deliciousness and caught up on our favorite shows. After taking an intermission to make brownies, we watched the whole first season of *Derry Girls* on Netflix.

We laughed hysterically over the crazy teenage drama while scarfing down brownies. Everything would be fine. Sure, Oz and I just needed to talk it out. Once we both knew where the other stood, we could find a way to muddle through.

Long after Val fell asleep in my guest bedroom, I lay in bed staring at the ceiling. Tiny glowing star stickers shined down on me. When I was young, Dad had put similar stars above my bed every time we moved.

A true sailor in his soul, Dad had said, "Whenever you feel lost or alone, know that the stars will always bring me home to you."

He hadn't known how comforting and then devastating those words would be. And even though I knew he was never coming back, I'd put stars up in every place I lived.

I tried to settle my brain as I had since childhood, counting the stars and my blessings. I had great friends, a clean apartment, a job, and my family. As my list grew longer, I thought about my students and hoped they were all safe and happy.

And Oz. How could one person fill me with such joy and despair at the same time? I couldn't say if I forever and ever loved him, but he made my heart sing. I felt alive when I was with him. As if all my life had been a dream, and Oz woke me up.

Stevie jumped up onto the bed. He curled up on the pillow by my head and started to purr. I rubbed his head as peace settled over me. My eyes closed. For the first time in days, a song began to play in my mind, and the soft melody of *Goodnight, My Angel* by Billy Joel soothed me to sleep.

Chapter 24: Oz

Mother Like Mine

Early Friday morning, I sat in my mom's kitchen. The dark sky only hinted at the start of the sun's return with a touch of color to the east. I tiptoed to the pantry to find where she'd hidden the coffee. I really didn't want to wake up the whole house. I could sense the inquisition coming and wanted to avoid it as long as possible.

Measuring the coffee grounds into the machine, I remembered Audrey's face in the rearview mirror. Her pale face, with her eyes turned down and tears on her cheeks, just about made me want to slam on the brakes. But I drove away and kept going, knowing I needed time and distance.

My heart tangled with thoughts of confident, sassy Audrey and sexy Red, and I knew I needed to find my own solid ground. I'd planned to head home, change my clothes, and have a snack before hitting the road, but since I had my duffel in the back, I hit the highway instead. I didn't want to take the chance I'd end up on her doorstep, begging. If she pushed me away again, I knew I'd have to end it and leave my heart outside her door.

So, I blasted my tunes and drove with the windows open. The roads were quiet, and the trip up the Delmarva Peninsula and into Seaford helped me find my balance. I let myself into my childhood home after midnight. The smells of lemon furniture polish and yeast bread washed over me like a comforting wave.

Mom stood up from the sofa. "Oz, Honey, is that you?"

"I texted you not to wait up, Mom."

She padded over to me in her fuzzy, plaid robe and matching slippers. Putting her hand on my cheek, she studied my eyes. She hugged me hard, and I braced myself for questions I didn't want to answer.

"I'm glad you're home, Sweetie."

"I am too," I said, a little roughly. I was relieved to be home.

We chatted briefly about her latest interior design job and the mile-long list of things she wanted me to fix. Before she went to bed, she kissed me on the cheek and gave me a big hug.

"Sleep as late as you want in the morning," she said, pushing me toward the stairs and my childhood bedroom.

Surrounded by signed baseballs and a few trophies from high school, I slept in my old twin bed, my feet hanging off the bottom. Before dropping off, my mind wandered to Red as it always did when I got horizontal these days.

***

On my first day home, I'd changed the lightbulbs in the ceiling fans, swept the pine needles off the roof, and cleaned out the gutters, about half the list.

I thought Mom would be ecstatic, but instead, her eyes were sharp and worried, like I was a puzzle and she needed to find the missing pieces. Sure, I didn't laugh a lot, and I might've been quieter than usual. Is it a crime to turn down a second helping of apple pie? Or take a nap in the middle of the day?

Stella, my little sister, arrived that evening. I met her outside our two-story Cape Cod house. The shrubs were a little overgrown and trimming them was near the bottom of my to-do list.

Stella's blond hair was up in one of those messy buns, and I tugged it playfully when I hugged her.

"How you doing, Shrimp?" I used the nickname I'd called her all her life.

She snorted. "Fine, Dumbass."

Sisters.

Hauling her bags up the driveway from her blue Toyota Camry, I compared the small duffel I'd brought with the four suitcases and laptop Stella had brought.

"What the hell, Stel?" The cases were heavy as lead.

"I need to do my laundry this weekend." She winked at me from the porch, and I was tempted to dump all her clothes out on the lawn.

"You brought home four suitcases of laundry?"

She crossed her arms over her chest. "If someone made plans to come home earlier, I would have done laundry last weekend."

Instead of carrying them up the stairs to her bedroom, I dumped them all in the laundry room that branched off the big kitchen. "So this is my fault?"

"It always is." Stella laughed and went to find Mom in the kitchen.

In the kitchen, Stella and I played sous chef and diced onions and peppers for Mom's famous marinara sauce. Mom and Stella talked about their work.

I didn't interject much. I was too wrapped up in thoughts of Audrey. I kept picturing her face, eyes shining with tears. Maybe crying was a good sign. It meant she cared. Or it meant she was resolved to say goodbye. My heart twisted a little.

I caught Mom and Stella throwing strange looks at me throughout the evening, and I wondered how long they'd wait before the questions began.

After dinner, Stella demanded we watch TV. I cued up *Die Hard.*

"I want to watch *Love Actually.*"

I knew was about to be outvoted. I surrendered the remote.

She started up the movie. It's one of those extremely complicated Christmas films with a thousand actors in it. However, by the end of it, I found myself wrapped up in the plot. When David finally kissed Natalie backstage and the audience saw it all, it made me think of Red in the garden with her hair down and her face under the stars, and I got a little choked up.

Stella passed the box of tissues to me without saying anything.

I went to bed after that. Some might call it escaping. I thought of it as a strategic retreat.

***

And that's why on Friday morning, I was up before the sun, brewing coffee in the dark. Savoring the peace and the quiet before Mom and Stella woke.

I'd barely sat down at the table when Mom breezed in. Her hair was a frizzy halo of sunlight as she beamed at me like a spider with a new web.

I needed caffeine because I knew that smile. She was the general and I was about to take artillery hits. She filled two mugs with coffee and set them down on the table. Not waiting, I burned my mouth with a bracing swallow.

I knew what was coming: the toughest game of twenty questions since my junior year of high school. I'd snuck out to meet Marcia Eberle and christened the backseat of my used Dodge Neon. Mom hadn't taken *I don't want to play* for an answer then, and she wouldn't now.

The game started long ago. At the doctor's office or driving around on errands, I'd beg her to play to beat down boredom or anxiety. She'd pick something random, and I'd ask her twenty questions to try to figure it out.

But as I got older, Mom used the game to break down the walls I built between us. More than once, I deflected twenty questions about my teenage sex life or lack thereof. Jesus, it still gives me nightmares!

After I joined the Army, she would send me twenty questions to answer in her emails. I loved those questions about nothing and everything. Bobby and I would spend hours coming up with funny answers to send back. Those questions were a taste of home, as sweet as ice-cold lemonade in the hot desert sun.

But now, she studied me with a calculating stare. When I didn't say anything, she asked, "So, is it a woman?"

"It's five thirty in the morning, Mom. I'm not playing twenty questions."

"I waited a whole day. You could make it easy and just tell me."

"I'm fine, Mom."

"Fine? Your mopey face proves that's a lie. Besides, I don't need twenty questions! I know it's a woman!"

"I love you, Mom, but–"

"But. But." She waved her hand in the air, dismissing my response. She got up, took cinnamon rolls from the pantry, and placed them in the warmer. "What I don't understand is why you never mentioned her. Bobby was the one to tell me."

"Bobby should keep her nose out of it," I growled.

"She cares about you."

Shouting at my mother wasn't an option, so I took a few deep breaths and checked the rolls. They were barely warm. "Bobby is blowing it out of proportion."

"I don't think so, Ozzie. Your poker face is better than it used to be, but I can still see the unhappiness."

Her brown eyes searched mine like a lie detector. I hadn't fibbed to her since she washed my mouth out with soap when I was seven. I just omitted details, which was not the same thing at all.

I slid the rolls out of the oven even though they were only lukewarm. I set a big plate of them on the table.

She bit into a roll, chewing slowly. "Tell me."

Resigned, I sighed. Like a pitbull with a rawhide stick, my mom would never stop chewing until she knew the truth. "Okay," I started.

A thud above our heads interrupted my train of thought. Footsteps raced down the stairs, and I winced.

Stella came sliding into the kitchen in hot pink socks and a nightshirt. Her round cheeks and brown eyes gave her a mouse-like expression. "Did you start without me? What did I miss?"

"Good morning, Darling," Mom said casually. "Bring more coffee and have a cinnamon roll. Ozzie only started to tell me about his woman."

I rolled my eyes. "Mom, she's not my woman."

Stella's head tilted in question, and she leaned in expectantly, vibrating with curiosity. "Did he tell you who she is?"

My sister grabbed the pot full of coffee, got her own mug, and refilled our cups. She sat down across the table from me. Her long, curly blond hair was messy from sleep. I read the saying on her nightshirt: Opera Singers Do It With Vibrato.

Mom sighed. "No, but he will."

I groaned and bowed my head until my chin hit my chest. Both women smiled as if my frustration only proved their point. I loved them deeply, but letting them twist my balls was too much. "I'm a grown man. I don't need the two of you butting in."

Stella rolled her eyes. "You cried during *Love Actually*."

That damn movie. I knew it would haunt me! "I didn't. My allergies acted up because of your dumb perfume."

Stella laughed. "I don't wear perfume. Admit it, you cried! My big brother, the war hero, crying at the end of a rom-com!"

I despised when she called me a hero. In my experience, all soldiers are cowards who do dumb shit in dangerous situations. "Shut up. There's a difference between surviving a war and being a hero."

"But you have a drawer full of medals," she insisted.

"Those medals aren't worth the minerals they're made from," I grumbled.

She started to argue, but Mom interrupted her. "Stella, love, leave your brother alone."

"Thanks, Mom." I smirked at my sister like a twelve-year-old. Mom played me right into the corner with her sneak attack. She whipped the rug out from under me with her next words.

"Tell me about Audrey."

My gut did a somersault. "How do you know her name? Are you spying on me?" I don't know why it surprised me. Of course, she spied on me, with Bobby as her fucking undercover agent.

"You come home, all quiet and sad. You don't talk to me; you mope, mope, mope. I had to do something, and you gave me Bobby's number."

Was I in some cheesy TV sitcom? I paused, waiting to hear the laugh track. "I gave you her number in case of an *emergency*, Mom."

"You weren't talking to me. Then you cried during the movie, Ozzie. Stella and I agreed you're in a crisis." Mom crossed her arms over her chest. Debate over.

What the hell? She was treating me as if I was eight. Most of the time, I regretted running off to join the Army, but now it seemed like the best decision I'd ever made.

Stella leaned forward. A smile lit her face, and she danced in her seat with eagerness to hear the details. No help would be coming from her corner.

I picked up a cinnamon roll and bit off a big chunk. Flavor exploded on my tongue, and cinnamon and sugar combined into bliss. I closed my eyes for a moment, savoring the taste. When I opened them, I met my mom's stare head-on.

She raised an eyebrow. "Bobby says you like Audrey."

Sighing, I put the roll down. "I work with her, Mom. It's complicated."

Stella laughed. "Complicated means he's slept with her."

I grabbed a paper napkin out of the holder, balled it up, and threw it at her. It bounced off Stella's forehead, making her laugh harder.

"Alright, since you two won't mind your own businesses, I'll tell you. Her name is Audrey Freemont, and I like her. There's chemistry, but as I said before, it's complicated."

Both women wore identical expressions of impatience. They drank their coffee, shooting glances at one another, talking without words. I ate the rest of my cinnamon roll and tried to relax.

After a minute, Mom spoke. "How is it complicated?"

I couldn't tell my mom that my principal had photographic evidence of how much I liked Audrey. She'd whap me with a ruler across my knuckles and threaten to cut off my balls.

"We met before the school year started before either of us knew we were co-workers. Audrey wants to stay just friends, but I like her."

Stella made kissy noises. "Bobby says you *LIKE* like her."

Fuck, Bobby, what the hell? I planned on chatting with her about her meddling when I got back.

I glared at Stella. "How old are you?"

"Twenty-six," she snickered. "But I'm not the one in the hot seat."

I glared at her. If looks could kill, Stella would've been dead.

"I like her, okay?" I repeated firmly. "Not that it's any of your business."

Mom gasped. "My baby comes home with a broken heart, and it's none of my beeswax?" She shook her finger at me.

"Mom, my heart isn't broken." I threw my hands up in frustration.

She drained the rest of her coffee, set the cup on the table, and gave me the MOM FACE. The same look she'd given me after I drove her car down the street to the 7-11 at age thirteen.

I took a deep breath. "Mom, I'm sorry; I know you love me and want to help, but I can figure this out on my own. Despite what you think, I'm a grown man."

"You'll always be my little boy." Mom squeezed my hand. "Tell me what's going on before I get out my rolling pin and hit you with it."

"I'll get the cast iron pan," Stella added.

I laughed like they intended me to. And that's how I found myself sitting at my mom's scarred kitchen table, pouring out my soul. Mom pushed more cinnamon rolls toward me while I told them about Audrey, school, and the mess I'd left there. I recounted stories I'd already told them, but this time I included Audrey. I described how we coached the Maidens together. How the bus broke down and I'd gotten to know her. How we threw axes, and she'd helped me get ready to dance at the tricycle basketball game.

"I wish I could have been there," Stella said wistfully. "Wait! Is there a video?"

I nodded, and Stella grabbed her phone, texting Bobby.

Why had I given her Bobby's number, too?

I hoped the phone woke my idiot friend. Bobby needed to share some of my pain.

Mom urged me to continue, so I explained that a teacher had complained to the principal about us and that Dr. Winters wanted to find new coaches to stop the rumors.

Stella threw her phone onto the table. "What a bitch!"

Mom threw the napkin at Stella this time. I grinned smugly until Mom turned her eyes back to me. "This teacher is wrong. You're always very professional, Ozzie."

I'd go back to Afghanistan before I told her how unprofessional I'd actually been in various parking lots and in the tiny, not-so-secluded garden. Bobby better keep her trap shut, too.

Skipping over those details, I said, "Audrey's career is important to her. The principal mentioned she might move us to different schools. Her dad was in the Navy, and she spent a lot of her childhood moving from town to town and school to school. She doesn't want to start over again."

Mom nodded, and I knew she understood Audrey's reluctance. She'd risen from the ashes herself after Dad died. Moving to Delaware, buying this house, and finishing her interior design degree, Mom had gotten Stella through school all while worrying over me.

Stella gave me an exasperated look. "Women don't want strong, silent men anymore. We're looking for equal partners."

I opened my mouth to sass Stella but closed it when Mom's face grew dark. She clenched her hands together, wringing them, and I knew she was thinking of Dad.

"Ozzie, you must talk to Audrey as soon as you get back. Life is short. Your father and I..."

And there it was. The reminder that men in my family die and leave the women to pick up the pieces.

I'd been hearing it all my life, and the closer I got to forty, my own mortality loomed over me. Anxiety crept up my throat.

"My doctor says I'm in excellent health."

Mom reached across the table and took my hand. "I just worry. Your father and grandad seemed fine, too."

"I know, Mom, but I'm okay." I squeezed her hand and then walked around to hug her. We stayed like that for a few moments.

We broke apart when Stella said, "You still need to tell Audrey how you feel."

I poured more coffee into my cup and sat down. "I told her already."

Mom sank down in her seat, gaping at me. "What did you specifically say?"

"I said, I liked her, and I might even love her."

Stella clutched her hands to her chest dramatically. "So romantic, bro."

"I'm afraid of scaring her away. I was trying to sugarcoat it."

"I'm guessing that backfired," Stella said softly.

A small smile curled at the corner of my lips. "It left her completely speechless for two days."

Stella giggled. "I like her. When can I meet Audrey?"

"No way am I introducing you. You'll gang up on me, and I'll never get any peace."

"If you're in love, you need to fight for her," Mom cut to the chase.

I'd fought for Red in Dr. Winter's office. Sure, maybe it was a skirmish and not a battle. I knew getting her to love me would be a longer campaign. Love and war were almost the same. People in love did dumb shit, only in less-dangerous situations.

I was lost in thought, trying to figure out my next move when Stella let out a squeal.

Bobby had sent the link to the video.

Stella immediately played it on her phone. "Oh, my God, Mom, you have to see him dance!" They laughed, shoulders shaking until tears ran down their faces.

Then they replayed the video five more times.

Mom fanned her pink face, trying to get her giggles under control. "Your legs are so good, Ozzie. Sexy legs. Just like your dad's."

"Gross, Mom!" Stella and I groaned together.

"You two are such prudes," she scolded us, even as she laughed.

If. She. Only. Knew!

I looked away, clearing my throat.

Stella patted me on the back as she went to refill her cup. "If you ever need extra income, you might have a future as a drag queen, bro."

"Gee thanks, Stel." I pulled a strand of her hair lightly like I'd done throughout our childhood.

Mom pushed another roll at me. "Can we do anything to help, baby?"

I suppressed a shudder at the thought of my mom getting involved. She'd call Audrey up, extol my virtues, and text her my baby pictures.

Thankfully, Stella jumped up, distracting me from that nightmare scenario. "Wait, that video gave me an idea. Remember that show I used to watch on MTV during college break?"

I nodded. "*Revenge Prank*? I'm seriously thinking of re-watching some episodes to get back at Bobby."

She rolled her eyes. "No, dummy. It was *Promposal!*"

I scoffed. "Wasn't that the show where guys jumped out of airplanes to get girls to go out with them?"

"Not quite." Stella snorted. "It's about the romance. Guys use their creativity to ask their girlfriends to go to prom."

"Same thing," I argued.

"You need a grand gesture, Oz. Something that will knock Audrey off her heels and show her how much you love her."

"And you think I should ask her to prom?"

"No! Let me get my laptop and I'll show you." She ran out of the room, her footsteps loud on the stairs as she retrieved her computer and raced back to the kitchen

"I don't understand what's happening," Mom said.

"Just wait." Stella opened her laptop and did a search on YouTube. "Promposals are all the rage. Look at this one with the marching band!"

She tilted the screen so Mom and I could see. The video panned over a high school band playing and dancing to Neil Simon's *Sweet Caroline*. Cheerleaders held up signs asking a girl in the stands to go to the prom with a guy who stood by her side. She nodded to the delight of the screaming and crying crowd.

"Isn't that great?" But Stella grabbed the laptop back before I could answer.

"There's this other one where the guy uses Post-Its." She flipped the laptop around to show a video of a young man putting thousands of sticky notes on a small hatchback. A girl came out of the school, broke down in tears, and accepted his invitation to the dance.

When the video ended, Mom said, "I don't think Ozzie wants to ask Audrey to the prom, Stella."

Damn right, Mom! Thanks for saying it, so I didn't have to.

"It doesn't have to be a dance. He could ask her on a date. It's all about the grand gesture," Stella insisted. "Every romance novel has one."

Mom nodded. "I see. One time, your father begged for my forgiveness. I guess you could say it was a grand gesture."

"I've never heard that story, Mom," I said.

"Oh, it was before you were born, Ozzie. Your dad and I broke up. But when he saw me out on a date with Franz Finkleman, he was eaten up with jealousy." Mom's laugh was a girlish giggle. "He showed up at my apartment with a guitar and serenaded me with Foreigner's *I Wanna Know What Love Is.*"

Stella clasped her hands to her heart. "I didn't think Dad could sing!"

"He couldn't." Mom's eyes sparkled. "He was terrible, but all the neighbors came out and clapped for him. I thought my heart was going to explode. I never went out with Franz again."

And just like that, an idea clicked into my head with the sound of a gong being struck. As the sound resonated, the idea grew. Music was the key to Audrey's heart. If I could get the whole school and even the parents involved, I could convince her that people supported us. I could make it a splashy statement, maybe sing a song. Whatever I did needed to be crazy enough that it was all anyone could talk about. Only then would Priscilla would lose her bargaining chip. No one would care about the past, and the two of us could start over.

I leaned forward. "Show me more of these videos, Stel."

Stella's eyes widened. She squealed and hugged me. "I'll cue up the best of the shows! This is going to be so much fun!"

Chapter 25: Oz

Complicated

The drive home on Sunday afternoon gave me a lot of time to think. It didn't take a math teacher to know that a promposal, or as I had started calling it, a dateposal had a fifty percent chance of blowing up in my face. If Audrey decided she wanted nothing to do with me, did I really want to risk embarrassing myself in front of a large crowd?

I liked the idea of a grand gesture, though. Proving my noble intentions to the fair maiden and all that. Could I risk opening my heart so completely to Audrey's emotional roller coaster? I wanted to, but I also longed for reassurance from her.

An hour from Marchfield, I hadn't made much progress in figuring out my romantic desires. When I stopped to get gas, I checked my phone. The only text I'd received was a reminder from the school system about resuming classes tomorrow.

Back behind the wheel, I wondered if I should try talking to Audrey before going for the big guns of the grand gesture. She might be home right now, missing me. If we talked, I knew we could figure out our relationship. And if we ended up in her bed again, all the better. The whole dateposal idea could go by the wayside.

I stopped off at Share With Your Buds on my way into town and bought a bouquet of daisies. I hoped Audrey would recognize the flowers as a peace offering. I also bought big, thick, gooey brownies down the street at Pat's Bakery. According to Bobby, chocolate is every girl's best friend, and a good brownie goes a long way toward healing all wounds.

Pulling into Red's apartment complex, I saw her ugly, green car sitting in front of her apartment. Gathering my offerings, I walked to the door and knocked.

Audrey opened the door. Her hair was knotted on top of her head, making her neck impossibly long. Unconsciously, she leaned toward me, and I breathed her in. She smelled of fresh flowers and vanilla cookies. The aroma teased my senses and made me smile. At four in the afternoon, she wore those pajamas, labeling her a Llama Reading Mama. I smiled, remembering them from our first night together. All the blood left my head for parts south. Flannel jammies should have been the opposite of sexy, but my cock stood at attention.

"Uh, hi, Audrey. I, uh… I brought these for you." I held out the flowers and brownies awkwardly. My blood-starved brain made witty banter next to impossible.

She accepted my offerings, holding up the flowers to smell. Her eyes burned a trail across my shoulders and chest up my neck to my eyes. We stood, eyes locked, not speaking. She lit a fire in my blood.

I stepped forward until we touched. My chest brushed against the tips of her breasts. Her nipples tightened, and I instantly wanted more. I nudged my knee between hers, guiding her inside the apartment. No more public displays of affection… for a while, anyway.

Movement from behind Red stopped me in my tracks, my senses going on high alert. Instinctively, I stepped around Red to block her from danger.

Val smiled brightly as she shouldered a purple overnight bag. Behind me, Audrey reached for Val's arm as she passed, but Val slid out of reach.

"Hey, Oz, good to see you. Did you have a nice break? Don't answer that; I'm headed out. Y'all have fun." She started the engine of her car and zipped out of the lot with a honk and wave.

Audrey poked me in the side, and I looked down at her. I hadn't even realized I was still holding a protective position.

She stepped around me. "You should come in."

I followed her into the apartment. Audrey went into the tiny kitchen and filled a large mason jar with water while I walked over to pet Stevie who sat on the coffee table. He reached out with one paw and snagged my jeans, clawing through the fabric to my leg. I supposed that was fair.

I sat on her pretty sofa, the cat and I staring at one another. Audrey padded across the floor, her feet bare. I noticed her toes were painted neon pink.

Setting the flowers on the coffee table, she sank into an armchair across from me. She took a second to adjust cross-legged in the chair.

I forced my eyes away from the pink toes that peeked out. "Did you have a good break?"

"Pretty good. Val and I watched movies and hung out."

Stevie sauntered over to the bouquet and stuck his head into the daisies. With eyes squinted shut, he chewed on the leaves and then sucked a flower into his mouth.

Were daisies poisonous? Killing Audrey's cat would be terrible.

"Please, don't eat the daisies," Audrey scolded, quickly moving the flowers to the top of a nearby bookcase. Stevie jumped down to sit on the floor in front of the shelves, plotting his next move. Audrey returned and sat in a chair rather than sitting next to me on the sofa.

"Good movie," I said.

"What movie?"

"*Please Don't Eat the Daisies.* Nineteen-sixties rom-com? Doris Day and David Nivon?"

She shook her head. "Never seen it."

"My mom and sister, Stella, are romantic-comedy nuts. I've watched every one ever made."

She absorbed this information, then changed the subject. "Did you have a good trip home?"

I rolled my shoulders and forced myself to relax. "My mom and sister are annoying, pushy, and in my business, but good."

Audrey laughed, and I flushed with relief.

I smiled for the first time since leaving home. "Bobby sent Stella a video of the halftime show. I swear they watched it five hundred times. They couldn't stop laughing at that part where Frank stepped on my foot, and I almost fell."

"You did look a little like a cartoon character whirling your arms around."

Audrey's smile reached her eyes. My heart raced, and my chest tightened. I sucked in a deep breath.

"They wouldn't shut up about how great my legs are."

Surprise made her eyes widen, and she burst out in a belly laugh.

The sound soothed my sharp edges and heated my blood with desire—not for her body, although I wanted her badly. But it was a sudden desire to come home to her every night and talk about our day. I wanted to hear her laugh for the rest of my life.

"Audrey, I'm so sorry about last week. I shouldn't have walked away without resolving the issues between us."

She sobered. "I-I'm sorry too."

I ached to reach out to her and hold her hand. but she held them clenched together in her lap.

"I also need you to know I don't regret a single second of the time I've spent with you."

She met my eyes. The deep green of them touched my soul. Her eyes widened as if she saw me for the first time, and I saw questions she was afraid to ask in their depths.

My hands fisted in my lap. Dr. Winters and Priscilla Henesey opened wounds. Both of us had bled, but we could heal each other.

"You know I was a soldier. I saw horrible things in the Middle East, and while I was there, I shut down parts of myself to survive. When I got out, I thought I could go back to being the person I was before."

She nodded, and I knew she understood. Every family touched by the military understood that war changed a person.

"It didn't happen," I continued. "I walked around feeling half asleep. My family treated me like I was fragile, or worse, like I might explode. I moved away, going to New York to teach, but my heart wasn't in it there."

Her cat seemed to sense I was baring my soul. He jumped up on the sofa next to me and curled up, purring by my leg.

"What you need to know though is when I saw you that first time in the bar, it was like I woke up. For the first time in years, I could breathe deeply. That night when I fell asleep in your bed like an asshole? It was the first night I slept without nightmares since getting out."

There were tears in her eyes. I gripped the arm of the sofa to stop myself from getting on my knees and begging her to let me hold her.

"I went to therapy for years, Audrey. But I don't talk about that time in my life much, not even with Bobby. But I wanted you to know."

"Thank you for telling me," Audrey spoke softly, her hands lay still in her lap now.

"I wanted you to know because what we have, our relationship is special. I'm a better person because of knowing you, and that's worth fighting for. Dr. Winters was out of line."

Audrey shook her head. "No, she was right. We took it way too far that night."

I nodded. "Maybe. But I can't regret making you come in my arms under the stars. We should probably stick to more private locations from now on though."

She untangled her legs and jumped to her feet. Her arms hugged hard around her chest. I stayed on the couch, giving her space.

"Oz, we need to slow down. This thing between us is like an out-of-control train. Neither of us has time for a relationship. You're a new teacher at Marchfield, and I've established my career and my reputation. We can't afford to mess this up."

I ignored the jab of pain in my heart. Audrey always pushed me away, but tonight I needed to push back. I breathed in deeply, resolving to not lose my cool no matter how she pushed my buttons. "We can go as slow or fast as you want, Audrey. I know your career is as important to you as it is to me. But I'm asking you to consider building a relationship with me."

"I don't trust myself when I'm around you. I lose my balance and do crazy things. I'm not sure if I can work with you and be in a relationship, too."

She lowered her head, looking lost, and I wanted desperately to cuddle her close and reassure her that she could have both. She could be respected in a challenging career and have a relationship.

"Being a teacher isn't your sole identity, Audrey. You're one of the strongest people I know. Lots of educators balance both a career and a relationship. I know we can, too."

Restlessly, she sat again, wrapping her arms around her knees as if she could disappear. "Being a teacher is my whole life. I drove my brothers crazy, playing school, giving them homework, even grading it. I would never be happy in another profession."

I didn't know how to help her past the edges of the box she'd sealed herself into, but I needed her to realize there was an infinite capacity to grow and be more.

I stood, moving to where she sat, bending down next to her chair, sitting on the floor at her feet. "I love that. I hope there are family photos of you schooling your brothers. I want to know everything about you."

"My family says I'm too rigid sometimes. That I can't see the forest through the trees."

Her family had a point, but I wasn't going to say it.

"I want to know more about your childhood and all the places you've lived. Where did you go to school? What hobbies help you relax? Who your favorite authors are?"

"You're missing the point."

I reached out to run my finger across her knee. "You can give me pop quizzes and grade me after."

She smiled, and my heart opened. The ground rippled beneath me, and I was happy I sat on the floor. Looking around, I wondered if it was an earthquake. Nothing moved, so I guessed that tectonic force was inside me.

I loved her. That genuine, beautiful smile wrecked me. It obliterated all my barriers, brought me to my knees, and then helped me up. I loved Red's craziness, determination, and strength. I loved that she overthought everything and kept me at arm's length even when she wanted to pull me closer. I loved the teacher and the coach. I loved the whole package no matter how frustrating, hard-headed, driven, and goal-oriented she was. My mind spun while my heart stuttered in my chest.

I took her wrists, pulled them away from her body, and eased her down onto my lap. Wrapping my arms around her, I held her close, my chin resting on the top of her head.

A moment later, she was wiggling out of my arms and off my lap. She stood and then paced away from me. I stood too, still reeling from my monumental discovery. I forced myself back to reality when she started to speak.

"You don't understand, Oz. All my life, I jumped from one school to another until being an outcast became my identity. By the time I was in middle school, I stopped making friends. I lived for every time Dad's ship came home. When he was home, then the world made sense. It was the only time we were all happy."

I waited for her to continue as she paced back and forth.

"Mom died a little with my dad. I'm not sure she's ever recovered. In one horrible swoop, everything was ripped from underneath us, and he was gone. Then we found out about the debt, and the world tilted off its axis at home. School was my safe space. There was food, warmth, and teachers who cared."

My heart hurt for the little girl who lost her dad too young. I'd been older, but losing my dad had driven me to join the Army. Losing a parent had a deep impact on both of our lives.

She stopped pacing and faced me. "I've worked so hard to build a stable life in Marchfield. What if Dr. Winters decides to transfer me? I would lose everything I've worked for here."

"We'd build a new life. Together. You wouldn't lose anything that mattered. Val and Bobby, all your friends would still be there..."

I wanted to say more but stopped when she held up her hand.

"I can't," she whispered. Her shoulders slumped, and I felt my heart cracking in my chest.

"We can fight Dr. Winters. We can go above her head."

"No, we can't, Oz." She threw her hands up in agitation. "I threw myself at you at the bar, in the school parking lot, and in the garden. It's a wonder I haven't stripped you naked in your classroom. Don't you see? You're my catnip and my kryptonite. Being so out of control is killing me."

"I wanted you from the moment I laid eyes on you. Keeping my hands off you is next to impossible, but we can find a way to fix all of this." I reached my hand out to her.

She stepped back, closing me off, and I knew there wasn't anything I could do about it. "We need to end this. I can't bear it anymore."

I shook my head. "But I love you."

Audrey's mouth opened and then closed. Then I watched her pink lips form the words I desperately wanted to hear. "I love you too, Oz..."

Music swelled through my mind. Whitney Houston's *I Will Always Love You* swelled to a crescendo. Was I channeling Audrey's playlist somehow? I saw lips move and tuned back in.

"But teachers are held to a higher standard than other people. Parents and students actually believe we sleep at the school behind our desks. If word got out about the two of us, or that camera footage got put on the internet, they would hate us.

We'd be two more disgusting teachers on the news. It would change everything."

I admitted, yes, we'd made a mistake. But scandals only lasted until the next one came along. People would forgive us and support us. "You're a living, breathing woman. The kids and parents don't expect you to marry the school like a nun marries the church."

She looked at me with wounded eyes and then pointed toward the door. "I can't do this anymore."

My eyes begged her to reconsider. "Don't let Priscilla win."

"What about Priscilla?" Her expression turned fierce.

"She went out of her way to assure me we'd made the right decision for the school to avoid negative publicity."

Audrey shook her head in confusion. "Why?"

"Why does anyone do something vindictive? Jealousy? Revenge?"

"I have to figure it out. It's gone on long enough."

I moved to kneel in front of her chair. "You're not alone. Let's puzzle this out together."

Her eyes were wet, her voice hard as she pushed her fist against my shoulder. "I don't need you to solve my problems."

Why didn't she understand? I wanted to work with her, by her side, support her, not settle her problems for her.

When Audrey said, "I need time, Oz. Please," I knew I had to go.

"I respect your feelings, Audrey. But this isn't over for me. I love you, and I'm not giving up."

Reluctantly, I walked to her door, closing it behind me. Sitting in my truck, my eyes felt gritty, and my head pounded. I tried to envision my next move, but my mind was blank.

When my phone buzzed, I picked it up off the passenger's seat. Someone started a new text thread between Bobby, Val, and me, and I had missed eight messages.

4:30 PM **Val: Oz, how did it go with Audrey?**
4:38 PM **Val: Text us when you see this message.**
4:39 PM **Bobby: You there, Sarge?**
4:45 PM **Bobby: Damn it, Oz. Text us back!**
4:45 PM **Val: They're probably still talking, Bobby.**
4:50 PM **Bobby: Message us when you're done, man.**
4:58 PM **Val: I already said that.**
5:00 PM **Bobby: It bears repeating.**

I drove home without responding. Audrey wasn't the only one who needed to think.

When I arrived, I sat outside on the front stoop for a few minutes. The sun set, and the sky went from pink to black. I rested my hands on my knees.

Audrey had pushed me away after admitting me she loved me. It was impossible to ignore that I loved her, too. Even now, the thought made my heart pound.

I couldn't go back, but she was afraid to go forward. There had to be some way to prove to her that we could have it all. Her friends, co-workers, students, and parents would support us, and we could have both stability and a relationship.

It looked like the dateposal was back on the table.

I picked up my phone to text Val and Bobby.

6:30 PM **Me: Hey, guys, I need your help.**

Chapter 26: Audrey

I'm Movin' On

The alarm went off at six on Monday morning, an hour and a half earlier than normal. I threw my phone across the room and pulled the covers over my head. My chest felt tight and heavy. My anxieties weighed a lot.

Peeping out from the covers, Stevie's round green eyes watched me. He stood, his feet digging painfully into my breasts as he circled a few times before plopping down again with his tail in my face. It twitched, tickling my nose.

I closed my eyes and composed an absentee note in my mind:

Dear Dr. Winters,

I am unable to teach today because my cat has crushed my ribcage. I'm certain you will understand that this may extend into a week-long absence.

Sincerely, Audrey Freemont

I'd take any excuse not to go to work today. The Sunday night gloomies haunted me with nightmares of returning to work. I understood the typical end of a holiday dread, but not this deep, gut-wrenching sense of doom. I'd woken five times from a dream where I was making out in the garden with Oz in front of Dr. Winters, Priscilla, and, oddly, Val. They were Olympic Orgasm judges and kept scoring us at two and a half out of ten.

Every time I jerked awake, I worried about getting through the day. Oz would be everywhere! He'd be across the hall in his classroom, out in the halls, eating at the same time as me in the cafeteria, and, of course, at our last regular season soccer match.

I threw the pillow over my head, trying to block out Taylor Swift's *I Knew You Were Trouble* as it played through my mind. Hearing Oz's voice or catching a glimpse of his shoulders above the heads of the students might destroy me. And if he looked at me like I'd broken his heart, I'd run out crying in front of everyone!

Dear Dr. Winters,

Please excuse my spur-of-the-moment absence. What can I say? I need therapy.

Sincerely, Crazy Audrey

After fifteen minutes of entertaining worst-case scenarios in my head, I gave up, hoping a magical sinkhole would open up beneath my bed. It was time to put on my big girl pants and face the music.

Stevie hopped off and allowed me to stumble into the bathroom.

In front of the mirror, I repeated my new mantra: I'm strong. I'm doing what's right for me and my students.

I said it over and over as I showered, only stopping when I questioned why breaking my own heart was the best thing to do. Protecting my career and staying at Marchfield Middle sounded like hollow excuses.

I shrugged it off and put on my hot-pink power underwear. Tough days called for sexy lingerie. Searching my closet, I inspected each item until goosebumps covered my body. Deciding on a pink shirt with puffy sleeves, I put it on. Then I took it off. None of my clothes felt right.

Dear Dr. Winters,

Please excuse my sweatpants and T-shirt. I'm aware they are against dress code, but I don't give a fuck.

Audrey, aka Red

In the end, I put on a black dress and boots. Dressing for my own funeral seemed appropriate.

The face in the mirror was a blotchy mess. A new pimple or two, hell, three, erupted overnight. Dark circles showed off my puffy, red eyes. I slathered on concealer and foundation.

And my hair wouldn't cooperate either. Twenty cowlicks popped up and refused to settle down. After wrestling with it for ten minutes, I yanked it back into a ponytail with a black elastic band to match my theme for the day.

Giving up on my appearance, I played with Stevie and then gave him breakfast while my coffee brewed. I poured the whole pot into a giant thermos and added cream and sugar. It's true what they say. Some days, teachers actually do run on coffee.

Juggling my coffee and bag full of essays, I walked to my car. Settling into the driver's seat, I turned over the engine, and Sinead O'Connor's silky, sweet voice filled the space. *Nothing Compares to You* hit me with a slap of emotion. Tears welled up in my eyes. I clicked the music off and drove in tortured silence.

Luckily, the students hadn't noticed. I shuddered to think of the feeding frenzy if they'd sensed the attraction between us. I imagined the giggling and pointing. Teens had no filter. Their comments, questions, and sing-song chanting of our names would've been unbearable, and I shuddered at the thought.

And yet, I couldn't forget the desolation in Oz's eyes last night and how the same emotion now echoed deep in my chest.

I arrived early and parked in the deserted lot. I didn't want to answer endless, well-meaning questions by my co-workers: What did you do over the weekend? Tell me about your break! I cringed at the thought of lying about it and pretending that I was okay.

I signed in and ran to the safety of my classroom. Behind the closed door, I breathed a sigh of relief. Settling into the morning routine, I turned on the computer, wrote the objectives on the board, pulled up my slideshow, and set out the graded essays. I loved today's lesson about the plot and character in *The Monkey's Paw*, a classic spooky story perfect for late October and Halloween. As a bonus, it matched my outfit and mood: dark, gloomy, and dread.

I sat down to inhale coffee from my thermos and check my emails when someone knocked. I jumped and splashed coffee across my desk. Cursing, I mopped it up with a wad of paper towels. Maybe whoever it was at the door would go away.

I imagined it was Oz, standing on the other side of my door with flowers and donuts. That was exactly the kind of spectacle that would make people talk. The mere thought of it made me want to hide.

But what if it was Dr. Winters? Maybe she needed to talk to me about the Literacy Committee meeting next week or to schedule the semester midterms. I couldn't leave my boss standing out in the hallway while I curled up in a fetal position under my desk.

Whoever it was knocked again. I tiptoed to the door and put my ear on the cool wood, listening for clues to his or her identity.

"It's Val, open up, Audrey. I know you're in there. I heard your salty language a minute ago."

I yanked the door open. Val's big smile erased some of my anxiety. She held two red and white pom poms in front of her red staff shirt.

"Go Girls' Soccer!" She punctuated the cheer with a little hop and kick.

I groaned, "I'm not in the mood."

She gave me a long stare. "Where's your teen spirit, Wednesday Addams?"

I sighed, "I don't have time this morning, Val."

Undeterred, she gave me a hug. "You didn't return my message last night. I'm guessing it didn't go well with Oz."

The lump in my throat made it impossible to respond. I shook my head and shrugged.

"I'm sorry, Aud. I'm here if you need to talk."

I hugged her, trying not to let the tears spill down my face. I swallowed hard. "I know."

She patted my shoulder, her face clouded with worry. Before she could say anything, the school bell rang.

We heard the cheerful sounds of students entering the building. Lockers opened and slammed shut. Students laughed, catching up after the short break. They'd be coming to class soon.

"I've gotta run," Val said, picking up her pompoms and heading toward the door. "See you at lunch."

My classes *loved The Monkey's Paw*. The old-fashioned horror story sparked great discussion, and I fed off their energy. By the end of the day, my emotions and my resolve steadied. The kids and my career mattered.

I avoided Oz all day. I ate lunch in my classroom and kept my head down in the hallway. Though I didn't see Oz, I heard him. During class change, he scolded some children for running down the hallway. Later, I heard him compliment others on their test scores. As time inched closer to the soccer match, I huddled behind my door, listening for the deep sound of his voice.

By 4:30, my nerves had twisted into a lump in my stomach. I arrived on the field with a huge case of water bottles and a bag of protein bars. Glancing around with trepidation, I spotted Oz across the field, watching the Maidens warm up. Co-captains, Haley and Adrienne, approached him, and I imagined them discussing plays and strategy.

As if sensing me, Oz met my eyes over the girls' heads. I turned away and set out the snacks as butterflies in my stomach began a frenzied jitterbug. With nothing left to do, I distracted myself by cheering the girls on as they practiced their plays.

Oz sent the girls in to hydrate and get a snack as Blakely Middle's bus arrived. While the opposing team ran out onto the field to warm up, Oz gathered the girls around him.

"It's been my pleasure all season to watch you girls grow into a team. Blakely may be full of strong players, but they can't compete with your heart, spirit, or loyalty. No matter what happens in today's match, Ms. Freemont and I will be right by your side. I know you want to go to the playoffs, so let's give it our best shot."

Once again, I met his eyes over the girls' heads. My smile felt tight and uncomfortable. He nodded and turned away.

When the referee called both teams to the field, I noticed Priscilla and Dr. Winters walking out of the school building together. They made their way to the stands and sat to watch the game. They smiled and clapped as the girls took their positions on the field.

Their stares felt like itchy hives on my neck. I knew my imagination had to be running on overtime. I glanced back toward where they were seated.

And burst out laughing.

Bobby and Mel had moved in front of Priscilla. They stood, cheering the girls, blocking Pree's view of the game. Val and Keith sat behind Dr. Winters, yelling encouragement and blowing into loud plastic vuvuzela horns. Dr. Winters's smile melted into one of irritation, and it delighted me.

The Maidens on the sidelines kept up a constant chatter. They cheered every good play and encouraged every player. Even when Blakely scored in the last few minutes of the half, their optimism and team spirit never faltered.

In the second half, Marchfield rallied. Haley scored a goal to tie the game. Reenergized, the team held off Blakely's attempts to score. They were tied at the end of regulation time.

Oz called a timeout to give the tired girls a short break before overtime began. "You're doing great. Blakely's reached their limit. Push them back hard."

"You've got this, girls." I slapped their hands, giving high-fives down the line.

When I got to Oz, he lifted his hand for a high-five. My palm touched his, and I felt a spark race down my arm. My head jerked up and I met his eyes. They burned with so much emotion, I wondered if my clothes might burn off.

He moved to say something to Bree, one of the forwards, before she ran onto the field. I glanced over my shoulder toward Val. And saw Bobby instead, partially blocking Pree's view. Her seething expression made me smile. I waved to Bobby, and she saluted.

Overtime lasted twenty minutes. Blakely stole the ball, almost scoring early on, but the shot went high, missing the goal. It seemed like neither team could win as the players became increasingly tired. In the last two minutes, Haley drove forward and passed the ball to Bree, who managed to get around Blakely's defense. Bree passed to Kimberley, who happened to be in the pocket. Kimberley kicked the ball hard toward the net. Their goalie, dove, brushing the ball with her fingertips, but it flew into the net.

The Maidens fell onto the field together like a pile of puppies, hugging and screaming. Then they broke apart, dancing, cheering, and waving to friends and family in the stands. With grins so wide they could've swallowed the moon, they rounded up Oz and me into a big hug.

Finally, Oz led the team over to shake hands with the girls on the other team. He stood with their coach, discussing the game.

The late afternoon sun shone down on him. His smile was confident and easy as he talked, nodding toward the girls. I remembered thinking he wasn't a good teacher all those months ago. I'd been such a fool. His style and methods were different from mine, but we both valued education and put the kids first.

That's what I love about him.

Romantic songs portray falling in love as something wild and elemental, uncontrollable. But as I stood there watching Oz from across the field, love gently wrapped itself around me.

I imagined launching myself at him. He would lift me up and swing me around. We would laugh, and the girls would cheer. Val, Bobby, and the rest of our friends would tease us. We'd go home together, lock the door, and–

Dr. Winters appeared at my side, startling me. "Great game, Ms. Freemont. The girls did a marvelous job!"

Reluctantly, I turned toward her. "They certainly did. But Oz is the one who deserves the congratulations. I'm just the snack wench and ball handler."

My face flooded with heat. That hadn't come out right.

Dr. Winters's eyes widened slightly. "Yes, well, I'll be sure to congratulate him, too."

I nodded, not trusting myself to speak. *Ball handler, indeed!*

She cleared her throat awkwardly. "I'm glad you came to your senses and did the right thing; the girls would thank you, too, if they knew."

Behind her, I could see Priscilla in the stands. Bobby was animatedly detaining her, preventing Pree from walking around by throwing out her hands.

Clouds covered the sun, and I shivered. Having them here sucked the joy away from the girls' victory. I squared my shoulders, unwilling to let Priscilla win.

Dr. Winters cleared her throat. I forced my focus back to her as she spoke. "I have some great news. I've been meaning to tell you that The City-Wide Teacher of the Year Committee made its final nominations, and you're on the shortlist."

I was a finalist for the Teacher of the Year Award?

My mouth fell open.

In Marchfield, students nominated teachers secretly, and the superintendent chose the finalists. After announcing the candidates, anyone living in the city had the opportunity to vote for the teacher they liked best.

"Wow, that's, uh, gr–great," I stuttered. "Thanks for letting me know."

Dr. Winters' hands were fisted at her sides, her back uncomfortably straight.

I bet this burns your ass.

I pretended I didn't see her outstretched hand and bent to pick up the mesh ball bag at my feet. A giggle tried to work its way up my throat, but I stifled it.

Dr. Winters coughed again, shifting her feet. "Marchfield Middle is especially honored because we have two outstanding teachers on the list this year."

The realization was like a basketball hitting me on the head. Here was the answer to the question I'd been asking since school started. Details clicked into place: first, the pregnancy rumor, then tattling on us. Priscilla Henesey was the other nominee.

I watched Dr. Winters walk back toward the school. Her short heels sunk into the turf with every step, and her shoes became muddy and grass-stained.

Hysterical giggles bubbled out of me. I scanned the field. More than anything, I wanted to share Dr. Winters's revelation with Oz.

But he was gone.

Chapter 27: Oz

Wanna Be Startin' Somethin'

My tiny living room was crammed with people because Bobby stopped short of calling out the National Guard. Most of my friends stood talking about school with an assortment of teachers I recognized but didn't know well.

Stella and Mom, who told me they wouldn't miss this for the world, passed around homemade meatballs on toothpicks and cookies on plates.

I stood back by the hallway that led to my bedroom. Large crowds made me nervous, and I gripped a cold Cola with enough force to dent the can.

Bobby met my eyes. It was time to get the show on the road.

"Thanks for coming, everybody," I started, then paused.

Standing here in front of this crowd, the dateposal seemed like a bad idea. I'd embarrass Audrey and look like a fool. The best thing would be to send everyone home.

But everyone smiled and nodded. They seemed excited to hear about my plan. Stella clapped her hands, grinning at me while doing a little dance.

My gut tightened. I needed to push through this, and then I could back out later. "Audrey and I didn't have the best start at Marchfield."

"Y'all got sent to the office an hour into the first day!" Keith laughed, and others joined in.

I smiled, but my body tensed. "Thanks, Keith, for reminding us all."

I set the can of soda down on a new side table my mom had brought with her. I tapped my hand on the side of my thigh, a habit I'd developed in the Army to deal with my anxiety. They all be laughing at me again soon enough.

"Over the past few weeks, I've gotten to know and like Audrey. I want to take her on a few dates."

"Are you asking our permission?" Pete Tenchly, the reading teacher, snickered.

"No, he only asked for mine," Mom interjected to much laughter.

"Let him finish," Bobby scolded everyone.

"What's the problem then?" Marnie asked.

I cleared my throat. Teachers were more rowdy than eighth-grade boys.

"Dr. Winters insists we keep our relationship platonic and has told us we may not date."

Mel kissed my bestie, and I couldn't help but smile. "That's silly! Bobby and I have a romantic relationship."

Sixth-grade teacher, Marsha Ingleside nodded. "I dated Carl a while back, and no one cared."

I bet y'all didn't make out and more on school grounds.

Dee rubbed her huge pregnant belly, and I prayed she didn't pop until after she left. "Our job is stressful enough without the boss butting into our social lives, too."

Every teacher in the room grumbled in agreement.

"I've spoken with Audrey and made these same points. Even though she likes me, she's uncomfortable breaking the rules."

Val grinned and wiggled her eyebrows. "Trust me, she more than likes you."

Dee and several other female teachers nodded and laughed. Their confidence made me feel more hopeful, even though I was still sweating bullets.

"She's also worried about how you and the students will react if we date."

Marnie sent me a look that made me squirm. "She's a lucky girl. Some of us might be envious, but we'd still support her."

Dee said, "That's why we're all here. Bobby said you were planning a grand gesture."

Every woman in the room sighed with a kind of squeal at the end. It seemed like a positive reaction, but I choked on my next words. They might all think a dateposal was a dumb idea. I threw a glance at my best friend.

Bobby patted my shoulder. "Stella, Oz's sister, came up with an idea. It's crazy and sounds ridiculously fun."

Stella stood and waved to everyone. "Oz wants to ask Audrey out with a promposal!"

The women made that noise again, and I took it as a sign to continue. "I'm calling it a dateposal. Honestly, I'm not completely convinced it's going to work, but I'm hopeful."

Frank winked at Oz. "Women love grand gestures."

"How do you know?" Marnie asked him. "You're a single, old man."

Frank chuckled and stroked his white beard. "I was young once."

"Val and I agree. Audrey will love it," Bobby said. "Women enjoy it when men horribly embarrass themselves."

"It's smoking hot." Val nodded seriously.

Keith laughed. He winked at Kate Mitchell, the cute single art teacher he was dating. "You're a hopeless romantic, Oz, willing to go the extra mile."

Dee snorted at Keith's comment, patting the baby that was thankfully still inside her belly. "I wish my husband made a gesture before we married."

Pat Collins, one of the P.E. teachers, groaned and slapped his forehead. "This will make it rough for all the rest of us guys. You're setting a precedent all women will expect us to top."

"This isn't about you, Pat," Mel scolded. "We're here to support Oz."

Bobby wrapped her arms around her waist. "I love it when you're sassy." Mel blushed and kissed Bobby, long and sweet.

Keith balled-up a napkin and threw it at them. "Get a room."

"Settle down, children." Val's stern teacher voice quieted the crowd.

Mom stepped up beside me and put her arm around my waist. "What exactly is the plan, Honey?"

I had outlined it all in my head countless times. This would put a spotlight on Audrey and make her the center of attention. She'd either appreciate it or it would make her run, but I needed to know. This was my last chance.

"Well, um." I hesitated for a second, wondering where to begin.

Val filled the silence. "My bestie has convinced herself she can't be with Oz."

"Because our principal is an ass," Keith interjected. Some of the teachers nodded in agreement. Dr. Winters was not universally liked.

Val nodded, "She has other reasons too."

I cleared my throat. "Audrey moved a lot as a kid. She never experienced the security many of us did by growing up in one place with friends and people to support her. I want to show her I have her back. That we all do."

Stella sighed dreamily. "He wants to do a halftime show at the soccer playoffs."

Marnie asked, "Are you asking her to marry you?"

I'd thought about proposing, but we'd only known each other a few months, and we'd never even had a real date. "No, I'm going to ask her to go out with me."

"Are you wearing the dress again? With those red shoes?" Frank laughed.

"I have a new costume for him," Stella interjected.

A small spike of fear straightened my spine. "I'm not sure..."

"I love the idea of a flashy costume and an embarrassing dance number." Bobby shot me a mischievous grin.

Kate giggled, "I can't wait to see this!"

"He's going to need help from all of us." Val put her hand on my shoulder, steadying me. I trusted her.

Dee nodded. "If we stand behind Audrey and Oz, Dr. Winters won't be able to do anything about it without the whole world knowing she's an unromantic jerk."

"I'm in," Frank said. "Anything to stick it to Winters. She's a thorn in my ass."

Pat nodded. "You can count on the P.E. Department, Oz."

"I'll make posters if you need them," Kate volunteered.

"Whatever you need, Oz," Mel said, and the rest of the teachers murmured their agreement.

Mom dabbed at her eyes with a tissue. "You've found an amazing community here, Ozzie."

I smiled. Marchfield had given me more than I'd ever imagined. Even after such a short time, the people here had embraced me. It truly felt like home.

Bobby leaned forward. "Okay, Sarge, tell us what you need us to do."

Taking a deep breath, I laid out my plan for the dateposal.

***

A week later, under the late afternoon sunshine, I gathered the Maidens around me. "All season long, you've been fierce soccer princesses. If we win today, we'll be the best team in the city, but if you ask me, we don't even need to play this game. You've proven again and again you deserve the title, and I'm so proud of you."

Haley squealed, "Aww!" The others joined in.

"I'm also participating in a special halftime show. I'd appreciate it if y'all cheer as loud as possible."

"Are you asking Ms. Freemont to marry you?" Haley elbowed Adrienne.

My mouth dropped open. Apparently, the girls weren't as oblivious as I'd thought. I jumped to set the record straight.

"Whoa, girls, that's jumping the gun. I've only known Ms. Freemont for a couple of months."

Adrienne lifted one eyebrow, imitating me.

I laughed. "Okay, you caught me, I like Ms. Freemont, but nobody's getting engaged today. Now remember, no loose lips. I'm counting on you."

They nodded, holding up their pinkies to promise, and I sent them onto the field to warm up.

Audrey arrived. The late-day sun made her skin glow and her hair turn to fire. Wearing tight skinny jeans and a Marchfield sweatshirt, she organized snacks and water on the sidelines. When she bent over, my eyes caressed her butt. Too soon, she stood and turned around, her eyes slipping past me to study the girls.

I took a deep breath and tried to focus on running the drills.

The first half of the match flew by. I heard Audrey's husky voice shouting encouragement, and my eyes found her again and again. When Bree collided with another player and walked off the field in tears, Audrey hugged her and whispered in her ear. Bree nodded and shook it off.

An enormous crowd of teachers, students, and parents filled the stands. My friends cheered for the girls alongside people I didn't recognize. Even Stella and Mom had taken the drive down for the game. I spotted a reporter and a photographer talking to Bobby and Val in the stands.

Priscilla Henesey and Dr. Winters sat on the edge of the second-row mid-field. They were both dressed in suits. They sat stiffly, their backs straight, and only clapped politely when Kya passed the ball to Haley, who scored the first goal of the game.

As time ran down toward halftime, my nerves made it harder to keep track of the plays. I couldn't stop checking my watch. Bobby came down and stood by me on the sidelines, offering me support through the last few minutes of the half.

When she left me just before time ran out, I wondered if I'd hyperventilate.

Knowing it was too late to call off Operation Dateposal, I took a deep breath, trying to slow my heart down. I tried to breathe in and out deeply as I walked over to Audrey. "I need to run into the school for a minute. I forgot the MVP award for the first half."

Her eyes traveled up my chest, across my neck. I felt little fires start where they touched. When she reached my eyes, she nodded. Our gazes locked, and electricity flowed between us. Her green eyes clung to mine, speaking volumes I didn't comprehend. Another smoky second ticked by before she turned back to the game.

Feeling more confident, I jogged off the sidelines as the buzzer sounded. Inside the school, I practically threw on the costume Stella gave me an hour earlier.

I jogged out to the parking lot as Bobby pulled up in a black convertible that we'd borrowed from Dee's husband. I jumped into the car.

Bobby paused, looking me over. She reached out and straightened my tie. Nodding, she patted my shoulder and then ruined the moment by saying:

"Damn! If I wasn't a queer, I'd drive off with you."

Looking down at my outfit, I knew I could've worn the black pants and button-down shirt any day, but the deep purple suit coat and matching dress shoes stole the show. Covered with sequins, they caught the sunlight and sent sparkling light dancing around me.

"You wish." I laughed, relaxing slightly for the first time in hours.

"This show will blow Audrey away."

I crushed the worries which tried to sprout in my mind, focusing only on breathing in and out. It was almost like preparing to go into battle.

Bobby put the car in gear and drove us onto the track. The lanes that wrapped around the field were just wide enough for the car.

She glanced at me. "No doubt. No surrender."

Our Army troop motto resonated in my heart, and I repeated it back to her. "No doubt. No Surrender."

Bobby stopped the car when we reached mid-field. This was Keith's cue to start playing Justin Timberlake's *CAN'T STOP THE FEELING* on the sound system.

As the music swept over the crowd, Dr. Winters and Priscilla stood. Their heads swiveled between the field and the stands, looking for the reason for the music.

The Maidens spread out on the sideline in front of my boss, singing along and jumping up and down.

I saw Audrey laugh from her spot near the snacks. She tossed her red hair back, shielding her eyes from the sun to watch the girls.

People in the stands could sense something was about to happen. They began clapping to the beat, standing up to catch the show. I made a mental note to thank Val for helping me pick a great song.

Keith, Mel, and Val ran out onto the field in front of the stands. They started the simple choreographed dance as we'd rehearsed. Val held a rolled poster in her hand and waved it above her head to the beat.

Bobby jumped out of the car, running around to open my door with a deep bow. This was it. Show time.

I jumped out, striking a pose like John Travolta in *Saturday Night Fever*. Then I strutted to center field to join the others.

Frank, Mack, and other teachers stood in the stands, dancing and mirroring the action on the field. Spectators screamed approvingly.

Bobby and I joined Val and the others dancing on the field. I caught a glimpse of Audrey shimmying on the sidelines. Priscilla stood a few yards behind her, craning her neck to look over the excited Maidens. Her unhappy face contrasted with everyone else's smiles.

The music swelled as Justin reached the chorus. I lifted the microphone and sang, belting out the words putting my heart and soul into them.

Bobby and Val joined in with other microphones. I danced as I sang, trying not to pant into the microphone. My heart pounded in my chest.

The Maidens clustered behind Audrey. Bree and Adrienne screamed, pointing at us on the field, like Elvis had come back from the dead.

In the midst of it all, Audrey's beauty stunned me. Her smile competed with the sun in brightness. Strands of her hair escaped her ponytail and blew around her face in the breeze. Her delicious neck was long, creamy, and bare. I swore I heard the tinkling bells of her laugh over the crowd. She was breathtaking.

As the song came to a close, I finished the dance with my arms above my head. Bobby and Val melted back, leaving me to bow alone to the crowd. Breathing hard, I brought the microphone down, waiting until people took their seats.

The moment of truth is here.

My stomach tightened. I felt a little lightheaded, but I would see this through. *No doubt. No surrender.*

"Thank you all for coming to support the best girls' soccer teams in the area. Your support means the world to everyone."

People in the stands clapped. Audrey gazed around with big eyes as the crowd showed their love. When she turned back to me with her face full of wonder, I knew.

Operation Dateposal was going to work.

"You might be wondering if there's another reason I'm dressed in sequins and dancing on the field. There's a special someone here today. I wanted her to know I can't stop the feeling."

I heard the squeals in the audience and knew that at least the women supported me. The Maidens jostled around Audrey, hands over their hearts.

I saw the moment the realization washed over Audrey's face. Her eyes locked with mine as her hands covered her mouth.

The team closed around her. Dee stood nearby, smiling. Behind them, Priscilla turned pale, almost green. Dr. Winters stood next to her. Her arms hung slack at her sides, her face blank.

"Someone once told me that as a role model, I couldn't date another teacher. That person didn't ask for our input or care about our feelings. Instead, she used threats to keep us apart."

"Boo," Frank yelled, and the crowd echoed him. I walked forward, toward the edge of the field, toward Audrey.

"But two adults in a solid relationship can be role models. I'm not perfect. I've made mistakes, but children can learn from people like me."

Audrey swayed back and forth, and I worried she might pass out. Dee stepped forward and wrapped her arms around her.

Tricia Drummold, one of my morning algebra students, called out, "Who is it, Mr. Taylor?"

I stopped about ten yards from Audrey. "I hope every student here learns that sometimes you have to do something crazy for those you love. Because today, I'm taking crazy by the horns. And if you believe in love and second chances, help me out by stomping your feet."

The metal bleachers amplified the sound of hundreds of pounding feet. Val and Bobby ran out onto the field again.

I shouted over the noise. "Ms. Freemont, Audrey, will you go out with me?"

Val and Bobby unrolled the giant poster:

Audrey,
Will You Go on a
Date With Oz?

That's when the world stopped. Time bent into a pretzel, and I held my breath.

The Maidens were nymphs, dancing in slow motion around their goddess. Audrey's head swiveled between me and the people in the bleachers.

Some held their hands to their hearts, others were crying. Many of the teachers raised signs over their heads.

Frank's said, "I SUPPORT OZ AND AUDREY!"

Dee's read, "LOVE CONQUERS ALL!"

Pat and the all P.E. teachers waved a long banner that stated, "LOVE IS SELF-CARE!"

Bobby, Dee, and Mel began chanting, "Date him! Date him!" The crowd joined them.

There was Mom. She dabbed her eyes with a tissue as Stella filmed everything on her phone.

Keith shouted, "Go out with him!" And time lurched forward.

I drew in the breath I'd been holding.

Val yelled, "We love you guys!"

I saw Dr. Winters separate herself from the crowd. She took a step toward the field.

My whole body bristled. *Bring it, bitch.*

Winters frowned, looking from me to Audrey and then back to the crowd of parents and teachers. The reporter interviewed Krissy from Barrel, and a photographer took pictures. Dr. Winters pasted a stern smile on her face and marched toward them.

I met Audrey's eyes and imagined her weighing the pros and cons.

Cons:
1. He loves dressing up a little too much.
2. He's making a spectacle of himself and me.
3. He dances like a rhythmic stork.

Pros:
1. Purple is my favorite color.
2. Oz must love me.
3. It's a date, so the stakes are low.
4. Or maybe I loved him too.

If the cons won out, I'd accept it, but my heart swelled with hope.

The energy shifted in the crowd. I lost sight of Audrey as the Maidens surrounded her again. The roar of the audience washed over me.

Just as I began to step forward, the circle of Maidens parted. And Red walked out onto the field.

Chapter 28: Audrey

Love on Top

My ears rang, and my heart raced to match the beat of the music. Colors flashed as if I rode a frantic merry-go-round. The girls' cheers of excitement wound around me, making me dizzy. People crowded the bleachers, clapping and stomping their feet.

When *Can't Stop This Feeling* played over the speakers, I smiled for the first time all day. The chance to sing and dance to Justin Timberlake relaxed me and filled my heart with a tiny bit of joy. I didn't realize how stiff and tense my muscles were until I started to dance with the team on the sideline.

But when Val and Keith ran onto the field and began moving in a choreographed dance, confusion swamped me. Why didn't they rope me into this show? Even Dee, her baby bump the size of a watermelon, shook her booty to the music. When more and more teachers joined in, I started to feel a little hurt. Why hadn't they included me?

All of this to surprise Haley with the MVP award?

Across the field, Oz jumped out of a car and ran onto the field. My heart squeezed a little at the sight. His blond hair and tall frame captured my attention, and my feet slowed as I stared at him. His jacket captured the light and threw it back in a dazzling display. It was as dark as the night sky, deep and velvety; a million shining sequins flashed like stars. His shoes matched, too. They glittered and sparkled in the sunlight, making tiny rainbows form all around him.

Did he know he wore my favorite color and sequins were a weakness of mine?

Dee handed Oz a microphone. He lifted it and sang the chorus of the song—not lip-syncing. He actually sang with Justin and joined the rest of the teachers in the dance. His voice resonated through me, strong and deep. My heart melted in a puddle of goo, and this song shot to my number one favorite song of all time. I knew I'd never hear it again without remembering this moment.

Heat washed over me. Oz was a glass of ice water in the hot desert. I wanted to drink him in, pour him over me. Streaks of gold and red highlighted his hair. My knees felt weak. I wanted him to sing to me. It was—he was—my personal catnip.

My body responded to him. My panties grew damp, and I crossed my arms over my chest to hide my nipples as they stood up like Oz's hard-core fans. Uncomfortable with my reaction, I glanced over my shoulder into the crowd.

Pree and Dr. Winters sat right above me, their hard faces carved into matching expressions of disapproval. Anger washed over me. They couldn't even enjoy a fun, spontaneous halftime show.

When the song ended, I looked for Haley, wanting to see her face as Oz gave her the MVP award. Using the microphone, he thanked everyone for coming out. He talked about the game and both teams' success. They were champions regardless of the outcome of the match. The crowd ate it up, shouting encouragement and cheering. His easygoing, caring nature won everyone over. And, of course, he was a hunk.

I absorbed the sound of his voice but not really listening to his words. So, when I heard my name echoing across the field, I froze. Immediately, the Maidens formed a tight circle around me, clutching their hearts and ooooo-ing and ahhh-ing. Why hadn't I paid attention?

"Mr. Taylor likeeess you," Haley drew out the word, grinning ear to ear.

"You need to go to him, Ms. Freemont," Adrienne squealed.

The crowd began chanting. I couldn't understand what they were saying.

Was it *Ate it* or *Fake him*?

"Say yes," Merry insisted. "You absolutely must."

And that's when it hit me. The crowd was chanting *Date him! Date him!*

Stunned, my knees felt loose, and I almost sank down on the cold ground. Oz had done all of this for me.

Dee appeared by my shoulder. "Everyone is behind you both, Audrey. You and Oz." She hugged me hard.

Dee's words and the sea of eager faces helped stiffen my spine. My friends and co-workers came together to support us. They'd helped him pull this whole thing together.

Oz loved me.

I loved him.

Acceptance surrounded me, a cozy blanket. People held signs: GIVE OZ A CHANCE and GO OUT WITH THE WIZARD OF OZ.

I glanced at where I'd seen Dr. Winters before. She was standing now, closer to me. Her face was stern as she looked at me and then up into the crowd.

Something caught her attention to my left. I turned to follow her line of sight to where a reporter interviewed Krissy and others in the crowd. A cameraman snapped pictures of the scene.

Keith's distinctive voice called out, "Go out with Oz."

I turned back. Oz stopped talking. I took a step forward, a foot nearer to a possible future—one where teaching and a relationship went hand in hand. I took another step.

From behind me, hard fingers clamped onto my shoulder. I spun around. Pree stood close, her cold eyes glaring.

"If only they knew you're only a slut."

Priscilla stood between me and my happy ending. Her rumors and nastiness had kept me from Oz for months.

Keeping a tight lid on my anger, I cut to the chase. "You had as much chance to win Teacher of the Year as I did. Couldn't you just let the committee decide without running a trash campaign?"

"And let you tarnish the reputation of the school if you win?"

"This wasn't about the school. It was all about you. Just admit you wanted to win so much, you sabotaged me."

Pree's face turned white before darkening to purple. "You don't deserve to be the Teacher of the Year. You're nothing but a whore."

She lifted her hand to slap me, but I caught her wrist. My calm eyes met her wild ones. "I don't care what you think of me, Pree. I'm done trying to be everything to everyone." Arianna Grande echoed my sentiment with *Break Free* playing in my mind.

I let go of her wrist, and her arm fell limply to her side.

She narrowed her eyes. "You won't win."

I smiled with all my teeth. "If you'll excuse me, I'm needed on the field."

I turned my back on her. And started toward the field and my happily ever after.

Val yelled, "We love you guys!"

My gaze returned to Oz, and I drank in the sight. His wide shoulders glinted with millions of shining sequins. They glowed like the stars on my ceiling at home, and I felt an urgency to hurry.

The ground shook from the cheers and foot-stomps. I walked past Bobby and Val, who gave me enthusiastic thumbs up. Etta James drowned out the crowd in my head, singing *At Last.*

With a sense of certainty, I walked faster. Oz shimmered ahead of me, pulling me toward him as if he controlled gravity. I began to run.

I was Baby in *Dirty Dancing* with *The Time of My Life* playing in my mind. I laughed, lighter than I'd been in months, leaping.

Oz caught me and swung me around. He broke into a laugh, too, and we were two crazy, laughing hyenas on the soccer field in front of the entire school.

Applause thundered in my ears. I hugged him hard, and I knew I could have it all. I could teach and date. I could even be the freaking Teacher of the Year.

I could love him and be everything I ever wanted.

I wrapped my arms around Oz and squeezed, resting my head against his chest. His heart hammered in time with mine. Creating the beat to a new song, one we made together.

The spicy scent of a forest by the sea enveloped me. He leaned down, his eyebrow quirked, making me melt. His lips brushed my cheek softly. "Will you go out with me, Red? We've never been on an official date."

"I'd love to date you." I stretched up onto my toes, holding on to his shoulders, and kissed him. The warmth of him seeped into me, opening me up to colors and sensations I'd never experienced before. I was more alive in this moment than I had in a long time.

His smile competed with the sun. We stared at one another with goofy, love-filled expressions until the ref came over to tell us to resume play within thirty seconds or forfeit the game.

We hurried off the field together as the Maidens raced past us.

Val ran over and hugged me, saying, "I'm so happy for you, Aud. Jealous too."

"We'll find you someone," I promised.

"Yes, please!" Val high-fived me with both hands.

The rest of the game flew by. Riding a wave of excitement, both teams played hard, but the Maidens won the match two to one.

He pulled me to his side. "Did you see that goal?"

"Um, no. I was too busy watching you."

He laughed, throwing his head back. "Well, it was amazing."

I opened my mouth to say something, but Keith and Dee appeared.

Keith smiled. "Congratulations, you two."

"Y'all are the cutest." Dee hugged me.

Haley and her mom came over together. "That was the sweetest thing, Mr. Taylor," Haley gushed.

Her mother nodded. "By far the most romantic dinner invitation out I've ever seen. Even better than the movies."

The three of us agreed while Oz's ears turned pink.

An older woman approached. She was taller than me and with Oz's blond hair and hazel eyes. A younger woman with similar features joined her.

"Honey, introduce us."

"Audrey, this is my mom and sister, Stella."

Audrey's eyes widened. "You loaned Oz those killer red shoes for the fundraiser."

"Yup."

Red's eyes sparkled. "I loved them so much. Any chance they come in a size eight?"

"I might be able to hook you up." Stella laughed.

Oz's mom smiled. "We need to head home, but we'd love for you to come to Thanksgiving or another weekend." She pulled me into a hug.

"I'll send you the video," Stella said, "You two are adorbs!"

"My mom would love to see it. Can you send it to her also?" We exchanged numbers before they headed toward their car.

Oz and I chatted with Adrienne and her dad. He'd removed the purple jacket and tossed it over his shoulder. His black shirt sleeves were rolled at his elbows, exposing his tanned forearms. He patted Adrienne on the shoulder. She hugged him before dragging her family away.

It seemed like hours before we were alone. Oz and I sat on the bleachers together, and he pulled me close.

His smoldering expression made me shiver and Lana Del Rey's *Love Song* washed over me. "I feel like you pushed the reset button, and we're free to start over."

"You have no idea how glad I am to hear you say that." He kissed me gently right there on school grounds where anyone could see.

I melted against him, hugging him close. A horn honked in the distance, and we broke apart, laughing.

"Do you have a plan for our date?" I asked.

"Red, do you think I'd do that whole song and dance and not have ideas?"

He quirked an eyebrow, and my insides melted on cue. Heat spread through my body, and I wanted him more than I'd ever wanted anything in my life.

I cupped his face with my palm. "Oh, yeah? What are these ideas?"

"I have reservations for seven thirty at three restaurants. I figured I'd let you choose and cancel the other two."

"Impressive," I whispered, trailing my fingers down his neck and along his collarbone.

"So, what shall it be, my lady? Fancy French cuisine at La Chaise Bleue? Perhaps a romantic candlelight dinner for two at Gustavo's, or do you want exotic and spicy Indian at Tandoori Twilight?"

All of these options sounded amazing, and I would love to go to any of those restaurants. But not tonight.

I batted my eyelashes. "Would you mind if we did something else tonight and saved our date for later?"

He leaned toward me, his sexy tone as delicious as a four-course meal. "You have something else in mind, Red?"

I kissed him. My pent-up urgency combined with a megaton of love poured out through my kiss. "Let's go home and reenact the night we met," I said.

"We can order a pizza." He grabbed my hand and pulled me toward the parking lot.

Chapter 29: Audrey

Lust for Life

I read somewhere that arguments over pizza toppings contributed to the increase in divorces. Oz insisted on The Caveman—all meat, extra cheese, but I wanted The Utopian— all veggies. Does it count as an argument if you laugh the whole time?

"I need meat," I mocked him with my best caveman grunt as he threw soccer equipment into the fieldhouse.

While locking up, he did an impression of the Queen of England in his best British falsetto. "Give me veggies, or I'll execute you all."

I snorted and placed the order for a large pie from Rustic Dough, half heart attack and half health freak.

"It'll be an hour," I told him as I hung up.

His eyes smoldered as he gave me a suggestive wink. Hallelujah, we were on the same wavelength. He squeezed my hand, and we raced to our cars for the short trip to his house.

When I pulled into his driveway and parked, my heart was pounding. I flipped down the visor to check my face in the mirror. Wide, twinkly eyes and rosy cheeks replaced the mopey, sad face I'd worn this morning. Twenty-four hours ago, I braced myself for a cold future alone. Now, excitement for tonight and tomorrow raced through me.

Oz opened the car door, giving me his arm. "My lady..."

"Why thank you, kind sir." I placed my palm on his arm, feeling the strength and heat of him.

Scooting out of the seat, he lifted me into his embrace. I ran my fingers from the side of his neck down to the waistband of his pants. He closed his hands on my hips and pulled me toward him. Reaching up, I ran my fingers through his hair as we kissed.

He scooped me up, kicking the car door closed. He spun me around until the cool metal of the car was hard against my back and kissed my neck. I moaned, loving the feel of Oz's hot body pinning me in place. I reached up to pull him closer, and the sound of his palm smacking against the window made me grin.

The simplest touch of his lips behind my ear set me on fire. I broke the kiss, panting.

"We should go inside," he suggested. "You never know who's watching."

Rockwell's *Somebody's Watching Me* flitted through my mind as I punched him lightly. He folded my fist into his hand, kissing my knuckles. We started up the path to his door.

The ability to think returned along with all the drama from the last few days. "Remind me to tell you something later." No way was I harshing the sexual buzz with it.

He put my hands around his neck and picked me up. My legs wrapped around him as he carried me up the steps to his porch. "Is it good or bad?"

"You'll have to wait and see." I wiggled to get free, but Oz held me tight. He wrapped an arm around my waist, refusing to let me go as he unlocked the door to his house.

"Can't get away from me that easy, Red." He opened the door, kicking it closed behind us with a bang.

Turning, he lowered me to the floor, but instead of stepping back, he wrapped his arms around me. His kind of conversation was better than mine, so I fused my mouth to his. His big hands roamed over my body. They skimmed up my back under my shirt to unhook my bra. My eyes drifted closed as his fingers followed the loose edge of the fabric around to cup and delightfully torment my breasts and nipples.

I moaned and arched into him. He reached down and pulled my shirt over my head, exposing my skin inch by inch to his rough hands. He threw my shirt and bra over his shoulder and covered my body with hungry kisses.

His gentle caresses and soft whispering touches drove me wild. I linked my arms around his neck and locked my legs around his waist, rubbing against the hard heat of his cock through his jeans. His hands slid under my butt, and I unbuttoned his shirt. I breathed in the warm scent of sun and grass on his skin with a frenzied urge for more.

His lips were too soft against my throat. "Harder. Oz, please."

He groaned, pinching my butt. He unlinked his fingers, and I pressed my bare breasts against his warm chest. Linking his fingers with mine, he tugged me toward his bedroom. I followed him eagerly, anticipating joining him in his enormous bed.

I fumbled with the buckle of his belt. George Michael whispered *I Want your Sex* in my head as I unzipped his pants and eased my fingers beneath the edge of his boxers.

"Audrey, damn, that feels good," Oz bit out.

I pushed his pants down and dropped to my knees, taking him in my mouth. The hard length pulsed against my tongue. The spicy musk of his body drove me wild. He tasted of fire, smoke, and a tantalizing saltiness. His fingers tangled in my hair. He leaned back and moaned.

Over the racing beat of my heart, I heard a muffled chime. I eased back a little, stroking his cock with my hands.

"Shit," Oz barked. He stepped away and turned an icy glare toward the living room. The doorbell rang again. Oz tensed, ready to murder anyone on the other side of the door.

"It's the pizza guy." I snickered at Oz's expression of loathing while Dean Martin crooned *That's Amore* to me.

Fumbling through his pants, he yanked out his wallet. Peeking down the hall, I watched him stalk naked through the house. He shoved the money through the mail slot and yelled, "Leave it on the porch."

Without hesitating, he stormed back, ignoring my hoots of laughter, pulling me after him toward his luxurious bed.

"Slow down, Caveman." I hiccupped with laughter as he herded me to the bed.

Oz pushed me back, and I bounced softly onto the bed. My laughter dried up as soon as Oz knelt in front of me. He took off my shoes, then pushed me back to slide down my pants.

"Cavemen make excellent lovers." Oz's husky voice sent shivers up my spine. His mouth traveled across the bare skin of my pussy, making me squirm and shiver. His fingers delved into the heat of my body and stroked. I felt myself coming apart, panting as I teased him. "Dragging women around by their hair? I'll pass, thanks."

I felt his smile against my sensitive skin. "You're wet for me, Red; you can't deny you like it when I go caveman on you." His busy mouth and fingers explored my body, finding places that drove me higher.

My hips shifted, begging for more, and I echoed the need in a voice I didn't recognize. "Please."

He wouldn't hurry. He caressed my overheated skin with kisses. His lips left my center to trail down the soft skin of my thighs. I thrashed my head when he returned to the crux of my thighs.

I gasped as he wound me tighter and tighter, his tongue and hands urging me on until I didn't know where I started, and he ended. I rose up from the bed, my muscles taut.

"Oz," I cried, reaching toward him as my world exploded, light shattering and pulsing around me.

He pulled me close, stroking my back with long sweeps of his hands, anchoring me while I drifted on pleasure. His fingers played with my hair, and I whispered, "I love how hard you make me come."

He smiled. "Cavemen had a lot of time in the dark to practice the art of love."

Michael Franks began singing *The Art of Love* in my mind. Smiling, I pushed him onto the pillows. "Cavewomen did, too."

His cock stood hard and inviting. I wrapped my hand around him, sliding across his hot skin. I found the rhythm that made him throw his head back and grit his teeth.

He pivoted, flipping me onto my back. His hand shot out to the pile of condoms on the nightstand. He ripped one open with his teeth and rolled it on. He lay back against the pillows next to me and quirked his eyebrow.

I straddled him. One of his hands cupped my breast as the other squeezed my butt. I lowered myself onto him and almost stopped breathing.

"You feel so good, Red." His hips arched, pushing deeper into me. My eyes closed, savoring the sensation of him inside me.

"Open your eyes," Oz demanded. My gaze met his while our bodies rocked together.

His dark eyes burned into mine as he stroked, taking control of the rhythm. His hands held my hips, moving me as he wanted. I panted with pleasure, moaning his name. My body moved instinctively as he pushed us higher, closer to the pinnacle. I felt myself losing control; the remnants of the world spun away as I climaxed. Oz thrust deep and came as my body squeezed him tight.

When I could think again, I nuzzled my lips against the side of his neck. "You make me melt under your hands."

He tightened his arms around me. "Wait till after our date. I promise to make your insides gooey."

I lifted my head and kissed him. "My insides are already gooey, but your decadent, scrumptious, insanely awesome promises remind me I have to keep my strength up."

My stomach growled, punctuating my sentence.

"I'll go get the pizza." Oz threw on his jeans and retrieved the pizza. We ate it cold with icy cold beer in bed. Nothing ever tasted so good.

Laughing, I reached toward his half of the pie. "I could eat this whole pizza."

Oz swatted my hand away. "Don't touch my Caveman."

I laughed. "I already did."

He wiggled his eyebrows. "You can touch my cock anytime, Red. But stay away from my half of the pizza."

I bit into a slice from my half. "Why would I want that? The Utopia is a combination of all the healthy foods on the pyramid. It's highly superior to the high cholesterol on a crust you're eating."

Oz tensed, his eyes clouding. I held my breath. Seconds ticked by, and I exhaled. "Did I say something wrong?"

Oz sighed. "It's a long story and one I'd rather not get into tonight."

I chewed on the inside of my mouth, wondering how far I should push. "I'm here when you want to tell me."

"I know you are," he said and kissed me. When he let me go, he picked up his slice and rolled his eyes. "I love you, but pizza without meat is wrong."

"I love you too, even though you're wrong." We laughed, and the tension evaporated, leaving only the giddy feeling of being in love.

A while later, I sighed happily, my belly full. Flopping back against the pillows, I spread my arms over my head and stretched.

Oz got up to put the rest of the food in the fridge. When he returned, I lay spread eagle, trying to take up the whole bed. I giggled.

"Whatcha doin'?" He stood over me, hands on his hips, amused.

"I'm recreating our first night together. When you stole my bed and fell asleep."

He winced. "I'm still sorry about that."

I rolled over and held my arms up to him. "You've made up for it."

Oz joined me under the covers. I snuggled up to him, lying with my head against his wide, hunky shoulder.

"You tried to tell me something earlier, but I was distracted by your luscious body," he said.

"I was nominated for City Teacher of the Year." There would be time later to tell him the rest.

His smile was dazzling. "That's amazing news. Congratulations, Darlin'."

Tears stung my eyes. Why had I ever pushed this man away?

"I wasted so much time pretending I didn't love you."

His arms tightened around me. "You were worth the wait, Red."

"Thanks for not giving up. Watching you out there on the field doing that sexy dance, you were my knight slaying my metaphorical dragons."

Oz laughed and tipped an imaginary hat. "At your service, ma'am."

"I'm serious. I might've spent my whole life living inside the box I'd made for myself. You opened me up to so much more." I kissed him, tasting spicy sausage and pepperoni. I couldn't get enough.

Tossing the covers back, I tasted his pepperoni and more.

Afterward, Oz lay back against the pillows, holding me. His fingers traced circles across the skin of my belly, lulling me to sleep. I snuggled into him and let my brain go blank.

His lips moved against my ear. "Red, will you go out on a date with me tomorrow night?"

I mumbled nonsense words, more asleep than awake. Under my cheek, his chest vibrated with silent laughter. When he pinched my butt and tickled the sensitive skin behind my knee, I shot up with a half scream and half laugh. "Stop! Okay, yes, I'll go out with you!"

He laughed, "Good."

"Good?" I grumbled, snuggling back down. "That's it? Good?"

"Yeah." He gathered me in his arms.

I sneaked my hand up and pinched him on his nipple. "Way to make a girl feel special, Caveman."

Oz flinched and caught my hand with his. He twined our fingers together. "What more do you want, Red? I sang my heart out for you. I even swiveled my hips in front of my mother."

"I'll remember it forever." I kissed him softly on the cheek and then the lips. Completely relaxed, I drifted off to sleep in his arms and dreamed of our happily ever after.

Epilogue: Audrey

One Year Later

Just the Way You Are

I slipped into the locker room as the first half of the tricycle basketball game ticked down. Oz stood in shorts and a tank top. His cheerleading dress lay on a bench next to a pair of tall, red, high-heeled boots and a long blond wig.

Stella had given them to him last Christmas. His mom and I thought it was hysterical.

"Hey." I walked into his arms and reached up to kiss him.

"Hi," Oz growled, kissing me back.

Out in the gym, the buzzer sounded, announcing the end of the half. Mr. Kline, Marchfield's new principal, announced on the loudspeaker, "The halftime show will begin in ten minutes. You don't want to miss it, folks!"

Last year, after Oz's halftime show, some of the parents' and students' comments on the news segment led to an investigation. I was surprised when the committee of supervisors found multiple cases suggesting Dr. Winters fostered a toxic work environment. The superintendent decided she would be better suited to a desk job at the school administration building. No one in the school missed her, and Mr. Kline was much more supportive and open.

This time I Know It's Real by Dionne Summers played in my mind with a montage of memories from last year. I helped Oz get dressed, and then he sat on the bench with his knees spread wide to zip up his boots.

"Those boots are killer, Oz. I wonder if Stella can get me a pair."

"You already have the other ones," Oz groused as he stood, arms spread wide for balance.

"True. Maybe I'll wear them to the Teacher of the Year celebration in Richmond."

Last March our superintendent announced that I'd won the City Teacher of the Year Award. I'd filled out the Virginia State application and written a ton of essays about my philosophy of the pedagogy. The winner would be announced next week, but I didn't care if I won. A lot had changed in a year.

"I'd love these boots a lot more on you." Oz stood gingerly.

I jumped up on the bench and helped him with his wig. I loved that he felt comfortable enough with himself to wear this costume for a second year. Hopping off the bench, I came around to hug him.

"I'll wear them for you tonight at home."

Now that soccer season had finished, I spent more time at Oz's house. Stevie loved Oz's place. The extra space and bigger windowsills were cat nirvana. Stevie also loved Oz's big shoulders as much as I did. I'll never forget coming home late one afternoon and finding the cat lying across his neck. His purr rumbled loud enough to shake the house.

His eyebrow quirked. "And nothing else?"

Taking a step back, I smiled wickedly. "Whatever you want, Queen."

He reached for me, but I shimmied away. Pausing at the door, I blew him a kiss. "Break a leg, Sweetie."

"Don't say that while I'm wearing these boots," Oz hollered as the door closed behind me.

Val was where I'd left her, but I noticed Evan Shurden had joined her. He was Marchfield's new technology education teacher, and he was tall with dark skin and shoulder-length black hair that he tied back. Rumor was he was Native American, which Val thought made him even sexier.

As I approached, he leaned close and said something in Val's ear. I watched my friend laugh. Rocking back on my heels, I didn't want to interrupt whatever was going on.

Val had been too quiet lately. I knew Logan, who'd been outside Barrel last year, was part of it, but Val wouldn't talk about it. If Evan could make her laugh again, I was all for it.

Val noticed me and waved, so I joined them. Evan smiled in welcome.

"Remember last year's show?" I asked.

"What I remember is you and Oz canoodled in the garden." Val poked me in the arm.

"You're never going to let me forget that, are you?"

Val pursed her lips and tapped her finger against them as if in deep thought. "Nope."

"I can't believe we volunteered for the second quarter. I was so sore last year."

Val nodded. "That's why we started that glute workout last month. It won't be as bad this year."

"I hope I don't get pegged with a ball again."

"Since Pree's gone, I'd say you're safe."

I was surprised when Priscilla quit last June. For all the trouble she'd made, I'd never wished she'd leave Marchfield Middle. "Marnie says Pree's driving everyone crazy in her husband's architecture office. I can't picture her as an administrative assistant."

"I saw the two of them running the other morning. I almost didn't recognize Pree with her hair a mess and her shirt all sweaty."

"I'm nice enough to hope the endorphins satisfy her."

"You should be proud of me, Aud. I didn't yell, 'loser' out my car window."

I laughed. "I'm overjoyed."

Val's laughter turned into a sigh. "I miss teaching on the same grade level as you."

Val and I still saw each other at work, but it wasn't the same. I'd taken Priscilla's vacant position in sixth-grade and moved to another hall.

"I really love little sixth-graders. Come teach the babies with me next year."

Val said something I didn't hear because the lights dimmed, and the music started. Rihanna's *Shut Up and Drive* poured through the gym's speakers.

Oz and the other male faculty members made their entrance, dressed in their red and white dresses. The crowd went wild as the four men started their routine.

It seemed so long ago that I'd kissed him at last August's happy hour.

***

Last Memorial Day weekend, we visited my family. Stella and Diane, Oz's mom, were invited too.

Our moms had become best friends after the dateposal and conspired through emails and phone calls. They were united in their desire for us to marry and have kids.

On the drive back home, Oz broke the news that even though he loved me, he didn't know if he would ever want kids of his own. He told me about his grandad and dad dying before the age of forty, and he didn't want to leave me in the same position if he died young.

The thought of Oz dying terrified me. I couldn't imagine my life without him. Together, we'd gone to a cardiologist, and I'd sat on the examining room table, holding him while we waited for the results of his echocardiogram.

We both breathed a sigh of relief when the test results confirmed Oz's excellent health, and we celebrated in bed for an entire weekend afterward.

Over the summer, we traveled together, visiting some of Oz's favorite places. We'd hiked a trail in the Grand Canyon, gambled in Vegas, and craned our necks up to peer at the giant Sequoia trees in California.

We'd already started planning a trip to Europe for this coming summer.

***

Back in the gym, Oz shimmied his hips and shoulders to the beat. He and the other men hammed it up, delighting the kids and parents with their hilarious show. By the end of the song, everyone jumped to their feet, dancing with them.

At the end of the song, the guys took their bows. I noticed Bobby waiting on the sidelines for them to finish. When she ran out and handed Oz a large poster, my heart stuttered.

What was he up to?

In Your Eyes by Peter Gabriel began to play as the other men walked off the court, leaving Oz behind.

I reached blindly for Val's hand. "What's he doing?"

"Shut up and pay attention," she suggested.

Oz stood alone in his loose dress and long, red stripper boots. His platinum blond hair streamed down over his very manly shoulders. He waited, his eyes on me until the song reached the chorus before lifting the poster over his head.

AUDREY FREEMONT,
WILL YOU MARRY ME?

The audience exploded with cheers. Val gave a happy scream and squeezed my hand hard.

Surprise held me immobile. I let the music flow over me. The crowd grew quiet, everyone holding their breath.

"Go get him, Audrey!" I heard Stella yell from somewhere behind me.

Keith yelled, "Put him out of his misery."

"Marry him! We want grandkids!"

That sounded like...*Wait! Both our moms were here?*

My knees wobbled as I stood.

He teetered on the heels of his crazy boots as he walked toward me.

My mental playlist shuffled to Nancy Sinatra's *These Boots Were Made for Walking*, but I was never walking away from Oz.

Standing right in front of me, he dropped the poster and reached out his hand. He'd never been more handsome, costume and all.

"Well, Red, what do you say?"

Adrenaline raced through me at the sound of his voice and my strength returned. I stepped up on the empty seat in front of me and launched myself toward him.

He stumbled back, but I caught his arm, steadying him. Then his arms wound tightly around my waist.

I stood on my tiptoes and reached up to brush the blond wig hair out of his face. "I love you, Oz."

It didn't seem possible, but he squeezed me harder, "I love you, too."

He bent over, and I wrapped my arms around his neck to kiss him. I poured my heart and all my love into that kiss. When the heat sizzled between us, I eased back, remembering the impressionable young people all around.

"Gross! That's our sister!" my brothers yelled in unison. Oz had apparently invited the whole family.

All around us, people roared their approval. I did a little curtsy. And when Oz imitated me, everyone laughed.

Then Oz took a ring from his pocket. A beautiful ruby surrounded by diamonds sparkled and flashed under the gym's lights. The room swayed.

"This ring belonged to my grandma. She told me to give it to the woman I loved," Oz told me while the whoops and hoots continued around us.

I nodded, swallowing hard to keep back the happy tears. John Legend sang *All of Me*, but I couldn't hear the words over my thundering heart.

He slipped the ring onto my finger, and I closed my hand over his.

Bobby shoved a microphone in my face. "Is that a yes?"

"Yes! Yes, I'll marry you!" My voice boomed through the gym, and *Can't Stop the Feeling*, my number one favorite song of all time, burst through the gym's speakers.

Oz swung me into his arms, and we danced. With our families, school, and community all around us.

About the Author

M. Jayne Ladow used to teach eleven to thirteen-year-olds how to write essays and diagram sentences. Like Audrey, she participated in several tricycle basketball games and couldn't walk afterward, and coached many sports at the principal's demand. Now she writes books about feisty women and the men who love them. She lives in Virginia in a tiny house with her husband, kids, three shelter cats, a tortoise, a beardy, and a bunny who rules them all.

See what I'm reading and join in the conversation on the Yram and Nerual Blog

Check out my website for more about me, my books, and sign up for my newsletter: mjladow.com

Acknowledgments

When I started writing this novel, I was caring for my mother-in-law, Mary Lou. I would sit in her room while we watched reruns of old shows on *Pluto* and zone out into my imaginary world where happy-ever-after was guaranteed. I miss my writing buddy greatly.

My husband, Jim, and my children, Megan and Miles—you are the rock under my feet and the spirits that guide me. Thank you for cheering me on and supporting me for the two years it took me to get this far. Miles, the cover you created for me and then recreated so Amazon could actually use it is amazing!

Liz, my big sister, thanks for being there when I told our mom I was writing explicit sex scenes and laughing during one of the hardest times in our lives. Your support is unending. I love you.

Lauren, my friend, you are my number one Alpha reader. Thank you so much for all the laughter, brainstorming, and encouragement. This book would not exist without you because I wrote it for us.

My heartfelt thanks also go out to Nancy and Mary. You believed in me from the beginning. Thank you for reading my work, being kind, sending me funny emojis, and a steady stream of joy.

Yvette, without your support, notes, Zoom meetings, advice, and laughter, this book would never have gotten published. I am so thankful our letter-writing addiction evolved into us becoming writing buddies.

To my Beta readers at Scribophile, especially Vivienne, Erin, Deb, and Rachael Anne, your comments and critiques were exactly what I needed to hear, especially the hard criticisms. Keep writing, my friends.

Countless students and teachers made me who I am today. I can't thank you enough for all you have taught me.